HORACE WALPOLE (1717–97) was born in Lon son of Sir Robert Walpole, and educated at Eton and King's College, Cambridge. Between 1739 and 1741 he toured France and Italy with the poet Thomas Gray. Before his return he had been elected a Member of Parliament and in 1748 he bought the villa at Twickenham he was leasing and renamed it Strawberry Hill. Remodelled, extended, and embellished over three decades in the 'Gothic' style, it became an acclaimed architectural attraction. He established a printing-press there and published many of his own works as well as those of others. In addition to *The Castle of Otranto* (1764) his books include *Anecdotes of Painting in England* (1762–80), *Historic Doubts on the Life of King Richard the Third* (1768), *The Mysterious Mother* (1768), and *Hieroglyphic Tales* (1785). He also left a vast collection of letters and memoirs which, in the mingling of his wide interests, and in the wit, penetration, and inside knowledge they display, gives one of the finest pictures of life in eighteenth-century upper-class society, as well as a history of contemporary taste.

NICK GROOM is Professor in English at the University of Exeter. He has published widely for both academic and popular readerships, and his many books include *The Forger's Shadow* (2002), *The Union Jack* (2006), *The Gothic: A Very Short Introduction* (2012), and editions of several eighteenth-century texts. His most recent book is *The Seasons: An Elegy for the Passing of the Year* (2013).

OXFORD WORLD'S CLASSICS

*For over 100 years Oxford World's Classics have brought
readers closer to the world's great literature. Now with over 700
titles—from the 4,000-year-old myths of Mesopotamia to the
twentieth century's greatest novels—the series makes available
lesser-known as well as celebrated writing.*

*The pocket-sized hardbacks of the early years contained
introductions by Virginia Woolf, T. S. Eliot, Graham Greene,
and other literary figures which enriched the experience of reading.
Today the series is recognized for its fine scholarship and
reliability in texts that span world literature, drama and poetry,
religion, philosophy, and politics. Each edition includes perceptive
commentary and essential background information to meet the
changing needs of readers.*

OXFORD WORLD'S CLASSICS

HORACE WALPOLE

The Castle of Otranto
A Gothic Story

Edited with an Introduction and Notes by
NICK GROOM

OXFORD
UNIVERSITY PRESS

OXFORD
UNIVERSITY PRESS

Great Clarendon Street, Oxford, OX2 6DP,
United Kingdom

Oxford University Press is a department of the University of Oxford.
It furthers the University's objective of excellence in research, scholarship,
and education by publishing worldwide. Oxford is a registered trade mark of
Oxford University Press in the UK and in certain other countries

Editorial material © Nick Groom 2014
The Castle of Otranto first published as a World's Classics paperback 1982
Reissued as an Oxford World's Classics paperback 1998, 2008

This edition first published 2014

The moral rights of the author have been asserted

Impression:16

Published in the United States of America by Oxford University Press
198 Madison Avenue, New York, NY 10016, United States of America

British Library Cataloguing in Publication Data

Data available

Library of Congress Control Number: 2014935112

ISBN 978-0-19-870444-7

Printed and bound in Great Britain by Clays Ltd, Elcograf S.p.A.

ACKNOWLEDGEMENTS

Judith Luna, who commissioned this edition, has been a wonderful ally throughout its development: an enthusiastic, encouraging, and patient editor, and a penetrating and insightful critic; her experience and assistance have been invaluable. I would also like to thank Dale Townshend for specific comments and advice. Some of the introductory material was aired in research seminars at the University of Exeter, and my colleagues in the Department of English were especially helpful. Finally, I would like to thank my family for their forbearance. This edition is dedicated to my students.

CONTENTS

INTRODUCTION

HORACE WALPOLE'S *The Castle of Otranto* is generally considered to be the first Gothic novel, and yet many modern readers find it by turns ludicrous and unreadable. The extraordinary literary effects that Walpole pioneered and which thrilled his readers in the 1760s have either been overworked in the hands of generations of his followers and so become clichés, or have been superseded as effectively failed literary experiments. The weird significance of dreams, the appearance of the animated dead, and the prevalence of secret passages, for instance, became staples of a new form of fiction that was eventually christened the 'Gothic' novel. In contrast, the sudden appearance of colossal fragments of statues, imitations of knockabout Shakespearean comedy, and a reliance on the conventions of sentimentality—a parade of blushes, tears, and swoons—strike modern audiences as at best embarrassingly archaic, at worse laughable. *The Castle of Otranto* is a striking example of a book that by inaugurating a new style within a few years made itself obsolete.

Previous editors have accordingly tended to dwell on the reception and subsequent influence of *Otranto*, and have been frank about the book's shortcomings. It is certainly true that within a generation Ann Radcliffe and Matthew Lewis were producing far more adept terror and horror fiction, but to judge Walpole's novel by his successors is to do *Otranto* a serious critical injustice. The appearance of *The Castle of Otranto* on 24 December 1764 is best understood not as the first rudimentary attempt in a new genre or as the genesis of the Gothic literary tradition in English, but rather as the climax of eighteenth-century discussion and debate about the Goths and 'Gothick'. Three distinct strands are tangled together here. First, the Goths' place in ancient history and their characteristic society and art; secondly, their contributions to political thought through Gothic polity or the Gothic system of government and its subsequent influence on the British constitution; and thirdly the culture of the Middle Ages and its effect on contemporary eighteenth-century taste. It is within these contexts that Walpole's novel takes its place within literary history; indeed, seen thus, it becomes clear that *The Castle of Otranto* was not only innovative, but succeeded in shifting an entire paradigm. In the context of eighteenth-century Gothic Walpole's novel was a game-changer: that was why it was so important—and why eighteenth-century readers read it in astonished awe.

Gothic Contexts

The ancient Goths were members of a Germanic tribe who in AD 376 crossed the Danube into the Roman Empire. After years of turbulent conflict and uneasy treaties, Alaric led the Goths to march on Rome and in 410 they sacked the Eternal City, eventually occupying and ruling southern Europe from Italy to Spain. With the advent of this Gothic ascendancy and their extensive territorial power came the need for a legitimating cultural history, and so Gothic historians such as the sixth-century statesman Jordanes developed a myth of racial purity and migration. The society and culture of the tribes of Germania had already been compared with classical values and civilization by Roman historians such as Tacitus in the *Agricola* and *Germania*, and by Caesar in his *Gallic War*, but Jordanes developed a complete ethnic myth for the Goths. His people were a northern race who had their origins in Scandza, an island not unlike Britain. This was the 'northern hive' or 'womb of nations', from where they migrated to Scythia (Eastern Europe) before moving inexorably westwards. The Goths, originating in the harsh climate and rugged landscapes of the north, were thus presented as a viable alternative to decadent Mediterranean culture: northern vigour was in marked contrast to Roman enervation and corruption.

Although the kingdoms and cultures of the Ostrogoths and Visigoths (eastern and western Goths, respectively) themselves rose and fell, the Goths' perceived role in history was primarily one of destruction: they were responsible for the collapse of the Roman Empire. Their reputation remained so for centuries, gradually extending into other regions and epochs inimical to classical civilization. Come the Italian Renaissance and the revival of classical learning and taste, commentators were quick to condemn any fashions of art and architecture of the past thousand years that were non-classical, and so building styles from ninth-century Carolingian in France to fifteenth-century perpendicular in England were all dismissed as 'Gothic'. In *Lives of the Artists* (1550), Giorgio Vasari claimed that this architecture was 'monstrous and barbaric, wholly ignorant of any accepted ideas of sense and order'. Its taste was 'confused and disordered', made up of 'portals with flimsy columns twisted like corkscrews . . . façades made up of one damned tabernacle on top of the other . . . and lots of pinnacles, gables, and foliage'. He concludes that 'This manner of building was invented by the Goths, who put up structures in this way after all the ancient buildings had been destroyed. . . . It was they who made vaults with pointed arches . . . and then filled the whole of Italy with their accursed buildings.'[1]

Presenting the Goths as non-Roman implied that their civilization was devoid of all the refinements and accoutrements of classical Rome, and so 'Gothic' became a synonym for everything crude, ignorant, vulgar, brutish, and ferine. Where the Romans were educated and urbane, the Goths were barbarous and rude; where the Romans built and cultivated, the Goths laid waste. Yet at the same time that the Goths were being reviled by artists and aficionados, they were also being slowly rehabilitated by scholars as an intriguing example of primitive society. By the beginning of the sixteenth century classical texts such as the *Agricola* and *Gallic War* had been rediscovered and reprinted, and these accounts strongly hinted that the barbarian tribes of late antiquity were far more sophisticated than had hitherto been recognized—and moreover embodied values of purity and liberty that had been lost to the Romans. The Goths were not simply savages; they also displayed signs of enlightenment. Hence their

[1] Quoted by Chris Brooks, *The Gothic Revival* (London: Phaidon, 1999), 10.

ruinous activities could be theorized in more nuanced intellectual and political ways.

In England, the possibility that the ancient Goths were more than mere barbarians became central to the process of national renewal following the Reformation. William Camden, one of the founding historians of racial migrations and settlements in Britain, argued in his epoch-making work *Britannia* (1586) that the Goths who overran Europe had resisted all attempts at invasion and subjugation, being 'a most ancient people . . . invincible themselves, and free from any foreign yoke'.[2] So while the Goths could certainly still be seen as a horde of destructive thugs who had razed classical civilization, they could also be understood as presenting an alternative to the imperial hegemony of ancient Rome—an alternative that resisted and rebelled against tyranny, one that was driven by its own values of liberty and freedom, one that had swept away centuries of Roman oppression and cruelty. These politically motivated Goths were, it was argued, one of the primal European races. Far from being a disastrous disruption of classical history the Goths became associated with abundance and freedom, exemplifying a different but credible model of society to that which had evolved around the Mediterranean. Their irrepressible vigour was nurtured by the northern regions to which they were drawn, and which they settled most successfully. Thus they were recognized as the ancestors of the Angles, Saxons, and Jutes—from whom the English were themselves descended.

The first sustained attention given to this positive analysis of the Gothic spirit was in the mid-seventeenth century, when antiquarians began to research Anglo-Saxon forms of government and sovereignty in an attempt to regulate and curb the powers of the king. These investigations into the ruling institutions of the Saxons and the Normans—primarily the Saxon *Witenagemot*, the early precursor of parliament—formed the core of the debates then seeking to establish and justify the extent of the monarch's power. Northern European forms of government were, it was claimed,

[2] William Camden, *Britannia: or A Chorographical Description of Great Britain and Ireland, together with the Adjacent Islands*, 2 vols (London, 1722), i, p. xlvii.

originally Gothic and had consequently developed under similar conditions of climate, temper, and inclination. They were all alike in being anti-tyrannical, contrasting sharply with autocratic forms of political order associated with the Romans. By the eighteenth century, 'Gothic polity' (being a 'Government of Freemen' and a model of parliamentary rule that resisted arbitrary power) was not only seen as the driving force of social progress but was central to the political ideology of the Whig Party—deliberately opposing the monarchical, crypto-Catholic despotism of Tory Royalists.

The Whigs accordingly acknowledged the 'Gothick Constitution' as a righteous form of governance founded on natural rights of freedom, and inimical to tyranny and absolutism. Where the Romans had invaded and imposed their rule, the Goths had resisted and rebelled, insisting on their natural liberties and freedoms. That was their bequest to the English, and its evidence was scattered throughout the nation's history, from Magna Carta to the Glorious Revolution. Neither was the Gothic resistance to tyranny confined to the theatre of politics. The Protestant Reformation was also apprehended as a rebellion against religious despotism and, like the Gothic constitution, was woven into the Gothic identity of the nation—eventually formalized in the Act of Settlement (1701) that secured the Protestant succession to the throne. Again the threat seemed to be from Rome —no longer classical Rome, now Catholic Rome. Hence Henry VIII's policy to dissolve the monasteries and bring about the English Reformation was given a Gothic spin as a rebellion against absolutist papal jurisdiction.

Gothic thinking inevitably identified monumental medieval architecture with the strange and sinister traces left centuries earlier by the Ancient Britons in the empty wildernesses of antiquity: the mysterious burial mounds and colossal megaliths that were thought to be the tombs and temples of sacrifice of a forgotten age. The notion, first promulgated in the Renaissance, was that English architectural history was essentially both continuous and Gothic, from prehistoric remains to the cathedrals and castles of the Middle Ages. The seventeenth-century historian and theologian Gilbert Burnet, for instance, explicitly associated the Goths of antiquity with Norman and medieval building styles—in short, with non-classical taste. Similarly, the eighteenth-century poet and literary scholar Thomas Warton traced English architecture from the Saxons to the Reformation, dividing the 'Gothic' into different orders and celebrating its indigenous, recognizable Englishness.[3] Megaliths and stone circles were considered 'ancient Gothic'—'massive, heavy, and coarse', and resonated with their own sublime power: 'those huge rude masses of stone, set on end, and piled on each other, turn the mind on the immense force necessary for such a work'.[4] 'Modern Gothic', in contrast, consisted of the characteristic medieval architecture of pointed arches, ribbed vaulting, and flying buttresses: 'light, delicate, and rich to Excess', characterized by an 'Abundance of little, whimsical, wild, and chimerical Ornaments'.[5] A growing element of national pride is also apparent here: British antiquities were comparable to the classical destinations visited on the Grand Tour.

But weaving the Gothic myth into English history was profoundly problematic. If, as the Whigs proposed, the primitive Gothic model of shared government had effectively constituted the modern progressive parliamentary system, it had come at a dire cost. The English constitution, claiming both to embody and promote the liberties and rights of the people against oppression and absolutism, had brought about the execution of Charles I, the Civil Wars, the invasion of William of Orange and the so-called 'Bloodless Revolution', and the ensuing ruthless repression and execution of Welsh, Irish, and Scottish rebels—not to mention a foreign policy predicated on colonialism and warfare. The evidence of this abidingly destructive Gothic spirit littered the English landscape in the broken abbeys and priories left by the Protestant Reformers. The Reformation, by attacking not only the spiritual values of Catholicism but also its worldly status,

---

[3] Thomas Warton, *Observations on The Fairy Queen of Spenser*, 2 vols, 2nd edn (London, 1762), ii. 185–98.

[4] Edmund Burke, *A Philosophical Enquiry into the Origin of our Ideas of the Sublime and Beautiful*, ed. Adam Phillips (Oxford: Oxford University Press, 1990), 71.

[5] *The Builder's Dictionary: or, Gentleman and Architect's Companion*, 2 vols (London, 1734), i, unpaginated [439].

had disbanded religious orders, seized their treasures, and abandoned their buildings to neglect and pillage. A millennium and a half of culture and civilization was overthrown and the medieval world was literally left in ruins. The removal of Catholicism was not enough for the Reformers: iconoclasm demanded that buildings were left deliberately derelict and images of saints remained permanently defaced as a perpetual reminder of the downfall of idolatry. Disturbingly, the ruination of this art and architecture was as Gothic as was the noble stand against tyranny.

An aesthetic of ruin thus emerged from this historical and religious carnage. A fascination with deterioration and decay pervades English culture, from the work of antiquarians such as William Camden and John Leland to the drama of the Elizabethan and Jacobean stage—especially in Revenge Tragedy—as well as in popular ballads and folklore. The past is inescapable, and ever threatening to return. If as a national religion Catholicism was ostensibly dead, it refused to lie down, and the superstitious imagination of the people populated all its architectural wreckage with ghosts—the revenants of a Catholic medieval past: vengeful spirits, shadowy monks and nuns, uncanny manifestations. The Gothic imagination—as it would be named centuries later—took shape therefore in the dilapidated wreck of ecclesiastical architecture, and was haunted by the inexorable violence that had powered the political and social progress of the nation. The Gothic myth was rooted in antiquity and antiquarian politics; it celebrated English history as progressive, Protestant, and parliamentarian; but it was also guiltily aware of its violent and bloody past.

From this complicated and contradictory mix a recognizable Gothic culture arose in the eighteenth century. The liberal instincts of the ancient Gothic tribes had not, it was argued, been confined to political and religious freedoms, but were also sublimated into the arts. Thus their culture was a product of the same forces of restlessness, passion, intensity, power, and resistance to tyranny. The Gothic offered a Whiggish alternative to Tory neoclassicism, and Whig grandees began to Gothicize their estates with medievalist garden houses and faux ruins. It was accordingly in architecture that the Gothic first began to flourish as a cultural form. The most stunning example of this fashion was undoubtedly Strawberry Hill in Twickenham, an opulent and rambling medievalist fantasy that began to take shape from 1749. The exterior of the building was upholstered with cloisters, crenellations, turrets, and pinnaces; the interior was trimmed with niches, canopies, stained glass, and ribbed vaulting, and bedecked with all manner of antiques—from suits of armour to *objets d'art*. Much of the lavishly overwhelming effect came from *trompe l'oeil* and pastiche effects—plasterboard arches, wallpaper painted to look like stonework, and columns that served no structural purpose—and the whole was concocted as if it were a book of architectural quotations: the chimney piece in the Little Parlour, for instance, was based on Bishop Ruthall's pre-Reformation tomb at Westminster Abbey. Strawberry Hill was a stunning vision of romantic caprice, a dream made flesh (or plaster). And it was the creation and brainchild of Horace Walpole: Strawberry Hill was where Walpole lived, and where he composed *The Castle of Otranto*.

Walpole and Gothic Style

Horatio (Horace) Walpole (1717–97) was the fifth child of Robert Walpole, the first minister of the Whig Party from 1721 to 1742 and leader of the government for some twenty years. Horace inherited from his father both his fortune and his political sympathies. He was also an apologist for his father's artistic taste (if not for his alleged corruption in public office and the subsequent satirical description of him as 'the Great Man' or 'the English Colossus'), and indeed Walpole's first published book, *Ædes Walpolianæ* (1747), was a catalogue of the paintings at his father's seat of Houghton Hall, Norfolk, detailing its extensive art collection. Horace Walpole was educated at Eton College and King's College, Cambridge, went on the Grand Tour with his schoolfriend and later scholar and poet Thomas Gray, and was already a Member of Parliament before he returned to Britain. During his career in the House of Commons he was a political fixer and the author of anonymous pamphlets, and the editor of the essay periodical *The World* and founder of the Strawberry Hill private press, as well as being an incorrigible socialite and an inveterate letter-writer, and ultimately a political memoirist and historian of his own life and times.

In Horace Walpole, the Gothic politics of the Whig Party and the Gothic aesthetics of medievalism came together in building Strawberry Hill and in writing *The Castle of Otranto*; in both, he was a pioneer. Strawberry, as Walpole called his home, started life as Chopp'd Straw Hall, a Thameside Georgian villa which he first leased, then in 1748 purchased. The next year he began transforming Chopp'd Straw Hall into Strawberry Hill. The project, which took many years, was overseen by 'The Committee of Taste': Walpole himself, the antiquarian John Chute, and Richard Bentley, son of the Master of Trinity College, Cambridge. They proposed and imported into Strawberry whatever Gothic architectural features and fragments of interior decoration arrested the attention. Walpole described the first phase of his highly imaginative re-creation of a monastic Gothic architectural style in a letter to the diplomat Horace Mann (12 June 1753). The wallpaper he had commissioned for Strawberry appeared to be anciently, authentically Gothic: 'it is impossible at first sight not to conclude that they contain the history of Attila [the Hun] or Tottila [King of the Ostrogoths], done about the very era'. From the outset, then, Walpole was keenly aware of the challenge he was presenting to classical taste and of the ancient heritage of the Gothic. He went on to describe the miscellany of objects with which the place was stuffed: 'lean windows fattened with rich saints in painted glass . . . and niches full of trophies of old coats of mail, Indian shields made of rhinoceros's hides, broadswords, quivers, long bows, arrows and spears'.[6] It was a heady mix of primordial Gothic with crusading medieval idolatry and the exotic and downright *outré*.

Walpole's preferred practice was casual connoisseurship, a delight in 'trifles' and curiosities. He coined the word 'gloomth' to describe the atmosphere he laboured to create—'one has

---

[6] *Horace Walpole's Correspondence*, ed. W. S. Lewis et al. (London: Oxford University Press, 1937–83), xx. 381.

a satisfaction in imprinting the gloomth of abbeys and cathedrals on one's house'. Just as his Ostrogothic wallpaper miniaturized and domesticated the ancient Goths, so Walpole sought for ways of incarcerating the barbaric and the archaic within the confines of his 'little Gothic castle': in his later illustrated guide, *A Description of the Villa of Mr. Horace Walpole* (1784), he stated that his intention was 'that of exhibiting specimens of Gothic architecture, as collected from standards in cathedrals and chapel-tombs, and shewing how they may be applied to chimney-pieces, cielings, windows, ballustrades, loggias, &c.'.[7] But it was not only in Gothic content but also in the tiny, efflorescing, and contradictory detail that Walpole realized his aim and Strawberry became properly Gothic in the eighteenth-century decorative sense. The effect of all his household Gothicism was deliberately miscellaneous: a heterogeneous jumble of northern architecture and antique artefacts that defied order, symmetry, and classification. Such a mood of disparate intermingling of styles and categorization would also characterize *The Castle of Otranto*.

In many ways, then, Gothic thinking was already at the heart of eighteenth-century politics and antiquarian research, and also in the home. Medievalist styles in architecture, interior decoration, gardening, and design were already well established by the mid-century and became the height of Whiggish fashion. The Goths were popularly agreed to be the bravest of the ancient races and had developed the medieval codes of chivalry; they were considered the originators of heraldic motifs, and enjoyed a battlefield culture of jousts and tournaments—which in the period was translated into a rising popularity of hunting for sport and a fashion for duels. For the more sedentary, this martial Gothic spirit could be played out without stirring from one's chair: as a game of strategy, chess was described as a '*Gothick* Game'.[8] 'Gothic' was also used in printing to describe the black-letter fount, which had

---

[7] *Correspondence*, xx. 111, 372; Horace Walpole, *A Description of the Villa of Mr. Horace Walpole, youngest son of Sir Robert Walpole Earl of Orford, at Strawberry-Hill near Twickenham, Middlesex* (Twickenham, 1784), i [italics reversed].

[8] William King, 'Animadversions on the Pretended Account of Danmark', *Miscellanies in Prose and Verse* (London, [1709]), 51–2.

associations of the earliest presses and medieval literature, as well as the Protestant Bible in English and the publication of Acts of Parliament.

In these rich political and architectural contexts—of anti-classicism, the politics of freedom, medievalism, and the impact of the Reformation—the influence of Gothic thinking on literature was inevitable. Predictably, Gothic literary style was another point of contention. As early as 1570 Roger Ascham had complained in *The Schoolmaster* that the English obsession with rhyming verses revealed the malign influence of the Goths, and a century later Dryden made the same complaint, attributing the introduction of rhyme in Romance verse (Italian, Spanish, French, and English) to the mingling of Gothic and Vandal languages with Roman Latin. Dryden was not at all sympathetic to the effect of the Gothic language on classical tongues. He describes modern Latin as 'rolling down thro' so many barbarous ages, from the Spring of *Virgil*', its linguistic purity polluted by the Goths: 'it bears along with it the filth and ordures of the *Goths* and *Vandals*'.[9] Even the eighteenth-century Whig aristocrat Anthony Ashley Cooper, Earl of Shaftesbury, despaired of 'the GOTHICK *Model* of Poetry' as 'the horrid Discord of jingling Rhyme'.[10] Indeed, elements of so-called 'Gothic' language and literary style were spoofed in *The Tatler* in the character of 'Ned Softly', an English poet noted for 'the little *Gothick* Ornaments of Epigrammatical Conceits, Turns, Points, and Quibbles, which are so frequent in the most admired of our *English* Poets'.[11]

Nevertheless, the rising vogue for Gothic decorative styles in home and garden decor helped to stimulate an increasing attention to the Gothic features of English literature: just as Thomas Warton's 'modern Gothic' architecture was characterized by a profusion of ornamentation, so English literature could be

---

[9] John Dryden (tr.), *The Works of Virgil: Containing his Pastorals, Georgics and Æneis*, 3 vols, 3rd edn (1709), i. 8 [italics reversed].

[10] Anthony Ashley Cooper, Earl of Shaftesbury, *Characteristicks of Men, Manners, Opinions, Times*, 3 vols, 5th edn (1732), i. 217.

[11] Richard Steele, *The Lucubrations of Isaac Bickerstaff Esq*, 4 vols (1716), iii. 243 (*The Tatler*, No. 163).

distinguished by a comparable elaboration of style. Indeed, according to Warton the original 'Gothic state' of St Paul's, 'one of the noblest patterns of that kind of architecture', had inspired John Milton's poem 'Il Penseroso'.[12] Similarly, the ecclesiastic and literary commentator Richard Hurd endeavoured to demystify the Middle Ages by contextualizing the attitudes and values of medieval society, connecting the unfamiliar, remote, and strange to the everyday and recognizable: linking romantic allegory, for instance, with gardening.[13] His aim is restorative, considering how chivalry, 'this *Prodigy*, which we now start at', emerged in the medieval period, and what societal purposes it served.[14] The implication is that contemporary social roles, such as masculinity, need to be tailored to current needs and that the Gothic spirit can be adapted to a modern version of chivalry and manners in the drawing rooms of England. Making the Gothic more homely chimed with Walpole's own vision for Strawberry, and presented modern writers with a possible new literary genealogy.

These more holistic models of Gothic style drew on Sir William Temple's influential essay 'Of Poetry' (1690). Temple, a political theorist, describes the advent of English poetry as the consequence of the conversion of the Gothic tribes to Christianity and their consequent social development. Accordingly, the Goths laid the foundations of culture—particularly of literary culture. While Temple agreed that the Goths invented rhyme, he placed this innovation within the powerful cultural context of literacy. The Goths, it was imagined, wrote in a Runic alphabet comparable in the development of written language to the Hieroglyphs of ancient Egypt. The practitioners of this literate art, the 'Runers', were therefore subsequently proposed to be an intellectual caste, who 'studied Nature, Astronomy and Magick, and without their Advice nothing of publick Importance was transacted; thus highly were they reverenced for their Familiarity with Devils, whom with

---

[12] Thomas Warton, *Observations on the Faerie Queene of Spenser* (London, 1754), 246 [1762 edn, ii. 135].

[13] Richard Hurd, *Letters on Chivalry and Romance* (1762), 67: see Appendix to the present edition.

[14] Hurd, *Letters on Chivalry and Romance*, 10.

supream Veneration they adored'.[15] The central position afforded
to the Runers meant that laws, governance, and literature, as well
as magic and prophecy, were embodied in the same figure.

Temple also considered the effect of the Gothic spirit on the
content of Runic poetry. Runic poetry was characterized by unrestrained flights of fancy, the sorcery of the Runers. This was the
literature of enchantments, the use of 'Incantation and Charms,
pretending by them to raise Storms, to calm the Seas, to cause
Terror in their Enemies, to transport themselves in the Air, to
conjure Spirits, to cure Diseases, and stanch bleeding Wounds,
to make Women kind or easy, and Men hard or invulnerable'.
The Runers were thus the originators of wizardry and witchcraft,
and hence from the Gothic imagination ('*Gothick* Wit') 'may be
derived, all the visionary Tribe of *Fairies*, *Elves*, and *Goblins*, of
Sprites and of *Bulbeggars* . . . '.[16] Temple went on to argue that
medieval Spanish Romances were likewise the product of '*Gothick*
Wit', identifying the tradition with the eerie Catholicism of the
Middle Ages. This version of Gothic literature was profoundly
political, violently martial, extravagantly magical, and resolutely
non-classical. Its savage primitivism and weird supernaturalism is
captured in Pope's early poem 'The Temple of Fame' (published
1715): his account of the distorting effects of the mirror-like walls
in the Gothic façade of the temple building is unnervingly dream-
like, and also evokes contemporary visual effects such as magic
lantern shows. The Gothic is already perceived to be the portal to
a realm of nightmare.

Nightmares could be conjured in other ways as well. The
crumbling abbeys and monasteries that lay strewn across the
countryside after the Reformation gradually became sites of
poetic reflection and meditation. They were an inspiration: physical embodiments of the shattered historical record and of human
futility, and they gave impetus to the later eighteenth-century

---

[15] John Webb, *A Vindication of Stone-Heng Restored: in which the Orders and Rules of Architecture Observed by the Ancient Romans, are Discussed*, 2nd edn (1725), 86.

[16] William Temple, 'Of Poetry', *The Works of Sir William Temple, Bart.*, 2 vols (1720), i. 243–4.

school of melancholy—Mark Akenside's *Pleasures of Imagination* (1744), Robert Blair's *The Grave* (1743), and Thomas Warton's *Pleasures of Melancholy* (1747)—writers who treated the 'dark backward and abyss of time' as an opportunity for meditation and the annihilation of subjectivity.[17] Yet later poets who found their inspiration in the past and in ancient British history, such as Walpole's friend and correspondent Thomas Gray, were confronted with the uneasy recognition of cruelty and violence that characterized history and drove forward the myths of civilization: national history itself became a burden for the poet to shoulder. The Battle of Culloden, in which the supporters of the Stuart claim to the throne had met defeat at the hands of the Hanoverian army, was fought in 1746 and had been followed by the ruthless massacre of the Jacobite clans. It was a reminder of the terrible secrets of bloodshed that lay at the heart of Whig history. Thus in Gray's poem 'The Bard' (1757) the aesthetics of the sublime and fashionable melancholia are mixed with an ominous fascination with the cost of English political progress and the gradual genesis of British identity, achieved through the liquidation of Welsh culture. And by addressing the horrors of the present through the mystical past these poems, and the sites that aroused them, did not remain confined in the depths of melancholy despair, but engaged and enlarged the soul: as such they were sublime.

The sublime was an aesthetic effect first analysed by the classical critic Longinus in his treatise *Peri Hypsos* as a grand style in writing concomitant with notions of freedom and hence political liberty. Through William Smith's 1739 translation the sublime became part of eighteenth-century culture, and in *A Philosophical Enquiry into the Origin of our Ideas of the Sublime and Beautiful* (1757) Edmund Burke, later to be the leading 'Old Whig' statesman, in turn identified and adapted the sublime as recognizably English and of course Whiggish. Burke argued that the sublime was experienced when the mind encountered and endeavoured to comprehend the infinite. The key to the sublime was the imagination, which worked most

---

[17] William Shakespeare, *The Tempest*, I. ii. 50.

powerfully when confronted with obscurity and losing itself in intimations of eternity and boundless immensity. For Burke, mistiness and murmured sounds, night and death, *Paradise Lost* and Stonehenge were mysterious, obscure, and potentially sublime, rousing the imagination to escape its own limitations. In its aesthetic extremism, Burke's *Philosophical Enquiry* became a template for the Gothic imagination.

The strange alchemy that blended sublimity with medieval architecture, social progress with the nightmare of history, ruins with ghosts, the defiance of classical convention with national identity, and ultimately politics with culture, was irresistibly potent, and Walpole was searching for a literary idiom that was recognizably Whiggish—a literature that reflected and scrutinized the political credo of the Whig Party. 'I . . . am a Whig to the backbone', he declared in 1755, and later wrote to the Revd William Cole on 10 June 1778,

We were never a great and happy country till the Revolution [i.e. of 1688]. The system of these days tended to overturn and has overturned that establishment, and brought on the disgraces that ever attended the foolish and wicked councils of the house of Stuart. If man is a rational being, he has a right to make use of his reason, and to enjoy his liberty. We, we alone almost, had a constitution that every other nation upon earth envied or ought to envy.[18]

In the 'gloomth' of Strawberry Hill he found what he sought. Gothic aesthetics and Gothic politics came together. Above Walpole's bed were copies of both the Magna Carta and the execution order for Charles I; it was in this bed that he dreamed of the castle of Otranto.[19]

'A Gothic Story'

It is clearly within the diverse contexts of constitutional monarchy, parliamentary union, the Reformation, medievalism, and anticlassicism, not to mention barbarity, savagery, freedom, chivalry,

[18] *Correspondence*, xxxvii. 406; 2. 89.   [19] Walpole, *Description*, 41.

the poetics of melancholy, and literary eccentricity that Walpole subtitled the second edition of *The Castle of Otranto* 'A Gothic Story'. But he had already formulated a working cultural definition of the Gothic before he ever envisaged *Otranto*. In his *Anecdotes of Painting in England* (first published in 1762), Walpole fundamentally reassessed the Gothic via the elusive concept of 'taste'. He laments the Reformation and Civil Wars on grounds of taste ('that destruction of ancient monuments and gothic piles and painted glass') and considers Gothic architecture as 'a species of modern elegance'. Most daringly, he declares that 'One must have taste to be sensible of the beauties of Grecian architecture; one only wants passions to feel Gothic. . . . Gothic churches infuse superstition; Grecian, admiration . . .'.[20]

Within two years of this combative declaration, Walpole had written *The Castle of Otranto*. The novel is set in Italy in the late Middle Ages, just before the English Reformation, drawing on the political machinations of thirteenth-century Sicily. Medievalist Gothic thus becomes the setting for an extreme family drama of legitimacy and inheritance, political intrigue and arranged marriages, sudden death, incest, and lust. The story is fixated with Gothic Whig imagery, mixing anxieties over succession and power politics with magical Catholicism and extreme and incredible occurrences, all set in a haunted and collapsing castle. The story begins with a dreadful and inexplicable calamity: the sudden, bizarre appearance of a huge, unearthly helmet, which kills the heir to the principality of Otranto on his wedding day. Following this macabre event the narrative is driven with demonic intensity by the tempestuous and tyrannical moods and stratagems of his father—Manfred, Prince of Otranto—who, rather than mourning his dead son, turns his malevolent attentions and frustrated desires on his adoptive step-daughter, Isabella. The culmination of this headlong plot, which takes place almost exclusively in shadows, twilight, or complete darkness, is in a supernatural revelation

---

[20] Horace Walpole, *Anecdotes of Painting in England; with Some Account of the Principal Artists; and Incidental Notes on Other Arts*, 4 vols (Twickenham, 1762–3 [1762–80]), i. 107–8: see Appendix.

and an ensuing and devastating melancholy. The novel frequently teeters on the verge of absurdity, but if one can grasp the imaginative preoccupations of the period, *Otranto* is utterly eerie.

The Castle of Otranto is intensely claustrophobic in its setting and entirely unrelenting in its passion. The action is split between seemingly capricious yet uncannily prescient external forces, and the psychological turmoil of the characters. Walpole's almost morbidly pathological sensitivity to the torrents and tides of emotion is characteristic of novels of sensibility of the time, seen most genially in Sterne's *A Sentimental Journey* (1768)—although such novels tend to focus on domestic travails rather than the stupendous events that take place in Walpole's forbidding castle, and *Otranto* is anything but genial. Likewise, the movement of the plot, which advances from one set piece to another, is a structural device taken from sentimental fiction as a way of focusing attention on mental states. In *Otranto*, however, sensibility is taken to an extreme, and the combination of supernatural event and mental anguish is magnified to create a stunning melodrama.

Even before *Otranto* had been published, fantastic medievalism had been dismissed as a lunatic dreamworld, antithetical to Enlightenment rationality. John Newbery's *Art of Poetry on a New Plan* (1762), for instance, gave a typical popular description of medievalist Gothic literature:

when the *Roman* empire was over-run by the barbarous and uncultivated nations of the North, polite literature gave way to *Gothic* ignorance and superstition . . . absurd and unmeaning tales of giants, champions, inchanted knights, witches, goblins, and such other monstrous fictions and reveries, as could only proceed from the grossest ignorance, or a distempered brain.[21]

Nevertheless, the Gothic imagination was also gaining credence through its association with the writings of Edmund Spenser, William Shakespeare, and John Milton. Warton and Hurd had argued the case for Spenser's Gothicism, and Burke did so for

---

[21] John Newbery, *The Art of Poetry on a New Plan*, rev. Oliver Goldsmith, 2 vols (London, 1762), ii. 154.

Milton by making the depiction of Death in *Paradise Lost* an exemplar of the sublime. However, it was Shakespeare's Gothic that really confirmed the style.

Walpole himself had already adapted *Macbeth* in his political parody *The Dear Witches* (1742), and in *Historic Doubts on the Life and Reign of Richard the Third* (1768) he discusses the Gothicism of *The Winter's Tale*, in which a statue animates to redress the wrongs of the past—the wrongs in this case being not Leontes' impetuosity but Shakespeare's own propagandist play *Richard III*. By then, Samuel Johnson's Preface to his edition of Shakespeare (1765) had characterized Shakespeare's use of supernatural folkloric elements as Gothic, recalling Sir William Temple's early invocation of 'all the visionary Tribe of *Fairies*': in *A Midsummer Night's Dream*, Johnson argues that 'we see the loves of *Theseus* and *Hippolyta* combined with the Gothick mythology of fairies'.[22] Shakespeare was Gothic in so far that he was English; wrote more English history plays than any other playwright of the time; virtually ignored the classical unities of action, time, and plot; and mixed high and low characters. His plays also include more ghosts and supernatural events than the dramas of any of his contemporaries (with the exception of Christopher Marlowe's *Dr Faustus*).

Otranto is drenched in Shakespearean allusion, as well as a more general sense of Shakespearean dynamics of character, scenes and plot. Walpole claimed in the Preface to the first edition of 1764 that 'Every thing tends directly to the catastrophe' and drew attention to the theatrical elements of the narrative, which takes place within an explicit five-act structure. Walpole therefore effectively canonizes Shakespeare as Gothic. Moreover, in the Preface to the second edition of 1765, Walpole mobilizes Shakespeare against the literary conventions and restrictions of European neo-classicism. In particular, his antipathy to the French rules is lucidly laid out in the second Preface to *Otranto*, and as he later argued in the Prologue to *The Mysterious Mother* (1768), 'Shall foreign critics teach you how to think?':

[22] William Shakespeare, *The Plays of William Shakespeare*, ed. Samuel Johnson, 8 vols (1765), i, p. xxi.

> Shakespeare's magic dignified the stage,
> If timid laws had school'd th' insipid age?
> Had Hamlet's spectre trod the midnight round?
> Or Banquo's issue been in vision crown'd?
> Free as your country, Britons, be your scene!
> Be Nature now, and now Invention, queen![23]

These thoughts were further reiterated in a letter to Mme Deffand written on 13 March 1767, in which he described the genesis of *Otranto*:

I gave reign to my imagination; visions and passions choked me. I wrote it in spite of rules, critics, and philosophers; it seems to me the better for that. I am even persuaded that in the future, when taste will be restored to the place now occupied by philosophy, my poor *Castle* will find admirers.[24]

If Walpole drew much from the escalating Gothic culture, his complaint to Mme Deffand also reveals his trailblazing innovation in *Otranto* in his integrated use of supernatural plot devices. The supernatural was already an established genre in the period—both Daniel Defoe and Samuel Johnson wrote prose on the subject, and Isaac Watts composed dream poetry—but Walpole was the first to blend the varieties of medievalist Gothic, from romance and Shakespeare to architecture and politics, with an eerie narrative permeated (and indeed partly inspired) by dreams. In doing so, he deliberately placed the Gothic within the realms of Burke's sublime and established it as a style that could analyse trauma and challenge taboos. As a literary genre, this would prove to have extraordinary longevity.

Walpole's primary innovation was to allow dreams to direct the action. The Horatian epigraph Walpole prefixed to the second and subsequent editions was subtly altered to read '*vanae* | *fingentur species, tamen ut pes, et caput uni* | *reddantur formae*': 'idle fancies shall be shaped [like a sick man's dream] so that neither head nor

---

[23] Horace Walpole, *The Castle of Otranto: A Gothic Story, and, The Mysterious Mother: A Tragedy*, ed. Frederick S. Frank (Peterborough, Ontario: Broadview, 2011), 175–6.
[24] *Correspondence*, iii. 260 (French original; standard translation).

foot can be assigned to a single shape'.[25] 'Do I dream?' ask both
Manfred and Matilda, while Frederic and Ricardo are successively
influenced by dreams. The whole work was in fact inspired by
a dream, as Walpole claimed in a letter to William Cole (9 March
1765):

Your partiality to me and Strawberry have I hope inclined you to excuse
the wildness of the story. You will even have found some traits to put you
in mind of this place. When you read of the picture quitting its panel, did
not you recollect the portrait of Lord Falkland all in white in my gallery?
Shall I even confess to you what was the origin of this romance? I waked
one morning in the beginning of last June from a dream, of which, all
I could recover was, that I had thought myself in an ancient castle (a very
natural dream for a head filled like mine with Gothic story) and that
on the uppermost banister of a great staircase I saw a gigantic hand in
armour. In the evening I sat down and began to write, without knowing
in the least what I intended to say or relate. The work grew on my hands,
and I grew fond of it—add that I was very glad to think of anything
rather than politics—In short I was so engrossed with my tale, which
I completed in less than two months, that one evening I wrote from the
time I had drunk my tea, about six o'clock, till half an hour after one
in the morning, when my hand and fingers were so weary, that I could
not hold the pen to finish the sentence, but left Matilda and Isabella
talking, in the middle of a paragraph. You will laugh at my earnestness,
but if I have amused you by retracing with any fidelity the manners of
ancient days, I am content, and give you leave to think me as idle as you
please.[26]

The romance tradition is evident here, as is modern Gothic architecture and martial culture as well as the immediate pressures of
politics—all submerged into a dream. Walpole later excused his
attraction to medievalism as it stimulated his dreams, writing
again to Cole (12 July 1778),

I like Popery, as well as you, and have shown I do. I like it as I do chivalry and romance. They all furnish one with ideas and visions, which

[25] Horace Walpole, *The Castle of Otranto*, ed. W. S. Lewis (Oxford: Oxford University Press, 1964), pp. xii–xiii.
[26] *Correspondence*, i. 88.

Presbyterianism does not. A Gothic church or convent fill one with romantic dreams . . .[27]

Yet just as the Gothic continued to retain its pejorative senses throughout the century, dreams were not held by all to be visionary experiences—they could just as easily be 'idle fancies'. Indeed, Walpole's circle of friends and correspondents discussed *Otranto* among themselves, and G. J. Williams wrote disparagingly to George Selwyn on 19 March 1765, less than three months after publication:

It consists of ghosts and enchantments; pictures walk out of their frames, and are good company for half an hour together; helmets drop from the moon, and cover half a family. He says it was a dream, and I fancy one when he had some feverish disposition in him.[28]

But by introducing dreams Walpole was able to give voice to the repressed that hung behind the Gothic myth like a nightmare—all that slaughter driving the granting of liberties, all that blood oiling the progress of the constitution. And by summoning images from dreams, Walpole showed that Gothic, far from being an antiquarian knot of historical, political, social, and cultural theories, could instead be a metaphor for the less tangible anxieties and traumas of the human condition. That is why dreams were dangerous—they could tell unpalatable truths. Hester (Thrale) Piozzi told a most sinister tale of Samuel Johnson's fear of dreams:

one day when my son was going to school, and dear Dr. Johnson followed as far as the garden gate, praying for his salvation, in a voice which those who listened attentively, could hear plain enough, he said to me suddenly, 'Make your boy tell you his dreams: the first corruption that entered into my heart was communicated in a dream.' What was it, Sir? said I. '*Do not ask me*,' replied he with much violence, and walked away in apparent agitation. I never durst make any further enquiries.[29]

---

[27] Ibid. ii. 100.
[28] Ibid. xxx. 177.
[29] Hester Lynch Piozzi, *Anecdotes of the Late Samuel Johnson, LL.D.* (London, 1786), 20.

Dreams also animate the supernatural aspects, enabling all that is unearthly. *Otranto* features ghostly figures, the walking dead, and spirits that emerge from painted panels and that slam doors. As Shakespeare's ghosts often direct the action—the ghost of King Hamlet, Banquo's ghost, the pageant of the dead who are manifested to Richard III—the spirits that haunt *Otranto* are active and interventionist. Ghost scenes were central to eighteenth-century stage adaptations of Shakespeare's plays, but there was also more serious work being performed in this unnatural realm, such as Dom Augustin Calmet's comprehensive antiquarian analysis of the conditions and extent of popular belief in supernatural figures published in French in 1746 and English in 1759: *Dissertations upon the Apparitions of Angels, Dæmons, and Ghosts, and Concerning the Vampires of Hungary, Bohemia, Moravia, and Silesia*. Despite this burgeoning scholarship, though, for Walpole the appearance of the Ghost in *Hamlet* was the degree zero of the supernatural, repeatedly replayed in *Otranto*. The novel dramatizes the soothsaying qualities of ghosts, the dead who still have truth to tell, the secrets that will come out. Writing to George Montagu on 5 January 1766, Walpole remarked,

Visions, you know, have always been my pasture; and so far from growing old enough to quarrel with their emptiness, I almost think there is no wisdom comparable to that of exchanging what is called the realities of life for dreams. Old castles, old pictures, old histories, and the babble of old people make one live back into centuries that cannot disappoint one. One holds fast and surely what is past. The dead have exhausted their power of deceiving—one can trust Catherine of Medicis now.[30]

It is this saturnine delight about which Thomas Gray wrote to Walpole within a week of publication (30 December 1764), saying that *Otranto* 'engages our attention here, makes some of us cry a little, and all in general afraid to go to bed o' nights. We take it for a translation, and should believe it to be a true story, if it were not for St Nicholas.'[31] Indeed, the publication of *Otranto* on

---

[30] *Correspondence*, x. 192.   [31] Ibid. xiv. 137.

Christmas Eve perhaps reflected the seasonal tradition of telling ghostly stories at this time of the year.

Gray had, in fact, been thought to be the author of *Otranto*. In the first edition, Walpole famously claimed that the work was a translation by William Marshall, Gentleman, of an Italian romance written by Onuphrio Muralto. Walpole's name did not appear anywhere, and he even had the work printed by Thomas Lowndes rather than using his own press at Strawberry Hill, to disguise his authorship further. This may have been simple modesty. Writing to the Earl of Hertford on 26 March 1765, three months after the book had been published and with the first edition of 500 copies sold out, Walpole admitted his authorship:

the success of [*Otranto*] has, at last, brought me to own it, though the wildness of it made me terribly afraid; but it was comfortable to have it please so much, before any mortal suspected the author: indeed, it met with too much honour far, for at last it was universally believed to be Mr Gray's. As all the first impression is sold, I am hurrying out another, with a new preface, which I will send you.[32]

The second edition, with a new Preface as promised, duly appeared in another run of 500 copies on 11 April 1765. There were at least ten further editions by the end of the century.

Walpole's anonymity and self-exclusion from the first edition has attracted much critical discussion—perhaps too much: E. J. Clery goes so far as to suggest that 'The significance of *Otranto* for literary history lies as much in the two Prefaces and their alternative constructions of the text as antiquity or innovation, as it does in the novel itself.'[33] This overstates the case, but the abdication of authorship not only to a pseudonym but also to a historical translation is suggestive of the authenticity debates surrounding James Macpherson's *Ossian* (first published in 1760) and the subsequent Rowley Controversy concerning Thomas Chatterton's medieval poetry (1777–82)—a controversy in which

---

[32] Ibid. xxxviii. 525–6.
[33] Horace Walpole, *The Castle of Otranto*, ed. W. S. Lewis, rev. E. J. Clery (Oxford: Oxford University Press, 1996), p. xi.

Walpole subsequently became embroiled. The issue with both Macpherson and Chatterton was one of literary forgery: they were forgeries of original material that challenged the definitions and conventions of literature and history at the time, and which subsequently metamorphosed into figures of inspiration—of absolute authenticity—for later writers. *Otranto* was certainly inspirational: Clara Reeve's *The Old English Baron* (1777) described itself as 'the literary offspring of the Castle of Otranto',[34] Robert Jephson's *The Count of Narbonne* (1781) successfully dramatized *Otranto* for the stage by internalizing the supernatural action, and by the 1790s Walpole's novel had been effectively canonized. But his authorial obfuscation did not last long—less than four months—and in that sense it was more of a hoax, a literary prank in which Walpole's authorship was in fact encoded in the half-translation of his name into 'Onuphrio Muralto'. However briefly, though, *Otranto* did, like *Ossian* and Rowley, challenge the validity of prefaces and authorial attribution; it also had a calculated political agenda. Just as *Ossian* comprised both a lament and a restitution of Scottish identity, Walpole challenged literature to accommodate Gothic supernaturalism and Whiggish sublimity in a prose narrative.

If Walpole's novel is an active, even risky, aestheticization of the ramifications of the Gothic myth, it is valuable to note that, as Michael Gamer has pointed out, the fictitious translator and editor William Marshall is a Tory, possibly even a Jacobite, republishing a Counter-Reformation narrative about the restoration of a rightful royal dynasty, retrieved from 'the library of an ancient catholic family in the north of England'.[35] Walpole was therefore perhaps positioning the text to be read in its first incarnation as a Tory justification for Stuart rebellion against the House of Hanover, as 'Jacobite Gothick'. The revelation that it was written by a Whig, however, reverses the politics of the novel, which then becomes a study of usurpation and the corrupting extension of a sovereign's

---

[34] Clara Reeve, *The Old English Baron*, ed. James Trainer (Oxford: Oxford University Press, 2008), 2.

[35] Horace Walpole, *The Castle of Otranto*, ed. Michael Gamer (London: Penguin, 2001), p. xxviii.

power. There is a pressing relevance here to the plight in which Walpole found himself in 1764 (and to which he obliquely refers in his confessional letter to Cole of 9 March 1765, quoted above). The novel was written during a period in which Walpole believed that the recently crowned George III was exceeding his powers in using the royal prerogative too frequently and imperiously. More specifically, the government's arguably illegal use of general warrants to imprison and silence the radical firebrand John Wilkes had encouraged Walpole, still an MP, to advise his cousin and political protégé General Henry Seymour Conway to vote against the administration. In consequence, Conway was dismissed both from his regiment and from his position in the Royal Household as Groom of the Bedchamber. Walpole was devastated and wrote a pamphlet to support his friend and relation. For his trouble he was viciously attacked in print: it was strongly insinuated that he was engaged in a homosexual affair with his cousin.

Walpole offered Conway his own inheritance to restore his fortunes—an impetuous act of generosity that would have meant the end of Strawberry Hill. So Walpole had brought about the ruin of Conway and now faced ruin himself. But that was not all: despite his defence of Wilkes's rights, like many commentators Walpole also feared that the riotous behaviour of Wilkesites could easily break out into open rebellion: 'My nature shuddered at the thought of blood.'[36] If Walpole claimed that he wrote *Otranto* to escape the political circus that had suddenly engulfed him, then that political dilemma is inscribed within the text in the plotlines of legitimacy and inheritance and the precariousness of the castle of Otranto itself, which is falling into ruin from almost the very first page. The shadow of losing Strawberry was hanging over Walpole, and hangs over the novel; likewise, the instability of rulers and the threat of civil strife looms over both England in the eighteenth century and Otranto in the twelfth century. Whig ideology is not an abstract feature of the novel, but a means of confronting arbitrary power and the iniquity of despots.

[36] Quoted by Clery, *Otranto*, ed. Lewis, rev. Clery, p. xxx.

Once Walpole admitted to his authorship, the politics of *Otranto* became bifurcated: it could be read either as the work of the Tory cipher 'William Marshall' or of the Whig scapegoat Walpole. In the Preface to the second edition, Walpole claimed that the book blended 'two kinds of romance, the ancient and the modern. In the former, all was imagination and improbability: in the latter, nature is always intended to be, and sometimes has been, copied with success.' His aim, he states, was to place his characters in extreme conditions: 'in short, to make them think, speak and act, as it might be supposed mere men and women would do in extraordinary positions'. And the result was 'a new species of romance'. The doubled politics—and Walpole's own ghastly predicament—have been transformed into a stylistic bind: more formal, more self-consciously literary. With Walpole's admission of authorship, *Otranto* shifts from being an antiquarian find such as Walpole might have displayed in one of his cabinets of curiosities to become a daringly experimental novel, inextricable from its contexts and dramatizing the author's fear of impending disgrace and the collapse of all his dreams—like his own characters he was *in extremis*.

Walpole's blend of 'two kinds of romance' proposed in the second Preface can also be read as alluding to unnatural union, echoing the perverse kinship relations and transgressions in the novel. The threat of parent–child incest (or rather, parent–adoptive child incest) is frequently referred to as *Otranto*'s heart of darkness. In one reading, parent–child incest is finally consummated by a fatal mistake, in another it is a form of sexual 'atrocity' that stands in for repressed homosexual desire and is thus an expression of the (unfounded) accusation of homosexuality against Walpole.[37] However, while *Otranto* was undeniably written against the background of the scandal involving his cousin—to whom Walpole admitted he was very close—homosexual desire is entirely absent from the novel. Manfred's incipient incest is not the repression of

---

[37] George Haggerty, 'Literature and Homosexuality in the Late Eighteenth Century: Walpole, Beckford, and Lewis', *Studies in the Novel* 18 (1986), 341–52. Haggerty covers the whole psychoanalytic gamut in his claim that the novel is a symptom of repressed and frustrated homosexual desire.

his desire for other men; rather it is a generational transgression: the unnerving lust of an older man for a younger woman (although even this reading is not entirely borne out by the text). And in any case, Walpole soon demonstrated in his play *The Mysterious Mother* (1768) that he was quite capable of writing explicitly about Oedipal desire and double-incest.

Although there is no evidence that Walpole was homosexual, nevertheless *Otranto* patently has elements of erotic fantasy. There are highly charged chance meetings and rendezvous, characters repeatedly find themselves in compromising situations (another conceit of the sentimental novel), women are hunted and pursued, as well as being courted, entangled in intrigue, and in receipt of declarations of chivalric love and devotion. With much of the action seeming to take place at night, or at least in twilight, and at times in underground tunnels and caves, the darkness becomes palpable. The threat of imminent sexual assault is almost overpowering, but again there is more to this than suggestively erotic metaphors of subterranean shafts—it is symptomatic of Walpole's Whiggish artistic creed. As one critic has pointed out, 'The maze of dark, twisting passageways underlying the Castle refers iconographically to the terminal "amazement" of the characters': the 'amazement' here is not simple incredulity or bewilderment, but is crucially the annihilating impact of a multiplied sublime.[38] The text is steeped in Burke's sublime—'that state of the soul, in which all its motions are suspended, with some degree of horror'—evident in the repetitions of words such as 'impetuous' and 'stupendous', the recurrence of phrases such as 'words cannot paint', and Manfred's moments of paralysed stupefaction.[39] The rhetoric of the eighteenth-century sublime is thus positioned as the central pillar of Whig aesthetics, and the union of poetic passion, originality, and spontaneity with political democracy and Protestant Christianity. It became the sacrament that reified the Gothic in literature. Walpole was, if not its pope, certainly its archbishop.

---

[38] *Otranto*, ed. Frank, 20.   [39] Burke, *Philosophical Enquiry*, 53.

Such sublime effects have since become standard Gothic fare, although the closest Walpole's readers would have come to them before *Otranto* would have been in the theatre, where charged encounters, murderous assailants, and the disorientating utility of trapdoors were regularly deployed. But even if incidents such as headlong flight through pitch-black passages, candles blowing out, and the unhoped-for salvation of secret doors have become formulaic, in *Otranto* they should be read as striking novelties. They are also the inescapable consequences of what could be called the 'Strawberry factor' in the novel. Walpole called Strawberry his 'Otranto', and concluded his Preface to his *Description* of Strawberry by remarking that his home was 'the scene that inspired, the author of the Castle of Otranto'.[40] The novel itself is packed with Strawberryisms, from the cloisters and dark passages to the metonymic projections of the funerary statue and Theodore's suggestive resemblance to Alfonso's portrait: character and destiny and life, in the novel, are forged from art, collecting, and antiquarianism. Enigmatic archaeological discoveries such as the massive sabre are reported, and pictures—real pictures, that Walpole had hanging in Strawberry—come to life. The statue of Alfonso, both a memorial and a work of art, is like a refrain that runs through the book, dismembered like so many antiquarian fragments, and yet an authentic relic through which the dead can act and utter. As Catholicism venerated its saintly relics, so eighteenth-century connoisseurs and antiquarians valued artefacts with suggestive associations and *bona fide* provenance; among his own collection Walpole himself had hair from the head of Edward IV. The supreme antiquarian artefact of the novel, the castle of Otranto itself—an early haunted house—may well also be the book's central protagonist. It is certainly an irresistible lure, and keeps drawing characters back to its baleful thrall. Its spell can only be broken when it is razed to the ground.

Just as Strawberry was as much a textual construct minutely described in Walpole's *Description* as it was a physical dwelling

---

[40] Walpole, *Description*, iv [italics reversed].

and tourist attraction, so *Otranto* is critically conscious of its own literary and linguistic being, and through his writing Walpole contemplates how meaning is amassed and collated. The language in which the tale is told is archaic and deliberately formal. Like Macpherson's *Ossian* (in which events also take place almost exclusively in the dark), the characters speak as if in translation, and like *Ossian* too, there are no similes—this is a world in which language is rooted in direct experience. Meaning comes unexpectedly—from an inscribed sword or from marks on the body. Terror and horror are inexorably 'imprinted' on minds and hearts over their palimpsests of feeling. An 'ancient prophecy' is quoted on the first page, the words of the past structuring the present, warning the reader of the inescapability of history made manifest, a history that will dwarf the present state of affairs by its gigantic implications and effects—thus dramatizing Whig fears of the cost of progress. There are competing narratives throughout: Manfred's account of his marriage is set against Jerome's doctrine, the story of his usurpation is contested by Theodore's true status. History is plainly not a grand narrative for Walpole. Instead it is a vast and intricately worked tapestry, tattered in many places, repaired in others, that does not illustrate so much as embody the fertile energy of Gothicism. This version of history, like the obliteratingly imprinted sensibilities of the protagonists, is sublime. And it cannot be ignored.

If the eighteenth century witnessed an increasingly wide application of the Gothic and its cognates in a bewildering array of different fields, they remained rooted in historical and archaeological researches, in political and constitutional theory, in an escalating medievalism, and in an aesthetic that mixed the sublime with melancholy, nostalgia with the repression of history, and mortality with the revival of the past. The months in which *The Castle of Otranto* was composed and published can be seen as the culmination of these concerns, and Walpole himself certainly saw his novel as a product of its time. As he wrote to Hannah More on 13 November 1784:

It was fit for nothing but the age in which it was written, an age in which much was known; that required only to be amused, nor cared whether its amusements were conformable to truth and the models of good sense; that could not be spoiled; was in no danger of being too credulous; and rather wanted to be brought back to imagination, than to be led astray by it.[41]

In the 1760s English literature was captivated first by the shadowy doom of *Ossianic* bards and Celts, and then by the resplendent majesty of the Middle Ages, and archaic Britain proved to be a fertile inspiration for pioneering work on cultural history. But it was also the decade in which the Gothic, as literary fiction, was forged; we are yet to escape its deadly embrace.

[41] *Correspondence*, xxxi. 221.

NOTE ON THE TEXT

THE copy text for this edition is the version prepared by Walpole for *The Works of Horatio Walpole, Earl of Orford*, published in five volumes in 1798 and seen through the press after his death by his close friend Mary Berry. The 1798 edition makes minor amendments and modifications to the text, such as dispensing with the italicization of proper nouns—a feature that remained until the sixth edition, published by James Dodsley in 1791. The text of the present edition is not modernized further beyond correcting minor typographical errors and regularizing the long 's', and contemporary conventions are thus preserved. The most notable of these is in the presentation of direct speech, which is not distinguished by quotation marks or paragraph breaks. Although this may create an obstacle for modern readers, the claustrophobic atmosphere of *The Castle of Otranto* is deepened by the headlong rapidity of dialogue, creating a clamour of voices that overlap and run into the narrative itself. To clarify this by distinguishing speakers with modern punctuation and layout would remove both a distinctive Walpolean feature and also stall the action; hence these elements have not been tampered with. In fact the seventh edition of the novel, published by Wenman and Hodgson in 1793, did comprehensively modernize Walpole's punctuation, but this innovation was evidently felt to be misguided and was not adopted in subsequent lifetime editions.

Care has been taken to ensure that the two varieties of long dashes deployed in the text are faithfully reproduced: these marks (— and ——) are used to herald direct speech, mark breaks and pauses, and distinguish parenthetical clauses or distinct phrases. Walpole's idiosyncratic use of square brackets is explained in the notes. An asterisk in the text signals the presence of a note in the Explanatory Notes at the back of the book.

SELECT BIBLIOGRAPHY

Life and Other Related Works

Alexander, Catherine M. S., '*The Dear Witches*: Horace Walpole's *Macbeth*', *Review of English Studies* n.s. 49.194 (1998), 131–44.

Baines, Paul, 'This Theatre of Monstrous Guilt: Horace Walpole and the Drama of Incest', *Studies in Eighteenth-Century Culture* 28 (1999), 287–309.

Coykendall, Abby, 'Chance Enlightenments, Choice Superstitions: Walpole's Historic Doubts and Enlightenment Historicism', *The Eighteenth Century* 54.1 (2013), 53–70.

Haggerty, George E., 'Walpoliana', *Eighteenth-Century Studies* 34.2 (2001), 227–49.

Harney, Marion, *Place-Making for the Imagination: Horace Walpole and Strawberry Hill* (Farnham: Ashgate, 2013).

Ketton-Cremer, R. W., *Horace Walpole: A Biography* (London: Methuen, 1964).

Langford, Paul, 'Horace Walpole', *ODNB*.

Lewis, W. S., 'The Genesis of Strawberry Hill', *Metropolitan Museum Studies* 5.1 (June 1934), 57–92.

—— *Horace Walpole: The A. W. Mellon Lectures in the Fine Arts, 1960* (London: Hart-Davis, 1961).

Lilley, James D., 'Studies in Uniquity: Horace Walpole's Singular Collection', *English Literary History* 80.1 (2013), 93–124.

Mowl, Timothy, *Horace Walpole: The Great Outsider* (London: John Murray, 1996).

Plumb, J. H., *Sir Robert Walpole*, 2 vols (London: Cresset Press, 1956–60).

Sabor, Peter (ed.), *Horace Walpole: The Critical Heritage* (London and New York: Routledge & Kegan Paul, 1987).

Silver, Sean R., 'Visiting Strawberry Hill: Horace Walpole's Gothic Historiography', *Eighteenth Century Fiction* 21.4 (2009), 535–64.

Snodin, Michael, and Roman, Cynthia Ellen, *Horace Walpole's Strawberry Hill* (New Haven: Yale University Press, 2009).

Architecture and Antiquarianism

Andrews, Malcolm, *The Search for the Picturesque: Landscape, Aesthetics, and Tourism in Britain, 1760–1800* (Stanford: Stanford University Press, 1989).

Baridon, Michel, 'Ruins as a Mental Construct', *Journal of Garden History* 5 (1985), 84–96.

Brooks, Chris, *The Gothic Revival* (London: Phaidon, 1999).

Charlesworth, Michael, *The Gothic Revival, 1720–1870: Literary Sources & Documents*, 3 vols (Mountfield: Helm Information, 2002).

Hebron, Stephen, *The Romantics and the British Landscape* (London: British Library, 2006).

Kidd, Colin, *British Identities before Nationalism: Ethnicity and Nationhood in the Atlantic World, 1600–1800* (Cambridge: Cambridge University Press, 1999).

Kliger, Samuel, *The Goths in England: A Study in Seventeenth and Eighteenth Century Thought* (Cambridge, Mass.: Harvard University Press, 1952).

Morrissey, Lee, *From the Temple to the Castle: An Architectural History of British Literature, 1660–1760* (Charlottesville: University Press of Virginia, 1999).

Pocock, J. G. A., *The Ancient Constitution and the Feudal Law* (Cambridge: Cambridge University Press, 1987).

Smith, R. J., *The Gothic Bequest: Medieval Institutions in British Thought, 1688–1863* (Cambridge: Cambridge University Press, 1987).

Stewart, David, 'Political Ruins: Gothic Sham Ruins and the '45', *Journal of the Society of Architectural Historians* 55.4 (1996), 400–11.

Sweet, Rosemary, *Antiquaries: The Discovery of the Past in Eighteenth-Century Britain* (London: Hambledon, 2004).

Womersley, David (ed.), *'Cultures of Whiggism': New Essays on English Literature and Culture in the Long Eighteenth Century* (Newark: University of Delaware Press, 2005).

Gothic Literary Criticism

Brown, Marshall, *The Gothic Text* (Stanford: Stanford University Press, 2005).

Castle, Terry, *The Female Thermometer: Eighteenth-Century Culture and the Invention of the Uncanny* (New York and Oxford: Oxford University Press, 1995).

Clery, E. J., *The Rise of Supernatural Fiction, 1762–1800* (Cambridge: Cambridge University Press, 1999).

Davenport-Hines, Richard, *Gothic: 400 Years of Excess, Horror, Evil and Ruin* (London: Fourth Estate, 1998).

Desmet, Christy, and Williams, Anne (eds), *Shakespearean Gothic* (Cardiff: University of Wales Press, 2009).

Drakakis, John, and Townshend, Dale (eds), *Gothic Shakespeares* (London: Routledge, 2008).

Ellis, Markman, *The History of Gothic Fiction* (Edinburgh: Edinburgh University Press, 2000).

Groom, Nick, *The Gothic: A Very Short Introduction* (Oxford: Oxford University Press, 2012).

Haggerty, George, *Queer Gothic* (Urbana: University of Illinois Press, 2006).

Kilgour, Maggie, *The Rise of the Gothic Novel* (Abingdon and New York: Routledge, 1995).

Mack, Ruth, *Literary Historicity: Literature and Historical Experience in Eighteenth-Century Britain* (Stanford: Stanford University Press, 2009).

Miles, Robert, *Gothic Writing, 1750–1820: A Genealogy* (Manchester: Manchester University Press, 2003).

Richter, David, *The Progress of Romance: Literary Historiography and the Gothic Novel* (Columbus: Ohio State University Press, 1996).

Watt, James, *Contesting the Gothic: Fiction, Genre and Cultural Conflict, 1764–1832* (Cambridge: Cambridge University Press, 1999).

Articles on The Castle of Otranto

Bedford, Kristina, ' "This Castle Hath a Pleasant Seat": Shakespearean Allusion in *The Castle of Otranto*', *English Studies in Canada* 14.4 (1988), 415–35.

Campbell, Jill, ' "I Am No Giant": Horace Walpole, Heterosexual Incest, and Love Among Men', *The Eighteenth Century* 39.3 (1998), 238–60.

Chaplin, Sue, ' "Written in the Black Letter": The Gothic and/in the Rule of Law', *Law and Literature* 17.1 (2005), 47–68.

Frank, Marcie, 'Horace Walpole's Family Romances', *Modern Philology* 100.3 (2003), 417–35.

Hamm, Robert B., Jr, '*Hamlet* and Horace Walpole's *The Castle of Otranto*', *Studies in English Literature, 1500–1900* 49.3 (2009), 667–92.

Hogle, Jerrold, 'The Ghost of the Counterfeit and the Genesis of the Gothic', in Allan Lloyd Smith and Victor Sage (eds), *Gothick Origins and Innovations* (Amsterdam and Atlanta: Rodopi, 1994), 23–33.

—— 'The Restless Labyrinth: Cryptonomy in the Gothic Novel', *Arizona Quarterly* 36 (1980), 330–58.

Miles, Robert, 'Nationalism and Abjection' in Fred Botting (ed.), *The Gothic: Essays and Studies 2001* (Cambridge: D. S. Brewer, 2001), 47–86.

Samson, John, 'Politics Gothicized: The Conway Incident and *The Castle of Otranto*', *Eighteenth-Century Life* 10.3 (1986), 145–58.

Further Reading in Oxford World's Classics

Burke, Edmund, *A Philosophical Enquiry into the Origin of our Ideas of the Sublime and Beautiful*, ed. Paul Guyer.

Lewis, Matthew, *The Monk*, ed. Emma McEvoy.

Radcliffe, Ann, *The Italian*, ed. Frederick Garber and E. J. Clery.

—— *The Mysteries of Udolpho*, ed. Bonamy Dobree and Terry Castle.

—— *The Romance of the Forest*, ed. Chloe Chard.

—— *A Sicilian Romance*, ed. Alison Milbank.

Reeve, Clare, *The Old English Baron*, ed. James Turner and James Watt.

A CHRONOLOGY
OF HORACE WALPOLE

	Life	Historical and cultural background
1717	Horatio Walpole born to Robert Walpole and his wife Catherine on 24 September (Old Style) in Arlington Street, London, the last of six children, four of whom survive infancy.	
1721		Robert Walpole becomes the principal ministerial figure and first lord of the Treasury; by the 1730s he is known as the 'prime minister' to George II. Walpole chooses to remain in the House of Commons for his political career; Charles Edward Stuart, the 'Young Pretender', born.
1725		Alexander Pope, edition of Shakespeare; Pope, *Odyssey* (1725–6).
1726		Jonathan Swift, *Gulliver's Travels*.
1727		Death of George I; accession of George II; death of Isaac Newton.
1727–34	Educated at Eton College.	
1728		John Gay, *The Beggar's Opera*; Pope, *The Dunciad*.
1732		Society of Dilettanti founded. William Hogarth, *A Harlot's Progress*.
1733		Excise crisis. Hogarth, *A Rake's Progress*; Pope, *Essay on Man*.
1735–8	Continues his education at King's College, Cambridge.	
1736	Visits father at his Palladian mansion, Houghton Hall, Norfolk, completed the previous year.	Porteous Riots; Gin Act and ensuing riots; statutes against witchcraft repealed.
1737	Death of mother, Lady Walpole. Sir Robert marries his mistress, Maria Skerrett, who herself dies a year later following a miscarriage.	

	Life	*Historical and cultural background*
1738	Leaves Cambridge without taking a degree. His father acquires sinecures for him, providing a secure income without any obligation to work; these include clerk of the estreates, comptroller of the pipe, and usher of the exchequer.	Herculaneum excavated. Samuel Johnson, *London*.
1739	Takes the poet Thomas Gray, his close friend from Eton and Cambridge, on the Grand Tour to France.	War of Jenkins' Ear with Spain; British victory at Porto Bello; Dick Turpin executed.
1740	HW and Gray continue to Italy, witnessing the Catholic rituals of Holy Week at St Peter's and encountering the Old and Young Stuart Pretenders, James III and Prince Charles Edward Stuart. Walpole starts forging the network of contacts that was to make him one of the century's most prolific and engaging correspondents; he also embarks upon a passionate friendship and possibly an affair with Elisabetta Capponi, wife of the Marchese Grifoni.	War of the Austrian Succession. John Dyer, *The Ruins of Rome*; William Stukeley, *Stonehenge*; David Mallet and James Thomson, *Alfred* (containing 'Rule, Britannia'); Samuel Richardson, *Pamela* (1740–2).
1741	HW succumbs to a quinsy (a complication of acute tonsillitis) at Reggio, in Italy; the trip ends in a rift with Gray. While still abroad, HW elected to parliament as MP for Callington in Cornwall (which he never visits); he returns to witness the parliamentary downfall of his father. By then, Robert Walpole has procured for his son sinecures and revenues from public sources that amount to some £3,400 per annum.	Robert Walpole survives 'The Motion', a vote of censure in Parliament; his ministry is weakened in the General Election. Henry Fielding, *Shamela*; David Hume, *Essays, Moral and Philosophical* (1741–2).

	Life	Historical and cultural background
1742	Maiden speech in House of Commons. Publishes the political parody *The Dear Witches*; his 'Sermon on Painting' preached by Sir Robert's chaplain.	Robert Walpole resigns from the House of Commons, is created Earl of Orford, and retires to Houghton Hall, Norfolk; Carteret ministry. Fielding, *Joseph Andrews*; Batty Langley, *Gothic Architecture Improved*; Edward Young, *Night Thoughts* (1742–5).
1743	Completes *Ædes Walpolianæ*, a catalogue of the paintings at Houghton Hall.	George II leads British army to victory over French at Dettingen. Robert Blair, *The Grave*; Fielding, *Jonathan Wild*.
1744	Compliments George II in Commons for valour on the field at Dettingen.	France declares war; 'Broad-Bottom' ministry, led by Pelham. Mark Akenside, *The Pleasures of Imagination*.
1745	Death of Sir Robert, who leaves property and legacies to HW. Reconciled with Gray.	Second Jacobite Rebellion under Prince Charles Edward Stuart. Hogarth, *Marriage-à-la-Mode*; Thomson, *Tancred and Sigismunda, A Tragedy*.
1746	Moves to Windsor.	Jacobites massacred at Culloden; Pelham ministry.
1747	Publishes *Ædes Walpolianæ*; writes anonymously for the press supporting opposition to Pelham ministry. Leases Chopp'd Straw Hall, Twickenham.	Thomas Gray, *Ode on a Distant Prospect of Eton College*; Thomas Warton, *The Pleasures of Melancholy*; Richardson, *Clarissa* (1747–8).
1748	Buys Chopp'd Straw Hall and renames it 'Strawberry Hill'; planning for its conversion into a Gothic pile commences in the next year. Has verses published in Robert Dodsley's miscellany *A Collection of Poems*.	Ruins of Pompeii uncovered. Tobias Smollett, *Roderick Random*; John Cleland, *Memoirs of a Woman of Pleasure* (1748–9).
1749		Fielding, *The History of Tom Jones*.
1750		London earthquakes. Johnson commences *Rambler* essays.
1751	Founds 'The Committee of Taste' to plan the first stage of the conversion of Strawberry, which lasts until 1753. Begins writing *Memoirs*, which are completed in 1791.	Gray, *An Elegy wrote in a Country Churchyard*; Smollett, *Peregrine Pickle*.

Life	Historical and cultural background
1752	Publishes revised edition of *Aedes Walpolianae*; anonymously warns in press of a Stuart plot concerning the heir to the throne, George III.	Gregorian calendar adopted. Fielding, *Amelia*; Charlotte Lennox, *The Female Quixote*.
1753	Begins contributing essays to periodical *The World*.	Charter of British Museum granted. Richard Glover, *Boadicea*; Smollett, *Ferdinand Count Fathom*; Richardson, *Sir Charles Grandison* (1753–4).
1754	Continues parliamentary career as MP for Castle Rising, his father's first seat.	Death of Fielding; Newcastle ministry; Society of Arts founded.
1755	Suffers an attack of the gout, which in time becomes chronic.	Lisbon earthquake. Johnson, *Dictionary* (1755–6).
1756		Seven Years War commences; Pitt–Devonshire ministry. Capitulation of British garrison at Minorca and subsequent arrest of Admiral John Byng. John Brown, *Athelstan*; John Home, *Douglas*; Alban Butler, *Lives of the Saints* (1756–9).
1757	Elected MP for King's Lynn, his father's seat. Establishes the Strawberry Hill printing press, the first private press in the country, to publish *Odes by Mr. Gray*; the press remains in operation until 1789. Publishes *A Letter from Xo Ho, a Chinese Philosopher at London, to his Friend Lien Chi at Peking* in defence of Byng.	Execution of Admiral Byng. Edmund Burke, *A Philosophical Enquiry into the Origin of our Ideas of the Sublime and Beautiful*; Gray, *Odes*.
1758	Second stage of the conversion of Strawberry, including adding the Round Tower, completed in 1763. Prints his Whiggish survey *A Catalogue of the Royal and Noble Authors of England, with Lists of their Works*, and *Fugitive Pieces in Verse and Prose*, dedicated to cousin Henry Seymour Conway.	

	Life	Historical and cultural background
1759		British Museum opens. Johnson, *Rasselas*; Voltaire, *Candide*; Sterne, *Tristram Shandy* (1759–67).
1760		Death of George II and accession of George III. James Macpherson, *Fragments of Ancient Poetry*.
1761		James Macpherson, *Fingal*; Smollett, *Sir Lancelot Greaves*.
1762	Prints the first two volumes of *Anecdotes of Painting in England*; a third volume appears in 1764, a fourth in 1780.	Bute ministry; Cock Lane Ghost; John Wilkes begins *North Briton*. Charles Churchill, *The Ghost*; Richard Hurd, *Letters on Chivalry and Romance*; Thomas Leland, *Longsword*; James Macpherson, *Temora*.
1763		Seven Years War ends with Treaty of Paris; Grenville ministry; Wilkes is arrested on general warrant for publishing the *North Briton*, no. 45.
1764	Conway stripped of his military and civil posts for opposing the issue of general warrants to imprison John Wilkes (11 April). William Guthrie defends the dismissal of Conway in a pamphlet *An Address to the Public, on the Late Dismission of a General Officer*; Walpole replies in *A Counter-Address to the Public*; Guthrie responds savagely in his *Reply to the Counter-Address*. *The Castle of Otranto* finished on 6 August and published by Thomas Lowndes on 24 December, dated '1765'.	Expulsion of Wilkes from House of Commons. Voltaire, *Dictionnaire philosophique*.
1765	*Otranto* abridged for the *Universal Magazine*; second edition published 11 April. Conway reinstated, but relations sour and Walpole winters in Paris, beginning long and intimate relationship with Mme Deffand.	Rockingham ministry. Johnson, edition of Shakespeare; Thomas Percy, *Reliques of Ancient English Poetry*; William Blackstone, *Commentaries on the Laws of England* (1765–9).

	Life	*Historical and cultural background*
1766	Third edition of *Otranto*. Last political tract, *Account of the Giants Lately Discovered*, published.	Grafton–Pitt (Chatham) ministry. Oliver Goldsmith, *The Vicar of Wakefield*; Sterne, *A Sentimental Journey*.
1767	First French translation of *Otranto* published as *Le château d'Otrante, histoire Gothique*.	American colonies taxed; Grafton ministry.
1768	Publishes the Ricardian apology *Historic Doubts on the Life of King Richard the Third*; *The Mysterious Mother* printed at Strawberry in a limited run of fifty copies. Retires from Parliament.	Wilkes prosecuted and sentenced for libel; Royal Academy founded; James Cook's first voyage. Gray, *Poems*; John Wilkes, *English Liberty* (1768–70).
1769	Thomas Chatterton sends samples of Thomas Rowley's work; HW initially accepts them as authentically medieval.	Wilkes expelled from Commons again; re-elected three times; Shakespeare Jubilee.
1770		North ministry. Death of Thomas Chatterton.
1771	Third stage of the conversion of Strawberry, completed in 1776.	Warren Hastings appointed Governor of Bengal. Percy, *The Hermit of Warkworth*; Smollett, *Humphry Clinker*; Henry Mackenzie, *The Man of Feeling*; Death of Gray; James Beattie, *The Minstrel* (1771–4).
1772		Cook's second voyage.
1773		Boston Tea Party.
1774	Prints *A Description of the Villa of Mr. Horace Walpole* at Strawberry, reprinted in 1784.	House of Lords ruling on 1711 Copyright Act, ending perpetual copyright. Johann von Goethe, *The Sorrows of Young Werther*.
1775		American War of Independence commences. Johnson, *Journey to the Western Islands of Scotland*.
1776		American Declaration of Independence; Cook's third voyage. Adam Smith, *Wealth of Nations*; Edward Gibbon, *Decline and Fall of the Roman Empire* (1776–89).

	Life	Historical and cultural background
1777		Chatterton, *Poems, supposed to have been written at Bristol, by Thomas Rowley, and Others*; Clara Reeve, *The Old English Baron.*
1778	His moralistic play *Nature will Prevail*, written in 1773, staged by George Colman.	France joins with American revolutionaries. Burney, *Evelina*; Chatterton, *Miscellanies in Prose and Verse*; Death of Voltaire.
1778–82		Rowley Controversy.
1779	Prints his account of his part in the Chatterton affair, *A Letter to the Editor of the Miscellanies of Thomas Chatterton*.	Britain declares war on Spain; siege of Gibraltar. Johnson, *Lives of the Poets* (1779–81).
1780	Fourth volume of *Anecdotes of Painting in England*, including 'Essay on Modern Gardening'.	Anti-Catholic protests culminate in the Gordon Riots; Newgate Gaol stormed.
1781	Robert Jephson's *The Count of Narbonne*, an adaptation of *Otranto* for the stage, runs for twenty-one nights; *Otranto* is republished again the following year and regularly thereafter for the remainder of the century.	
1782		Rockingham ministry. Frances Burney, *Cecilia*; William Cowper, *Poems*; William Gilpin, *Observations on the River Wye*.
1783		Peace of Versailles: American independence conceded; Fox–North coalition followed by Pitt ministry.
1784		Death of Samuel Johnson.
1785	Publishes collection of fairy stories, *Hieroglyphic Tales*, written in 1772.	Cowper, *The Task*.
1786		William Beckford, *Vathek*; William Gilpin, *Observations, Relative Chiefly to Picturesque Beauty . . . particularly the Mountains, and Lakes of Cumberland, and Westmoreland.*

	Life	*Historical and cultural background*
1788	Befriends new neighbours, Mary and Agnes Berry; becomes particularly close to Mary.	Warren Hastings impeached for corruption in India; George III succumbs to bout of madness.
1789		Storming of the Bastille and the beginning of the French Revolution; Declaration of the Rights of Man and of the Citizen; mutiny on the *Bounty*. William Blake, *Songs of Innocence*; Ann Radcliffe, *The Castles of Athlin and Dunbayne*.
1790		Blake, *The Marriage of Heaven and Hell*; Burke, *Reflections on the Revolution in France*; Radcliffe, *A Sicilian Romance*.
1791	Succeeds as 4th Earl of Orford, but does not take seat in the House of Lords.	James Boswell, *The Life of Samuel Johnson*; Thomas Paine, *The Rights of Man*; Radcliffe, *The Romance of the Forest*.
1792		France declared a republic; September Massacres in Paris; Warren Hastings acquitted. Mary Wollstonecraft, *A Vindication of the Rights of Woman*.
1793		Execution of Louis XVI of France and Marie Antoinette; Reign of Terror grips Paris; Britain declares war on France.
1794		Execution of Robespierre. Blake, *Songs of Experience*; William Godwin, *Caleb Williams*; Uvedale Price, *Essays on the Picturesque*; Radcliffe, *The Mysteries of Udolpho*.
1796		Burney, *Camilla*; Samuel Taylor Coleridge, *Poems on Various Subjects*; Matthew Lewis, *The Monk*; Regina Maria Roche, *Children of the Abbey*.
1797	Dies at home in Berkeley Square on 2 March. Buried in Houghton church in family tomb, 13 March.	Napoleon Bonaparte appointed commander of French military forces; French invasion force lands in Wales and is repelled. Radcliffe, *The Italian*.
1798	*The Works of Horatio Walpole, Earl of Orford* published in five volumes.	William Wordsworth and S. T. Coleridge, *Lyrical Ballads*.

THE

CASTLE of OTRANTO,

A

STORY.

Tranſlated by

WILLIAM MARSHAL, Gent.

From the Original ITALIAN of

ONUPHRIO MURALTO,

CANON of the Church of St. NICHOLAS
at OTRANTO.

LONDON:

Printed for THO. LOWNDS in Fleet-Street.
MDCCLXV.

Title-page of the first edition

THE

CASTLE of OTRANTO,

A

GOTHIC STORY.

———— *Vanæ*
Fingentur fpecies, tamen ut Pes, & Caput uni
Reddantur formæ. ————

HOR.

THE SECOND EDITION.

L O N D O N:
Printed for WILLIAM BATHOE in the *Strand*,
and THOMAS LOWNDS in *Fleet-Street*.

M. DCC. LXV.

Title-page of the second edition

PREFACE

TO THE FIRST EDITION

THE following work was found in the library of an ancient catholic family in the north of England.* It was printed at Naples, in the black letter, in the year 1529.* How much sooner it was written does not appear. The principal incidents are such as were believed in the darkest ages of christianity; but the language and conduct have nothing that favours of barbarism. The style is the purest Italian.* If the story was written near the time when it is supposed to have happened, it must have been between 1095, the æra of the first crusade, and 1243, the date of the last, or not long afterwards.* There is no other circumstance in the work that can lead us to guess at the period in which the scene is laid: the names of the actors are evidently fictitious, and probably disguised on purpose: yet the Spanish names of the domestics seem to indicate that this work was not composed until the establishment of the Arragonian kings in Naples* had made Spanish appellations familiar in that country. The beauty of the diction, and the zeal of the author, [moderated however by singular judgment]* concur to make me think that the date of the composition was little antecedent to that of the impression. Letters were then in their most flourishing state in Italy, and contributed to dispel the empire of superstition, at that time so forcibly attacked by the reformers. It is not unlikely that an artful priest might endeavour to turn their own arms on the innovators; and might avail himself of his abilities as an author to confirm the populace in their ancient errors and superstitions. If this was his view, he has certainly acted with signal address. Such a work as the following would enslave a hundred vulgar minds beyond half the books of controversy that have been written from the days of Luther* to the present hour.

The solution of the author's motives is however offered as a mere conjecture. Whatever his views were, or whatever effects the execution of them might have, his work can only be laid before the public at present as a matter of entertainment. Even as such, some apology for it is necessary. Miracles, visions, necromancy, dreams, and other preternatural events, are exploded now even from romances. That was not the case when our author wrote; much less when the story itself is supposed to have happened. Belief in every kind of prodigy was so established in those dark ages, that an author would not be faithful to the *manners* of the times who should omit all mention of them. He is not bound to believe them himself, but he must represent his actors as believing them.

If this *air* of the *miraculous* is excused, the reader will find nothing else unworthy of his perusal. Allow the possibility of the facts, and all the actors comport themselves as persons would do in their situation. There is no bombast, no similies, flowers,* digressions, or unnecessary descriptions. Every thing tends directly to the catastrophe. Never is the reader's attention relaxed. The rules of the drama* are almost observed throughout the conduct of the piece. The characters are well drawn, and still better maintained. Terror, the author's principal engine, prevents the story from ever languishing; and it is so often contrasted by pity, that the mind is kept up in a constant vicissitude of interesting passions.*

Some persons may perhaps think the characters of the domestics too little serious for the general cast of the story; but besides their opposition to the principal personages, the art of the author is very observable in his conduct of the subalterns. They discover many passages essential to the story, which could not well be brought to light but by their *naïveté* and simplicity: in particular, the womanish terror and foibles of Bianca, in the last chapter, conduce* essentially towards advancing the catastrophe.

It is natural for a translator to be prejudiced in favour of his adopted work. More impartial readers may not be so much struck with the beauties of this piece as I was. Yet I am not blind to my author's defects. I could wish he had grounded his plan on a more useful moral than this; that *the sins of fathers are visited on their children to the third and fourth generation.** I doubt whether in his time, any more than at present, ambition curbed its appetite of dominion from the dread of so remote a punishment. And yet this moral is weakened by that less direct insinuation, that even such anathema may be diverted by devotion to saint Nicholas. Here the interest of the monk plainly gets the better of the judgment of the author. However, with all its faults, I have no doubt but the English reader will be pleased with a sight of this performance. The piety that reigns throughout, the lessons of virtue that are inculcated, and the rigid purity of the sentiments, exempt this work from the censure to which romances are but too liable.* Should it meet with the success I hope for, I may be encouraged to re-print the original Italian, though it will tend to depreciate my own labour. Our language falls far short of the charms of the Italian, both for variety and harmony.* The latter is peculiarly excellent for simple narrative. It is difficult in English *to relate* without falling too low or rising too high; a fault obviously occasioned by the little care taken to speak pure language in common conversation. Every Italian or Frenchman of any rank piques himself on speaking his own tongue correctly and with choice. I cannot flatter myself with having done justice to my author in this respect: his style is as elegant as his conduct of the passions is masterly. It is pity that he did not apply his talents to what they were evidently proper for, the theatre.*

I will detain the reader no longer but to make one short remark. Though the machinery is invention, and the names of the actors imaginary, I cannot but believe that the ground-work of the story is founded on truth. The scene is undoubtedly laid in some real castle.* The author seems frequently, without design, to describe particular parts. *The chamber*, says he, *on the right hand; the door on the left hand; the distance from the chapel to Conrad's apartment:* these and other passages are strong presumptions that the author had some certain building in his eye. Curious persons, who have leisure to employ in such researches, may possibly discover in the Italian writers the foundation on which our author has built. If a catastrophe, at all resembling that which he describes, is believed to have given rise to this work, it will contribute to interest the reader, and will make The Castle of Otranto a still more moving story.

PREFACE

TO THE SECOND EDITION

THE favourable manner in which this little piece has been received by the public,* calls upon the author to explain the grounds on which he composed it. But before he opens those motives, it is fit that he should ask pardon of his readers for having offered his work to them under the borrowed personage of a translator. As diffidence of his own abilities, and the novelty of the attempt, were his sole inducements to assume that disguise, he flatters himself he shall appear excusable. He resigned his performance to the impartial judgment of the public; determined to let it perish in obscurity, if disapproved; nor meaning to avow such a trifle, unless better judges should pronounce that he might own it without a blush.

It was an attempt to blend the two kinds of romance, the ancient and the modern.* In the former all was imagination and improbability: in the latter, nature is always intended to be, and sometimes has been, copied with success. Invention has not been wanting; but the great resources of fancy have been dammed up, by a strict adherence to common life. But if in the latter species Nature has cramped imagination, she did but take her revenge, having been totally excluded from old romances. The actions, sentiments, conversations, of the heroes and heroines of ancient days were as unnatural as the machines employed to put them in motion.

The author of the following pages thought it possible to reconcile the two kinds. Desirous of leaving the powers of fancy at liberty to expatiate through the boundless realms of invention, and thence of creating more interesting situations, he wished to conduct the mortal agents in his drama* according to the rules of probability;* in short, to make them think, speak and act, as it might be supposed mere men and women would do in extraordinary positions. He had observed, that in all inspired writings, the personages under the dispensation of miracles, and witnesses to the most stupendous phenomena, never lose sight of their human character: whereas in the productions of romantic story, an improbable event never fails to be attended by an absurd dialogue. The actors seem to lose their senses the moment the laws of nature have lost their tone. As the public have applauded the attempt, the author must not say he was entirely unequal to the task he had undertaken: yet if the new route he has struck out shall have paved a road for men of brighter talents, he shall own with pleasure and modesty, that he was sensible the plan was capable of receiving greater embellishments than his imagination or conduct of the passions could bestow on it.

With regard to the deportment of the domestics, on which I have touched in the former preface, I will beg leave to add a few words. The simplicity of their behaviour, almost tending to excite smiles, which at first seem not consonant to the serious cast of the work, appeared to me not only not improper, but was marked designedly in that manner. My rule was nature.* However grave, important, or even melancholy, the sensations of princes and heroes may be, they do not stamp the same affections* on their domestics: at least the latter do not, or should not be made to express their passions in the same dignified tone. In my humble opinion, the contrast between the sublime* of the one, and the *naïveté* of the other, sets the pathetic of the former in a stronger light. The very impatience which a reader feels, while delayed by the coarse pleasantries of vulgar actors from arriving at the knowledge of the important catastrophe he expects, perhaps heightens, certainly proves that he has been artfully interested in, the depending event. But I had higher authority than my own opinion for this conduct. That great master of nature, Shakespeare, was the model I copied.* Let me ask if his tragedies of Hamlet and Julius Cæsar would not lose a considerable share of their spirit and wonderful beauties, if the humour of the grave-diggers, the fooleries of Polonius, and the clumsy jests of the Roman citizens were omitted, or vested in heroics?* Is not the eloquence of Antony, the nobler and affectedly-unaffected oration of Brutus, artificially exalted by the rude bursts of nature from the mouths of their auditors? These touches remind one of the Grecian sculptor, who, to convey the idea of a Colossus within the dimensions of a seal, inserted a little boy measuring his thumb.*

No, says Voltaire* in his edition of Corneille,* this mixture of buffoonery and solemnity is intolerable*—Voltaire is a genius[1]— but not of Shakespeare's magnitude. Without recurring to disputable authority, I appeal from Voltaire to himself. I shall not avail myself of his former encomiums on our mighty poet; though the French critic has twice translated the same speech in Hamlet, some years ago in admiration, latterly in derision;* and I am sorry to find that his judgment grows weaker, when it ought to be farther matured. But I shall make use of his own words, delivered on the general topic of the theatre, when he was neither thinking to recommend or decry Shakespeare's practice; consequently at a moment when Voltaire was impartial. In the preface to his Enfant prodigue,* that exquisite piece of which I declare my admiration, and which, should I live twenty years longer, I trust I should never attempt to ridicule, he has these words, speaking of comedy, [but equally applicable to tragedy, if tragedy is, as surely it ought to be, a picture of human life; nor can I conceive why occasional pleasantry ought more to be banished from the tragic scene, than pathetic seriousness from the comic] *On y voit un mel- ange de serieux et de plaisanterie, de comique et de touchant*; souvent

---

[1] The following remark is foreign to the present question, yet excusable in an Englishman, who is willing to think that the severe criticisms of so masterly a writer as Voltaire on our immortal countryman, may have been the effusions of wit and precipitation, rather than the result of judgment and attention. May not the critic's skill in the force and powers of our language have been as incorrect and incompetent as his knowledge of our history? Of the latter his own pen has dropped glaring evidence. In his preface to Thomas Corneille's Earl of Essex, monsieur de Voltaire allows that the truth of history has been grossly perverted* in that piece. In excuse he pleads, that when Corneille wrote, the noblesse of France were much unread in English story; but now, says the commentator, that they study it, such misrepresentation would not be suffered—— Yet forgetting that the period of ignorance is lapsed, and that it is not very necessary to instruct the knowing, he undertakes from the overflowing of his own reading to give the nobility of his own country a detail of queen Elizabeth's favourites—of whom, says he, Robert Dudley was the first, and the earl of Leicester the second.——Could one have believed that it could be necessary to inform monsieur de Voltaire himself, that Robert Dudley and the earl of Leicester were the same person?*

même une seule avanture *produit tous ces contrastes. Rien n'est si commun qu'une maison dans laquelle* un pere gronde, une fille occupée de sa passion pleure; *le fils se moque des deux, et quelques parens prennent part differemment à la scene, &c.* Nous n'inferons pas de là que toute comedie doive avoir des scenes de bouffonnerie et des scenes attendrissantes: il y a beaucoup de tres bonnes pieces où il ne regne que de la gayeté; d'autres toutes serieuses; d'autres melangées: d'autres où l'attendrissement va jusques aux larmes: il ne faut donner l'exclusion à aucun genre: *et si l'on me demandoit, quel genre est le meilleur, je repondrois, celui qui est le mieux traité.** Surely if a comedy may be *toute serieuse*, tragedy may now and then, soberly, be indulged in a smile. Who shall proscribe it? Shall the critic, who in self-defence declares that *no kind* ought to be excluded from comedy, give laws to Shakespeare?

I am aware that the preface from whence I have quoted these passages does not stand in monsieur de Voltaire's name, but in that of his editor; yet who doubts that the editor and author were the same person? Or where is the editor, who has so happily possessed himself of his author's style and brilliant ease of argument? These passages were indubitably the genuine sentiments of that great writer. In his epistle to Maffei,* prefixed to his Merope, he delivers almost the same opinion, though I doubt with a little irony. I will repeat his words, and then give my reason for quoting them. After translating a passage in Maffei's Merope, monsieur de Voltaire adds, *Tous ces traits sont naïfs: tout y est convenable à ceux que vous introduisez sur la scene*, et aux mœurs que vous leur donnez. *Ces familiarités naturelles eussent été, à ce que je crois, bien reçues dans Athenes; mais Paris et notre parterre veulent une autre espece de simplicité.** I doubt, I say, whether there is not a grain of sneer in this and other passages of that epistle; yet the force of truth is not damaged by being tinged with ridicule. Maffei was to represent a Grecian story: surely the Athenians were as competent judges of Grecian manners, and of the propriety of introducing them, as the parterre of Paris. On the contrary, says Voltaire [and I cannot but admire his reasoning] there were but ten thousand citizens at Athens, and Paris has near eight hundred thousand inhabitants, among whom one may reckon thirty thousand judges of dramatic works.—Indeed!—But allowing so numerous a tribunal, I believe this is the only instance in which it was ever pretended that thirty thousand persons, living near two thousand years after the æra in question, were, upon the mere face of the poll, declared better judges than the Grecians themselves of what ought to be the manners of a tragedy written on a Grecian story.

I will not enter into a discussion of the *espece de simplicité*,* which the *parterre** of Paris demands, nor of the shackles with which *the thirty thousand judges* have cramped their poetry, the chief merit of which, as I gather from repeated passages in The New Commentary on Corneille, consists in vaulting in spite of those fetters; a merit which, if true, would reduce poetry from the lofty effort of imagination, to a puerile and most contemptible labour—*difficiles nugæ** with a witness! I cannot help however mentioning a couplet, which to my English ears always sounded as the flattest and most trifling instance of circumstantial propriety; but which Voltaire, who has dealt so severely with nine parts in ten of Corneille's works, has singled out to defend in Racine;*

> *De son appartement cette porte est prochaine,*
> *Et cette autre conduit dans celui de la* reine.

In English,

> *To* Cæsar's *closet through this door you come,*
> *And t'other leads to the queen's drawing-room.*

Unhappy Shakespeare! hadst thou made Rosencraus* inform his compeer Guildenstern of the ichnography* of the palace of Copenhagen, instead of presenting us with a moral dialogue between the prince of Denmark and the grave-digger*, the illuminated pit of Paris would have been instructed a *second time** to adore thy talents.

The result of all I have said, is to shelter my own daring under the cannon of the brightest genius this country, at least, has produced. I might have pleaded, that having created a new species of romance, I was at liberty to lay down what rules I thought fit for the conduct of it: but I should be more proud of having imitated, however faintly, weakly, and at a distance, so masterly a pattern, than to enjoy the entire merit of invention, unless I could have marked my work with genius as well as with originality. Such as it is, the public have honoured it sufficiently, whatever rank their suffrages allot to it.*

SONNET

LADY MARY COKE.*

THE gentle maid, whose hapless tale
These melancholy pages speak;
Say, gracious lady, shall she fail
To draw the tear adown thy cheek?

No; never was thy pitying breast
Insensible to human woes;
Tender, though firm, it melts distrest
For weaknesses it never knows.

Oh! guard the marvels I relate
Of fell ambition scourg'd by fate,
   From reason's peevish blame:
Blest with thy smile, my dauntless sail
I dare expand to fancy's gale,
   For sure thy smiles are fame.

H. W.

THE CASTLE OF OTRANTO,
A GOTHIC STORY

CHAPTER I

MANFRED, prince of Otranto, had one son and one daughter: the latter, a most beautiful virgin, aged eighteen, was called Matilda. Conrad, the son, was three years younger, a homely youth, sickly, and of no promising disposition; yet he was the darling of his father, who never showed any symptoms of affection to Matilda. Manfred had contracted a marriage for his son with the marquis of Vicenza's daughter, Isabella;* and she had already been delivered by her guardians into the hands of Manfred, that he might celebrate the wedding as soon as Conrad's infirm state of health would permit. Manfred's impatience for this ceremonial was remarked by his family and neighbours. The former, indeed, apprehending the severity of their prince's disposition, did not dare to utter their surmises on this precipitation.* Hippolita,* his wife, an amiable lady, did sometimes venture to represent the danger of marrying their only son so early, considering his great youth, and greater infirmities; but she never received any other answer than reflections on her own sterility,* who had given him but one heir. His tenants and subjects were less cautious in their discourses: they attributed this hasty wedding to the prince's dread of seeing accomplished an ancient prophecy, which was said to have pronounced, *That the castle and lordship of Otranto should pass from the present family, whenever the real owner should be grown too large to inhabit it.* It was difficult to make any sense of this prophecy; and still less easy to conceive what it had to do with the marriage in question. Yet these mysteries, or contradictions, did not make the populace adhere the less to their opinion.

Young Conrad's birth-day was fixed for his espousals. The company was assembled in the chapel of the castle, and every thing ready for beginning the divine office, when Conrad himself was missing. Manfred, impatient of the least delay, and who had not observed his son retire, dispatched one of his attendants to summon the young prince. The servant, who had not staid long enough to have crossed the court to Conrad's apartment, came running back breathless, in a frantic manner, his eyes staring, and foaming at the mouth. He said nothing, but pointed to the court. The company were struck with terror and amazement.* The princess Hippolita, without knowing what was the matter, but anxious for her son, swooned away. Manfred, less apprehensive than enraged at the procrastination of the nuptials, and at the folly of his domestic, asked imperiously, what was the matter? The fellow made no answer, but continued pointing towards the court-yard; and at last, after repeated questions put to him, cried out, Oh, the helmet! the helmet! In the mean time some of the company had run into the court, from whence was heard a confused noise of shrieks, horror, and surprise. Manfred, who began to be alarmed at not seeing his son, went himself to get information of what occasioned this strange confusion. Matilda remained endeavouring to assist her mother, and Isabella staid for the same purpose, and to avoid showing any impatience for the bridegroom, for whom, in truth, she had conceived little affection.

The first thing that struck Manfred's eyes was a group of his servants endeavouring to raise something that appeared to him a mountain of sable plumes. He gazed without believing his sight. What are ye doing? cried Manfred, wrathfully: Where is my son? A volley of voices replied, Oh, my lord! the prince! the prince! the helmet! the helmet! Shocked with these lamentable sounds, and dreading he knew not what, he advanced hastily—But what a sight for a father's eyes!—He beheld his child dashed to pieces, and almost buried under an enormous helmet, an hundred times more large than any casque* ever made for human being, and shaded with a proportionable* quantity of black feathers.

The horror of the spectacle, the ignorance of all around how this misfortune happened, and above all, the tremendous phænomenon before him, took away the prince's speech. Yet his silence lasted longer than even grief could occasion. He fixed his eyes on what he wished in vain to believe a vision; and seemed less attentive to his loss, than buried in meditation on the stupendous object that had occasioned it. He touched, he examined the fatal casque; nor could even the bleeding mangled remains of the young prince divert the eyes of Manfred from the portent before him. All who had known his partial* fondness for young Conrad, were as much surprised at their prince's insensibility,* as thunderstruck themselves at the miracle of the helmet. They conveyed the disfigured corpse into the hall, without receiving the least direction from Manfred. As little was he attentive to the ladies who remained in the chapel: on the contrary, without mentioning the unhappy princesses his wife and daughter, the first sounds that dropped from Manfred's lips were, Take care of the lady Isabella.

The domestics, without observing the singularity of this direction, were guided by their affection to their mistress to consider it as peculiarly addressed to her situation, and flew to her assistance. They conveyed her to her chamber more dead than alive, and indifferent to all the strange circumstances she heard, except the death of her son. Matilda, who doted on her mother, smothered her own grief and amazement, and thought of nothing but assisting and comforting her afflicted parent. Isabella, who had been treated by Hippolita like a daughter, and who returned that tenderness with equal duty and affection, was scarce less assiduous about the princess; at the same time endeavouring to partake and lessen the weight of sorrow which she saw Matilda strove to suppress, for whom she had conceived the warmest sympathy of friendship. Yet her own situation could not help finding its place in her thoughts. She felt no concern for the death of young Conrad, except commiseration; and she was not sorry to be delivered from a marriage which had promised her little felicity, either from her destined bridegroom, or from the severe temper of Manfred, who, though he had distinguished her by great indulgence, had imprinted her mind with terror, from his causeless rigour to such amiable princesses as Hippolita and Matilda.

While the ladies were conveying the wretched* mother to her

bed, Manfred remained in the court, gazing on the ominous casque, and regardless of the crowd which the strangeness of the event had now assembled round him. The few words he articulated tended solely to enquiries, whether any man knew from whence it could have come? Nobody could give him the least information. However, as it seemed to be the sole object of his curiosity, it soon became so to the rest of the spectators, whose conjectures were as absurd and improbable as the catastrophe itself was unprecedented. In the midst of their senseless guesses a young peasant, whom rumour had drawn thither from a neighbouring village, observed that the miraculous helmet was exactly like that on the figure in black marble of Alfonso the Good, one of their former princes, in the church of St. Nicholas.* Villain! What sayest thou? cried Manfred, starting from his trance in a tempest of rage, and seizing the young man by the collar: How darest thou utter such treason? Thy life shall pay for it. The spectators, who as little comprehended the cause of the prince's fury as all the rest they had seen, were at a loss to unravel this new circumstance. The young peasant himself was still more astonished, not conceiving how he had offended the prince: yet recollecting himself, with a mixture of grace and humility, he disengaged himself from Manfred's gripe,* and then, with an obeisance* which discovered more jealousy* of innocence, than dismay, he asked with respect, of what he was guilty! Manfred, more enraged at the vigour, however decently exerted, with which the young man had shaken off his hold, than appeased by his submission, ordered his attendants to seize him, and, if he had not been withheld by his friends whom he had invited to the nuptials, would have poignarded* the peasant in their arms.

During this altercation some of the vulgar* spectators had run to the great church which stood near the castle, and came back open-mouthed, declaring the helmet was missing from Alfonso's statue. Manfred, at this news, grew perfectly frantic; and, as if he sought a subject on which to vent the tempest within him, he rushed again on the young peasant, crying, Villain! monster! sorcerer! 'tis thou hast slain my son! The mob,* who wanted some object within the scope of their capacities on whom they might discharge their bewildered reasonings, caught the words from the mouth of their lord, and re-echoed, Ay, ay, 'tis he, 'tis he: he has stolen the helmet from good Alfonso's tomb, and dashed out the brains of our young prince with it:—never reflecting how enormous the disproportion was between the marble helmet that had been in the church, and that of steel before their eyes; nor how impossible it was for a youth, seemingly not twenty, to wield a piece of armour of so prodigious a weight.

The folly of these ejaculations* brought Manfred to himself: yet whether provoked at the peasant having observed the resemblance between the two helmets, and thereby led to the farther discovery of the absence of that in the church; or wishing to bury any fresh rumour under so impertinent a supposition; he gravely pronounced that the young man was certainly a necromancer, and that till the church could take cognizance of the affair, he would have the magician, whom they had thus detected, kept prisoner under the helmet itself,* which he ordered his attendants to raise, and place the young man under it; declaring he should be kept there without food, with which his own infernal art might furnish him.

It was in vain for the youth to represent against this preposterous sentence: in vain did Manfred's friends endeavour to divert him from this savage and ill-grounded resolution. The generality were charmed with their lord's decision, which to their apprehensions carried great appearance of justice, as the magician was to be punished by the very instrument with which he had offended: nor were they struck with the least compunction at the probability of the youth being starved, for they firmly believed that by his diabolical skill he could easily supply himself with nutriment.

Manfred thus saw his commands even cheerfully obeyed; and appointing a guard with strict orders to prevent any food being conveyed to the prisoner, he dismissed his friends and attendants, and retired to his own chamber, after locking the gates of the castle, in which he suffered none but his domestics to remain.

In the mean time, the care and zeal of the young ladies had brought the princess Hippolita to herself, who amidst the transports of her own sorrow frequently demanded news of her lord, would have dismissed her attendants to watch over him, and at last enjoined* Matilda to leave her, and visit and comfort her father. Matilda, who wanted* no affectionate duty to Manfred, though she trembled at his austerity, obeyed the orders of Hippolita, whom she tenderly recommended to Isabella; and enquiring of the domestics for her father, was informed that he was retired to his chamber, and had commanded that nobody should have admittance to him. Concluding that he was immersed in sorrow for the death of her brother, and fearing to renew his tears by the sight of his sole remaining child, she hesitated whether she should break in upon his affliction; yet solicitude for him, backed by the commands of her mother, encouraged her to venture disobeying the orders he had given; a fault she had never been guilty of before. The gentle timidity of her nature made her pause for some minutes at his door. She heard him traverse his chamber backwards and forwards with disordered steps; a mood which increased her apprehensions. She was however just going to beg admittance, when Manfred suddenly opened the door; and as it was now twilight,* concurring with the disorder of his mind, he did not distinguish the person, but asked angrily who it was? Matilda replied trembling, My dearest father, it is I, your daughter. Manfred, stepping back hastily, cried, Begone, I do not want a daughter; and, flinging back abruptly, clapped the door against the terrified Matilda.

She was too well acquainted with her father's impetuosity to venture a second intrusion. When she had a little recovered the shock of so bitter a reception, she wiped away her tears, to prevent the additional stab that the knowledge of it would give to Hippolita, who questioned her in the most anxious terms on the health of Manfred, and how he bore his loss. Matilda assured her he was well, and supported his misfortune with manly fortitude. But will he not let me see him? said Hippolita mournfully: Will he not permit me to blend my tears with his, and shed a mother's sorrows in the bosom of her lord? Or do you deceive me, Matilda? I know how Manfred doted on his son: Is not the stroke too heavy for him? Has he not sunk under it?—You do not answer me—Alas, I dread the worst!—Raise me, my maidens: I will, I will see my lord. Bear me to him instantly; he is dearer to me even than my children. Matilda made signs to Isabella to prevent Hippolita's rising; and both these lovely young women were using their gentle violence to stop and calm the princess, when a servant on the part* of Manfred arrived, and told Isabella that his lord demanded to speak with her.

With me! cried Isabella. Go, said Hippolita, relieved by a message from her lord: Manfred cannot support the sight of his own family. He thinks you less disordered than we are, and dreads the shock of my grief. Console him, dear Isabella, and tell him I will smother my own anguish rather than add to his.

It was now evening; the servant who conducted Isabella bore a torch before her. When they came to Manfred, who was walking impatiently about the gallery, he started and said hastily, Take away that light, and begone. Then shutting the door impetuously, he flung himself upon a bench against the wall, and bade Isabella sit by him. She obeyed trembling. I sent for you, lady, said he,—and then stopped under great appearance of confusion. My lord!—Yes, I sent for you on a matter of great moment, resumed he:—Dry your tears, young lady—you have lost your bridegroom:—yes, cruel fate, and I have lost the hopes of my race!—But Conrad was not worthy of your beauty.—How! my lord, said Isabella; sure you do not suspect me of not feeling the concern I ought? My duty and affection would have always— Think no more of him, interrupted Manfred; he was a sickly puny child, and heaven has perhaps taken him away that I might not trust the honours of my house on so frail a foundation. The line of Manfred calls for numerous supports. My foolish fondness for that boy blinded the eyes of my prudence—but it is better as it is. I hope in a few years to have reason to rejoice at the death of Conrad.

Words cannot paint the astonishment of Isabella. At first she apprehended that grief had disordered Manfred's understanding. Her next thought suggested that this strange discourse was designed to ensnare her: she feared that Manfred had perceived her indifference for his son: and in consequence of that idea she replied, Good my lord, do not doubt my tenderness; my heart would have accompanied my hand. Conrad would have engrossed all my care; and wherever fate shall dispose of me, I shall always cherish his memory, and regard your highness and the virtuous Hippolita as my parents. Curse on Hippolita! cried Manfred: forget her from this moment, as I do. In short, lady, you have missed a husband undeserving of your charms: they shall now be better disposed of. Instead of a sickly boy, you shall have a husband in the prime of his age,* who will know how to value your beauties, and who may expect a numerous offspring. Alas, my lord, said Isabella, my mind is too sadly engrossed by the recent catastrophe in your family to think of another marriage. If ever my father returns, and it shall be his pleasure, I shall obey, as I did when I consented to give my hand to your son: but until his return permit me to remain under your hospitable roof, and employ the melancholy hours in assuaging yours, Hippolita's, and the fair Matilda's affliction.

I desired you once before, said Manfred angrily, not to name that woman; from this hour she must be a stranger to you, as she must be to me:—in short, Isabella, since I cannot give you my son, I offer you myself.—Heavens! cried Isabella, waking from her delusion, what do I hear! You, my lord! You! My father in law! the father of Conrad! the husband of the virtuous and tender Hippolita!—I tell you, said Manfred imperiously, Hippolita is no longer my wife; I divorce her from this hour. Too long has she cursed me by her unfruitfulness: my fate depends on having sons,—and this night I trust will give a new date* to my hopes. At those words he seized the cold hand of Isabella, who was half-dead with fright and horror. She shrieked, and started from him. Manfred rose to pursue her; when the moon, which was now up, and gleamed in at the opposite casement, presented to his sight the plumes of the fatal helmet, which rose to the height of the windows, waving backwards and forwards in a tempestuous manner, and accompanied with a hollow and rustling sound. Isabella, who gathered courage from her situation, and who dreaded nothing so much as Manfred's pursuit of his declaration, cried, Look, my lord! see heaven itself declares against your impious intentions!—Heaven nor hell shall impede my designs, said Manfred, advancing again to seize the princess. At that instant the portrait of his grandfather, which hung over the bench where they had been sitting, uttered a deep sigh and heaved its breast.* Isabella, whose back was turned to the picture, saw not the motion, nor knew whence the sound came, but started and said, Hark my lord! what sound was that? and at the same time made towards the door. Manfred, distracted between the flight of Isabella, who had now reached the stairs, and his inability to keep his eyes from the picture, which began to move, had however advanced some steps after her, still looking backwards on the portrait, when he saw it quit its pannel,* and descend on the floor with a grave and melancholy air. Do I dream?* cried Manfred returning, or are the devils themselves in league against me? Speak, infernal spectre! Or, if thou art my grandsire, why dost thou too conspire against thy wretched descendant, who too dearly pays for—Ere he could finish the sentence the vision sighed again, and made a sign to Manfred to follow him. Lead on! cried Manfred; I will follow thee to the gulph of perdition.* The spectre marched sedately, but dejected, to the end of the gallery, and turned into a chamber on the right hand. Manfred accompanied him at a little distance, full of anxiety and horror, but resolved. As he would have entered the chamber, the door was clapped-to with violence by an invisible hand.* The prince, collecting courage from this delay, would have forcibly burst open the door with his foot, but found that it resisted his utmost efforts. Since hell will not satisfy my curiosity, said Manfred, I will use the human means in my power for preserving my race; Isabella shall not escape me.

That lady, whose resolution had given way to terror the moment she had quitted Manfred, continued her flight to the bottom of the principal staircase. There she stopped, not knowing whither to direct her steps, nor how to escape from the impetuosity of the prince. The gates of the castle she knew were locked, and guards placed in the court. Should she, as her heart prompted her, go and prepare Hippolita for the cruel destiny that awaited her, she did not doubt but Manfred would seek her there, and that his violence would incite him to double the injury he meditated, without leaving room for them to avoid the impetuosity of his passions. Delay might give him time to reflect on the horrid measures he had conceived, or produce some circumstance in her favour, if she could for that night at least avoid his odious purpose.—Yet where conceal herself! How avoid the pursuit he would infallibly make throughout the castle! As these thoughts passed rapidly through her mind, she recollected a subterraneous passage* which led from the vaults of the castle to the church of saint Nicholas. Could she reach the altar before she was overtaken, she knew even Manfred's violence would not dare to profane the sacredness of the place; and she determined, if no other means of deliverance offered, to shut herself up for ever among the holy virgins, whose convent was contiguous* to the cathedral. In this resolution, she seized a lamp that burned at the foot of the staircase, and hurried towards the secret passage.

The lower part of the castle was hollowed into several intricate cloisters;* and it was not easy for one under so much anxiety to find the door that opened into the cavern. An awful silence reigned thoughout those subterraneous regions, except now and then some blasts of wind that shook the doors she had passed, and which grating on the rusty hinges were re-echoed through that long labyrinth of darkness.* Every murmur struck her with new terror;—yet more she dreaded to hear the wrathful voice of Manfred urging his domestics to pursue her. She trod as softly as impatience would give her leave,—yet frequently stopped and listened to hear if she was followed. In one of those moments she thought she heard a sigh. She shuddered, and recoiled a few paces. In a moment she thought she heard the step of some person. Her blood curdled; she concluded it was Manfred. Every suggestion that horror could inspire rushed into her mind. She condemned her rash flight, which had thus exposed her to his rage in a place where her cries were not likely to draw any body to her assistance.—Yet the sound seemed not to come from behind;— if Manfred knew where she was, he must have followed her: she was still in one of the cloisters, and the steps she had heard were too distinct to proceed from the way she had come. Cheered with this reflection, and hoping to find a friend in whoever was not the prince; she was going to advance, when a door that stood a-jar, at some distance to the left, was opened gently; but ere her lamp, which she held up, could discover who opened it, the person retreated precipitately on seeing the light.

Isabella, whom every incident was sufficient to dismay, hesitated whether she should proceed. Her dread of Manfred soon outweighed every other terror. The very circumstance of the person avoiding her, gave her a sort of courage. It could only be, she thought, some domestic belonging to the castle. Her gentleness had never raised her an enemy, and conscious innocence made her hope that, unless sent by the prince's order to seek her, his servants would rather assist than prevent her flight. Fortifying herself with these reflections, and believing, by what she could observe, that she was near the mouth of the subterraneous cavern, she approached the door that had been opened; but a sudden gust of wind that met her at the door extinguished her lamp, and left her in total darkness.

Words cannot paint the horror of the princess's situation. Alone in so dismal a place, her mind imprinted with all the terrible events of the day, hopeless of escaping, expecting every moment the arrival of Manfred, and far from tranquil on knowing she was within reach of somebody, she knew not whom, who for some cause seemed concealed there-abouts, all these thoughts crowded on her distracted mind, and she was ready to sink under her apprehensions. She addressed herself to every saint in heaven, and inwardly implored their assistance. For a considerable time she remained in an agony of despair. At last, as softly as was possible, she felt for the door, and, having found it, entered trembling into the vault from whence she had heard the sigh and steps. It gave her a kind of momentary joy to perceive an imperfect ray of clouded moonshine gleam from the roof of the vault, which seemed to be fallen in, and from whence hung a fragment of earth or building, she could not distinguish which, that appeared to have been crushed inwards. She advanced eagerly towards this chasm, when she discerned a human form standing close against the wall.

She shrieked, believing it the ghost of her betrothed Conrad. The figure advancing, said in a submissive voice, Be not alarmed, lady; I will not injure you. Isabella, a little encouraged by the words and tone of voice of the stranger, and recollecting that this must be the person who had opened the door, recovered her spirits enough to reply, Sir, whoever you are, take pity on a wretched princess standing on the brink of destruction: assist me to escape from this fatal castle, or in a few moments I may be made miserable for ever. Alas! said the stranger, what can I do to assist you? I will die in your defence; but I am unacquainted with the castle, and want—Oh! said Isabella, hastily interrupting him, help me but to find a trap-door that must be hereabout, and it is the greatest service you can do me; for I have not a minute to lose. Saying these words she felt about on the pavement, and directed the stranger to search likewise for a smooth piece of brass inclosed in one of the stones. That, said she, is the lock, which opens with a spring, of which I know the secret. If I can find that, I may escape—if not, alas, courteous stranger, I fear I shall have involved you in my misfortunes: Manfred will suspect you for the accomplice of my flight, and you will fall a victim to his resentment. I value not my life, said the stranger; and it will be some comfort to lose it in trying to deliver you from his tyranny. Generous youth, said Isabella, how shall I ever requite—As she uttered those words, a ray of moonshine streaming through a cranny of the ruin above shone directly on the lock they sought—Oh, transport! said Isabella, here is the trap-door! and taking out a key, she touched the spring, which starting aside discovered an iron ring. Lift up the door, said the princess. The stranger obeyed; and beneath appeared some stone steps descending into a vault totally dark.* We must go down here, said Isabella: follow me; dark and dismal as it is, we cannot miss our way; it leads directly to the church of saint Nicholas—But perhaps, added the princess modestly,* you have no reason to leave the castle, nor have I farther occasion for your service; in a few minutes I shall be safe from Manfred's rage—only let me know to whom I am so much obliged. I will never quit you, said the stranger eagerly, till I have placed you in safety—nor think me, princess, more generous than I am: though you are my principal care—The stranger was interrupted by a sudden noise of voices that seemed approaching, and they soon distinguished these words: Talk not to me of necromancers; I tell you she must be in the castle; I will find her in spite of enchantment.—Oh, heavens! cried Isabella, it is the voice of Manfred! Make haste, or we are ruined! and shut the trap-door after you. Saying this, she descended the steps precipitately; and as the stranger hastened to follow her, he let the door slip out of his hands: it fell, and the spring closed over it. He tried in vain to open it, not having observed Isabella's method of touching the spring, nor had he many moments to make an essay.* The noise of the falling door had been heard by Manfred, who, directed by the sound, hastened thither, attended by his servants with torches. It must be Isabella, cried Manfred before he entered the vault; she is escaping by the subterraneous passage, but she cannot have got far.—What was the astonishment of the prince, when, instead of Isabella, the light of the torches discovered to him the young peasant, whom he thought confined under the fatal helmet! Traitor! said Manfred, how camest thou here? I thought thee in durance* above in the court. I am no traitor, replied the young man boldly, nor am I answerable for your thoughts. Presumptuous villain! cried Manfred, dost thou provoke my wrath? Tell me; how hast thou escaped from above? Thou hast corrupted thy guards, and their lives shall answer it. My poverty, said the peasant calmly, will disculpate* them: though the ministers of a tyrant's wrath, to thee they are faithful, and but too willing to execute the orders which you unjustly imposed upon them. Art thou so hardy as to dare my vengeance? said the prince—but tortures shall force the truth from thee. Tell me, I will know thy accomplices. There was my accomplice! said the youth smiling, and pointing to the roof. Manfred ordered the torches to be held up, and perceived that one of the cheeks of the enchanted casque had forced its way through the pavement of the court, as his servants had let it fall over the peasant, and had broken through into the vault, leaving a gap through which the peasant had pressed himself some minutes

before he was found by Isabella. Was that the way by which thou
didst descend? said Manfred. It was, said the youth. But what
noise was that, said Manfred, which I heard as I entered the cloister? A door clapped, said the peasant: I heard it as well as you.
What door? said Manfred hastily. I am not acquainted with your
castle, said the peasant; this is the first time I ever entered it, and
this vault the only part of it within which I ever was. But I tell thee,
said Manfred, [wishing to find out if the youth had discovered the
trap-door] it was this way I heard the noise: my servants heard it
too.——My lord, interrupted one of them officiously, to be sure it
was the trap-door, and he was going to make his escape. Peace!
blockhead,* said the prince angrily; if he was going to escape, how
should he come on this side? I will know from his own mouth what
noise it was I heard. Tell me truly; thy life depends on thy veracity.
My veracity is dearer to me than my life, said the peasant; nor
would I purchase the one by forfeiting the other. Indeed! young
philosopher! said Manfred contemptuously: tell me then, what
was the noise I heard? Ask me what I can answer, said he, and put
me to death instantly if I tell you a lie. Manfred, growing impatient at the steady valour and indifference of the youth, cried, Well
then, thou man of truth! answer; was it the fall of the trap-door
that I heard? It was, said the youth. It was! said the prince; and
how didst thou come to know there was a trap-door here? I saw
the plate of brass by a gleam of moonshine, replied he. But what
told thee it was a lock? said Manfred: How didst thou discover
the secret of opening it? Providence,* that delivered me from the
helmet, was able to direct me to the spring of a lock, said he.
Providence should have gone a little farther, and have placed thee
out of the reach of my resentment, said Manfred: when Providence
had taught thee to open the lock, it abandoned thee for a fool, who
did not know how to make use of its favours. Why didst thou not
pursue the path pointed out for thy escape? Why didst thou shut
the trapdoor before thou hadst descended the steps? I might ask
you, my lord, said the peasant, how I, totally unacquainted with
your castle, was to know that those steps led to any outlet? but
I scorn to evade your questions. Wherever those steps lead to,

perhaps I should have explored the way—I could not have been in a worse situation than I was. But the truth is, I let the trap-door fall: your immediate arrival followed. I had given the alarm—what imported it to me whether I was seized a minute sooner or a minute later? Thou art a resolute* villain for thy years, said Manfred—yet on reflection I suspect thou dost but trifle with me: thou hast not yet told me how thou didst open the lock. That I will show you, my lord, said the peasant; and taking up a fragment of stone that had fallen from above, he laid himself on the trap-door, and began to beat on the piece of brass that covered it; meaning to gain time for the escape of the princess. This presence of mind, joined to the frankness of the youth, staggered Manfred. He even felt a disposition towards pardoning one who had been guilty of no crime. Manfred was not one of those savage tyrants who wanton in cruelty unprovoked. The circumstances of his fortune had given an asperity to his temper, which was naturally humane; and his virtues were always ready to operate, when his passion did not obscure his reason.

While the prince was in this suspense, a confused noise of voices echoed through the distant vaults. As the sound approached, he distinguished the clamour of some of his domestics, whom he had dispersed through the castle in search of Isabella, calling out, Where is my lord? Where is the prince? Here I am, said Manfred, as they came nearer; have you found the princess? The first that arrived replied, Oh, my lord! I am glad we have found you.—Found me! said Manfred: have you found the princess? We thought we had, my lord, said the fellow looking terrified—but—But what? cried the prince: has she escaped?—Jaquez* and I, my lord—Yes, I and Diego, interrupted the second, who came up in still greater consternation—Speak one of you at a time, said Manfred; I ask you, where is the princess? We do not know, said they both together: but we are frightened out of our wits.—So I think, blockheads, said Manfred: what is it has scared you thus?—Oh, my lord! said Jaquez, Diego has seen such a sight! your highness would not believe our eyes.—What new absurdity is this? cried Manfred—Give me a direct answer, or by heaven—Why, my lord,

if it please your highness to hear me, said the poor fellow; Diego
and I—Yes, I and Jaquez, cried his comrade—Did not I forbid
you to speak both at a time? said the prince: You, Jaquez, answer;
for the other fool seems more distracted than thou art; what is the
matter? My gracious lord, said Jaquez, if it please your highness
to hear me; Diego and I, according to your highness's orders, went
to search for the young lady; but being comprehensive* that we
might meet the ghost of my young lord, your highness's son, God
rest his soul, as he has not received christian burial—Sot!* cried
Manfred in a rage, is it only a ghost then that thou hast seen? Oh,
worse! worse! my lord! cried Diego: I had rather have seen ten
whole ghosts.—Grant me patience! said Manfred; these blockheads distract me—Out of my sight, Diego! And thou, Jaquez,
tell me in one word, art thou sober? art thou raving? Thou wast
wont* to have some sense: has the other sot frightened himself
and thee too? Speak; what is it he fancies he has seen? Why, my
lord, replied Jaquez trembling, I was going to tell your highness,
that since the calamitous misfortune of my young lord, God rest
his soul! not one of us your highness's faithful servants, indeed
we are, my lord, though poor men; I say, not one of us has dared
to set a foot about the castle, but two together:* so Diego and I,
thinking that my young lady might be in the great gallery, went
up there to look for her, and tell her your highness wanted something to impart to her.—O blundering fools! cried Manfred: and
in the mean time she has made her escape, because you were afraid
of goblins! Why, thou knave! she left me in the gallery; I came
from thence myself.—For all that, she may be there still for aught*
I know, said Jaquez; but the devil shall have me before I seek her
there again!—Poor Diego! I do not believe he will ever recover
it! Recover what? said Manfred; am I never to learn what it is has
terrified these rascals? But I lose my time; follow me, slave! I will
see if she is in the gallery.—For heaven's sake, my dear good lord,
cried Jaquez, do not go to the gallery! Satan himself I believe is
in the great chamber next to the gallery.—Manfred, who hitherto had treated the terror of his servants as an idle panic, was
struck at this new circumstance. He recollected the apparition of

the portrait, and the sudden closing of the door at the end of the gallery—his voice faltered, and he asked with disorder, what is in the great chamber? My lord, said Jaquez, when Diego and I came into the gallery, he went first, for he said he had more courage than I. So when we came into the gallery, we found nobody. We looked under every bench and stool; and still we found nobody.—Were all the pictures in their places? said Manfred. Yes, my lord, answered Jaquez; but we did not think of looking behind them.—Well, well! said Manfred; proceed. When we came to the door of the great chamber, continued Jaquez, we found it shut.—And could not you open it? said Manfred. Oh! yes, my lord, would to heaven we had not! replied he—Nay, it was not I neither, it was Diego: he was grown foolhardy, and would go on, though I advised him not—If ever I open a door that is shut again—Trifle not, said Manfred shuddering, but tell me what you saw in the great chamber on opening the door.—I! my lord! said Jaquez, I saw nothing; I was behind Diego;—but I heard the noise.—Jaquez, said Manfred in a solemn tone of voice, tell me, I adjure* thee by the souls of my ancestors, what it was thou sawest; what it was thou heardest. It was Diego saw it, my lord, it was not I, replied Jaquez; I only heard the noise. Diego had no sooner opened the door, than he cried out and ran back—I ran back too, and said, Is it the ghost? The ghost! No, no, said Diego, and his hair stood on end*—it is a giant, I believe; he is all clad in armour, for I saw his foot and part of his leg,* and they are as large as the helmet below in the court. As he said these words, my lord, we heard a violent motion and the rattling of armour, as if the giant was rising; for Diego has told me since, that he believes the giant was lying down, for the foot and leg were stretched at length on the floor. Before we could get to the end of the gallery, we heard the door of the great chamber clap behind us, but we did not dare turn back to see if the giant was following us—Yet now I think on it, we must have heard him if he had pursued us—But for heaven's sake, good my lord, send for the chaplain and have the castle exorcised, for, for certain, it is enchanted. Ay, pray do, my lord, cried all the servants at once, or we must leave your highness's service.—Peace, dotards!

said Manfred, and follow me; I will know what all this means. We!
my lord! cried they with one voice; we would not go up to the gallery for your highness's revenue.* The young peasant, who had
stood silent, now spoke. Will your highness, said he, permit me
to try this adventure? My life is of consequence to nobody: I fear
no bad angel, and have offended no good one. Your behaviour is
above your seeming, said Manfred; viewing him with surprise and
admiration—hereafter I will reward your bravery—but now, continued he with a sigh, I am so circumstanced, that I dare trust no
eyes but my own—However, I give you leave to accompany me.

Manfred, when he first followed Isabella from the gallery, had
gone directly to the apartment of his wife, concluding the princess
had retired thither. Hippolita, who knew his step, rose with anxious fondness to meet her lord, whom she had not seen since the
death of their son. She would have flown in a transport mixed of
joy and grief to his bosom; but he pushed her rudely off, and said,
Where is Isabella? Isabella! my lord! said the astonished Hippolita.
Yes, Isabella; cried Manfred imperiously; I want Isabella. My
lord, replied Matilda, who perceived how much his behaviour had
shocked her mother, she has not been with us since your highness summoned her to your apartment. Tell me where she is, said
the prince; I do not want to know where she has been. My good
lord, said Hippolita, your daughter tells you the truth: Isabella
left us by your command, and has not returned since:—but, my
good lord, compose yourself: retire to your rest: this dismal day
has disordered you. Isabella shall wait your orders in the morning. What, then you know where she is? cried Manfred: tell me
directly, for I will not lose an instant—And you, woman, speaking
to his wife, order your chaplain to attend me forthwith. Isabella,
said Hippolita calmly, is retired I suppose to her chamber: she
is not accustomed to watch at this late hour. Gracious my lord,
continued she, let me know what has disturbed you: has Isabella
offended you? Trouble me not with questions, said Manfred, but
tell me where she is. Matilda shall call her, said the princess—sit
down, my lord, and resume your wonted fortitude.—What, art
thou jealous of Isabella, replied he, that you wish to be present

at our interview? Good heavens! my lord, said Hippolita, what is it your highness means? Thou wilt know ere many minutes are passed, said the cruel prince. Send your chaplain to me, and wait my pleasure here. At these words he flung out of the room in search of Isabella; leaving the amazed ladies thunder-struck with his words and frantic deportment, and lost in vain conjectures on what he was meditating.

Manfred was now returning from the vault, attended by the peasant and a few of his servants whom he had obliged to accompany him. He ascended the stair-case without stopping till he arrived at the gallery, at the door of which he met Hippolita and her chaplain. When Diego had been dismissed by Manfred, he had gone directly to the princess's apartment with the alarm of what he had seen. That excellent lady, who no more than Manfred doubted of the reality of the vision, yet affected to treat it as a delirium of the servant. Willing, however, to save her lord from any additional shock, and prepared by a series* of grief not to tremble at any accession to it; she determined to make herself the first sacrifice, if fate had marked the present hour for their destruction. Dismissing the reluctant Matilda to her rest, who in vain sued for leave to accompany her mother, and attended only by her chaplain, Hippolita had visited the gallery and great chamber; and now, with more serenity of soul than she had felt for many hours, she met her lord, and assured him that the vision of the gigantic leg and foot was all a fable; and no doubt an impression made by fear, and the dark and dismal hour of the night, on the minds of his servants: She and the chaplain had examined the chamber, and found every thing in the usual order.

Manfred, though persuaded, like his wife, that the vision had been no work of fancy, recovered a little from the tempest of mind into which so many strange events had thrown him. Ashamed too of his inhuman treatment of a princess, who returned every injury with new marks of tenderness and duty, he felt returning love forcing itself into his eyes—but not less ashamed of feeling remorse towards one, against whom he was inwardly meditating a yet more bitter outrage, he curbed the yearnings of his heart, and did not

dare to lean even towards pity. The next transition of his soul was
to exquisite* villainy. Presuming on the unshaken submission of
Hippolita, he flattered himself that she would not only acquiesce
with patience to a divorce, but would obey, if it was his pleasure,
in endeavouring to persuade Isabella to give him her hand—But
ere he could indulge this horrid hope, he reflected that Isabella
was not to be found. Coming to himself, he gave orders that every
avenue to the castle should be strictly guarded, and charged his
domestics on pain of their lives to suffer nobody to pass out. The
young peasant, to whom he spoke favourably, he ordered to remain
in a small chamber on the stairs, in which there was a pallet-bed,*
and the key of which he took away himself, telling the youth he
would talk with him in the morning. Then dismissing his attendants, and bestowing a sullen kind of half-nod on Hippolita, he
retired to his own chamber.

CHAPTER II

MATILDA, who by Hippolita's order had retired to her apartment, was ill-disposed to take any rest. The shocking fate of her brother had deeply affected her. She was surprised at not seeing Isabella: but the strange words which had fallen from her father, and his obscure menace to the princess his wife, accompanied by the most furious behaviour, had filled her gentle mind with terror and alarm. She waited anxiously for the return of Bianca,* a young damsel that attended her, whom she had sent to learn what was become of Isabella. Bianca soon appeared, and informed her mistress of what she had gathered from the servants, that Isabella was no where to be found. She related the adventure of the young peasant, who had been discovered in the vault, though with many simple additions from the incoherent accounts of the domestics; and she dwelled principally on the gigantic leg and foot which had been seen in the gallery-chamber. This last circumstance had terrified Bianca so much, that she was rejoiced when Matilda told her that she would not go to rest, but would watch till the princess should rise.

The young princess wearied herself in conjectures on the flight of Isabella, and on the threats of Manfred to her mother. But what business could he have so urgent with the chaplain? said Matilda. Does he intend to have my brother's body interred privately in the chapel? Oh! madam, said Bianca, now I guess. As you are become his heiress, he is impatient to have you married: he has always been raving for more sons; I warrant he is now impatient for grandsons. As sure as I live, madam, I shall see you a bride at last. Good madam, you won't cast off your faithful Bianca: you won't put Donna Rosara* over me, now you are a great princess? My poor Bianca, said Matilda, how fast your thoughts amble! I a great princess! What hast thou seen in Manfred's behaviour since my brother's death that bespeaks any increase of tenderness to me? No, Bianca, his heart was ever a stranger to me—but he is my father, and I must not complain. Nay, if heaven shuts my father's heart against me, it over-pays my little merit in the tenderness of my mother—O that dear mother! Yes, Bianca, 'tis there I feel the rugged temper of Manfred. I can support his harshness to me with patience; but it wounds my soul when I am witness to his causeless severity towards her. Oh, madam, said Bianca, all men use their wives so, when they are weary of them.*—And yet you congratulated me but now, said Matilda, when you fancied my father intended to dispose of me. I would have you a great lady, replied Bianca, come what will. I do not wish to see you moped* in a convent, as you would be if you had your will, and if my lady your mother, who knows that a bad husband is better than no husband at all, did not hinder you.—Bless me! what noise is that? Saint Nicholas forgive me! I was but in jest. It is the wind, said Matilda, whistling through the battlements in the tower above: you have heard it a thousand times. Nay, said Bianca, there was no harm neither in what I said: it is no sin to talk of matrimony—And so, madam, as I was saying; if my lord Manfred should offer you a handsome young prince for a bridegroom, you would drop him a curtsy, and tell him you would rather take the veil. Thank heaven! I am in no such danger, said Matilda: you know how many proposals for me he has rejected.—And you thank him, like a dutiful daughter, do you, madam?—But come, madam; suppose, to-morrow morning he was to send for you to the great council-chamber, and there you should find at his elbow a lovely young prince, with large black eyes, a smooth white forehead, and manly curling locks like jet; in short, madam, a young hero resembling the picture of the good Alfonso in the gallery, which you sit and gaze at for hours together.—Do not speak lightly of that picture, interrupted Matilda sighing: I know the adoration with which I look at that picture is uncommon—but I am not in love with a coloured pannel. The character of that virtuous prince, the veneration with which my mother has inspired me for his memory, the orisons* which I know not why she has enjoined me to pour forth at his tomb, all have concurred to persuade me that somehow or other my destiny is linked with something relating to him.—Lord! madam, how should that be? said Bianca: I have always heard that your family was no way related to his: and I am sure I cannot conceive why my lady, the princess, sends you in a cold morning, or a damp evening, to pray at his tomb: he is no saint by the almanack.* If you must pray, why does not she bid you address yourself to our great saint Nicholas?* I am sure he is the saint I pray to for a husband. Perhaps my mind would be less affected, said Matilda, if my mother would explain her reasons to me: but it is the mystery she observes, that inspires me with this—I know not what to call it. As she never acts from caprice, I am sure there is some fatal secret at bottom—nay, I know there is: in her agony of grief for my brother's death she dropped some words that intimated as much.—Oh, dear madam, cried Bianca, what were they? No, said Matilda: if a parent lets fall a word, and wishes it recalled, it is not for a child to utter it. What! was she sorry for what she had said? asked Bianca—I am sure, madam, you may trust me.—With my own little secrets, when I have any, I may, said Matilda; but never with my mother's: a child ought to have no ears or eyes but as a parent directs. Well! to be sure, madam, you was born to be a saint, said Bianca, and there's no resisting one's vocation:* you will end in a convent at last. But there is my lady Isabella would not be so reserved to me: she will let me talk to her of young men; and when a handsome cavalier has come to the castle, she has owned to me that she wished your brother Conrad resembled him. Bianca, said the princess, I do not allow you to mention my friend disrespectfully. Isabella is of a cheerful disposition, but her soul is pure as virtue itself. She knows your idle babbling humour,* and perhaps has now and then encouraged it, to divert melancholy, and to enliven the solitude in which my father keeps us.—Blessed Mary! said Bianca starting, there it is again!—Dear madam, do you hear nothing?—This castle is certainly haunted!*—Peace! said Matilda, and listen! I did think I heard a voice—but it must be fancy; your terrors I suppose have infected me. Indeed! indeed! madam, said Bianca, half-weeping with agony, I am sure I heard a voice. Does any body lie in the chamber beneath? said the princess. Nobody has dared to lie there, answered Bianca, since the great astrologer that was your brother's tutor drowned himself.

For certain, madam, his ghost and the young prince's are now met in the chamber below—for heaven's sake let us fly to your mother's apartment! I charge you not to stir, said Matilda. If they are spirits in pain, we may ease their sufferings by questioning them.* They can mean no hurt to us, for we have not injured them—and if they should, shall we be more safe in one chamber than in another? Reach me my beads;* we will say a prayer, and then speak to them. Oh, dear lady, I would not speak to a ghost for the world, cried Bianca.—As she said those words, they heard the casement of the little chamber below Matilda's open. They listened attentively, and in few minutes thought they heard a person sing, but could not distinguish the words. This can be no evil spirit, said the princess in a low voice: it is undoubtedly one of the family—open the window, and we shall know the voice. I dare not indeed, madam, said Bianca. Thou art a very fool, said Matilda, opening the window gently herself. The noise the princess made was however heard by the person beneath, who stopped, and, they concluded, had heard the casement open. Is any body below? said the princess: if there is, speak. Yes, said an unknown voice. Who is it? said Matilda. A stranger, replied the voice. What stranger? said she; and how didst thou come there at this unusual hour, when all the gates of the castle are locked? I am not here willingly, answered the voice—but pardon me, lady, if I have disturbed your rest: I knew not that I was overheard. Sleep had forsaken me: I left a restless* couch, and came to waste the irksome hours with gazing on the fair approach of morning, impatient to be dismissed from this castle. Thy words and accents, said Matilda, are of a melancholy cast: if thou art unhappy, I pity thee. If poverty afflicts thee, let me know it; I will mention thee to the princess, whose beneficent soul ever melts for the distressed; and she will relieve thee. I am indeed unhappy, said the stranger; and I know not what wealth is: but I do not complain of the lot which heaven has cast for me: I am young and healthy, and am not ashamed of owing my support to myself— yet think me not proud, or that I disdain your generous offers. I will remember you in my orisons, and will pray for blessings on your gracious self and your noble mistress—If I sigh, lady, it is for others, not for myself. Now I have it, madam, said Bianca whispering the princess. This is certainly the young peasant; and by my conscience he is in love!——Well, this is a charming adventure!—— Do, madam, let us sift* him. He does not know you, but takes you for one of my lady Hippolita's women. Art thou not ashamed, Bianca? said the princess: what right have we to pry into the secrets of this young man's heart? He seems virtuous and frank, and tells us he is unhappy: are those circumstances that authorize us to make a property of him?* How are we entitled to his confidence? Lord! madam, how little you know of love! replied Bianca: why, lovers have no pleasure equal to talking of their mistress. And would you have *me* become a peasant's confidante? said the princess. Well then, let me talk to him, said Bianca: though I have the honour of being your highness's maid of honour, I was not always so great: besides, if love levels ranks, it raises them too: I have a respect for any young man in love.——Peace, simpleton!* said the princess. Though he said he was unhappy, it does not follow that he must be in love. Think of all that has happened to-day, and tell me if there are no misfortunes but what love causes. Stranger, resumed the princess, if thy misfortunes have not been occasioned by thy own fault, and are within the compass of the princess Hippolita's power to redress, I will take upon me to answer that she will be thy protectress. When thou art dismissed from this castle, repair to holy father Jerome* at the convent* adjoining the church of saint Nicholas, and make thy story known to him, as far as thou thinkest meet: he will not fail to inform the princess, who is the mother of all that want her assistance. Farewell: it is not seemly for me to hold farther converse with a man at this unwonted hour. May the saints guard thee, gracious lady! replied the peasant——but oh, if a poor and worthless stranger might presume to beg a minute's audience farther——am I so happy?—— the casement is not shut——might I venture to ask——Speak quickly, said Matilda; the morning dawns apace:* should the labourers come into the fields and perceive us——What wouldst thou ask—— I know not how——I know not if I dare, said the young stranger faltering——yet the humanity with which you have spoken to me emboldens—Lady! dare I trust you?—Heavens! said Matilda, what dost thou mean? with what wouldst thou trust me? Speak boldly, if thy secret is fit to be entrusted to a virtuous breast.— I would ask, said the peasant, recollecting himself, whether what I have heard from the domestics is true, that the princess is missing from the castle? What imports it to thee to know? replied Matilda. Thy first words bespoke a prudent and becoming gravity. Dost thou come hither to pry into the secrets of Manfred? Adieu. I have been mistaken in thee.—Saying these words, she shut the casement hastily, without giving the young man time to reply. I had acted more wisely, said the princess to Bianca with some sharpness, if I had let thee converse with this peasant: his inquisitiveness seems of a piece with thy own. It is not fit for me to argue with your highness, replied Bianca; but perhaps the questions I should have put to him, would have been more to the purpose, than those you have been pleased to ask him. Oh, no doubt, said Matilda; you are a very discreet personage! May I know what you would have asked him? A by-stander often sees more of the game than those that play,* answered Bianca. Does your highness think, madam, that his question about my lady Isabella was the result of mere curiosity? No, no, madam; there is more in it than you great folks are aware of. Lopez told me, that all the servants believe this young fellow contrived my lady Isabella's escape—Now, pray, madam, observe——You and I both know that my lady Isabella never much fancied the prince your brother.—Well! he is killed just in the critical minute—I accuse nobody. A helmet falls from the moon—so my lord your father says; but Lopez and all the servants say that this young spark* is a magician, and stole it from Alfonso's tomb.—Have done with this rhapsody* of impertinence, said Matilda. Nay, madam, as you please, cried Bianca—yet it is very particular though, that my lady Isabella should be missing the very same day, and that this young sorcerer should be found at the mouth of the trap-door—I accuse nobody—but if my young lord came honestly by his death—Dare not on thy duty, said Matilda, to breathe a suspicion on the purity of my dear Isabella's fame.—Purity, or not purity, said Bianca, gone she is: a stranger is found that nobody knows: you question him yourself: he tells you he is in love, or unhappy, it is the same thing—nay, he owned he was unhappy about others; and is any body unhappy about another, unless they are in love with them? And at the very next word he asks innocently, poor soul! if my lady Isabella is missing.—To be sure, said Matilda, thy observations are not totally without foundation—Isabella's flight amazes me: the curiosity of this stranger is very particular—yet Isabella never concealed a thought from me.—So she told you, said Bianca, to fish out your secrets*—but who knows, madam, but this stranger may be some prince in disguise?—Do, madam, let me open the window, and ask him a few questions. No, replied Matilda, I will ask him myself, if he knows aught of Isabella: he is not worthy that I should converse farther with him. She was going to open the casement, when they heard the bell ring at the postern-gate* of the castle, which is on the right hand of the tower, where Matilda lay. This prevented the princess from renewing the conversation with the stranger.

After continuing silent for some time; I am persuaded, said she to Bianca, that whatever be the cause of Isabella's flight, it had no unworthy motive. If this stranger was accessary to it, she must be satisfied of his fidelity and worth. I observed, did not you, Bianca? that his words were tinctured with an uncommon infusion of piety. It was no ruffian's speech: his phrases were becoming a man of gentle birth. I told you, madam, said Bianca, that I was sure he was some prince in disguise.—Yet, said Matilda, if he was privy to her escape, how will you account for his not accompanying her in her flight? Why expose himself unnecessarily and rashly to my father's resentment? As for that, madam, replied she, if he could get from under the helmet, he will find ways of eluding your father's anger. I do not doubt but he has some talisman* or other about him.—You resolve every thing into magic, said Matilda—but a man who has any intercourse with infernal spirits does not dare to make use of those tremendous and holy words which he uttered. Didst thou not observe with what fervour he vowed to remember *me* to heaven in his prayers? Yes, Isabella was undoubtedly convinced of his piety.—Commend me to the piety

of a young fellow and a damsel that consult to elope! said Bianca.
No, no, madam; my lady Isabella is of another-guess mould* than
you take her for. She used indeed to sigh and lift up her eyes in
your company, because she knows you are a saint—but when
your back was turned—You wrong her, said Matilda; Isabella is
no hypocrite: she has a due sense of devotion, but never affected
a call she has not. On the contrary, she always combated my inclination for the cloister: and though I own the mystery she has made
to me of her flight confounds me; though it seems inconsistent
with the friendship between us; I cannot forget the disinterested
warmth with which she always opposed my taking the veil: she
wished to see me married, though my dower* would have been
a loss to her and my brother's children. For her sake I will believe
well of this young peasant. Then you do think there is some liking
between them? said Bianca.—While she was speaking, a servant
came hastily into the chamber, and told the princess that the lady
Isabella was found. Where? said Matilda. She has taken sanctuary
in saint Nicholas's church, replied the servant: father Jerome has
brought the news himself: he is below with his highness. Where is
my mother? said Matilda. She is in her own chamber, madam, and
has asked for you.

Manfred had risen at the first dawn of light, and gone to
Hippolita's apartment, to enquire if she knew ought* of Isabella.
While he was questioning her, word was brought that Jerome
demanded to speak with him. Manfred, little suspecting the cause
of the friar's arrival, and knowing he was employed by Hippolita in
her charities, ordered him to be admitted, intending to leave them
together, while he pursued his search after Isabella. Is your business with me or the princess? said Manfred. With both, replied
the holy man. The lady Isabella—What of her? interrupted
Manfred eagerly—is at saint Nicholas's altar, replied Jerome.
That is no business of Hippolita, said Manfred with confusion:
let us retire to my chamber, father; and inform me how she came
thither. No, my lord, replied the good man with an air of firmness
and authority that daunted even the resolute Manfred, who could
not help revering the saint-like virtues of Jerome: my commission

is to both; and, with your highness's good-liking,* in the presence of both I shall deliver it—But first, my lord, I must interrogate the princess, whether she is acquainted with the cause of the lady Isabella's retirement from your castle.—No, on my soul, said Hippolita; does Isabella charge me with being privy to it?—Father, interrupted Manfred, I pay due reverence to your holy profession; but I am sovereign here, and will allow no meddling priest to interfere in the affairs of my domestic. If you have aught to say, attend me to my chamber—I do not use* to let my wife be acquainted with the secret affairs of my state; they are not within a woman's province. My lord, said the holy man, I am no intruder into the secrets of families. My office is to promote peace, to heal divisions, to preach repentance, and teach mankind to curb their headstrong passions. I forgive your highness's uncharitable apostrophe: I know my duty, and am the minister of a mightier prince than Manfred. Hearken to him who speaks through my organs. Manfred trembled with rage and shame. Hippolita's countenance declared her astonishment, and impatience to know where this would end: her silence more strongly spoke her observance of Manfred.

The lady Isabella, resumed Jerome, commends herself to both your highnesses; she thanks both for the kindness with which she has been treated in your castle: she deplores the loss of your son, and her own misfortune in not becoming the daughter of such wise and noble princes, whom she shall always respect as *parents*: she prays for uninterrupted union and felicity between you: [Manfred's colour changed]* but as it is no longer possible for her to be allied to you, she entreats your consent to remain in sanctuary till she can learn news of her father; or, by the certainty of his death, be at liberty, with the approbation of her guardians, to dispose of herself in suitable marriage. I shall give no such consent, said the prince; but insist on her return to the castle without delay: I am answerable for her person to her guardians, and will not brook her being in any hands but my own. Your highness will recollect whether that can any longer be proper, replied the friar. I want no monitor, said Manfred colouring. Isabella's conduct leaves room for strange suspicions—and that young villain, who was at least the accomplice of her flight, if not the cause of it—The cause! interrupted Jerome: was a *young* man the cause? This is not to be borne! cried Manfred. Am I to be bearded* in my own palace by an insolent monk? Thou art privy, I guess, to their amours. I would pray to heaven to clear up your uncharitable surmises, said Jerome, if your highness were not satisfied in your conscience how unjustly you accuse me. I do pray to heaven to pardon that uncharitableness: and I implore your highness to leave the princess at peace in that holy place, where she is not liable to be disturbed by such vain and worldly fantasies as discourses of love from any man. Cant* not to me, said Manfred, but return, and bring the princess to her duty. It is my duty to prevent her return hither, said Jerome. She is where orphans and virgins are safest from the snares and wiles of this world; and nothing but a parent's authority shall take her thence. I am her parent, cried Manfred, and demand her. She wished to have you for her parent, said the friar; but heaven, that forbad that connexion, has for ever dissolved all ties betwixt you: and I announce to your highness— Stop! audacious man, said Manfred, and dread my displeasure. Holy father, said Hippolita, it is your office to be no respecter of persons: you must speak as your duty prescribes: but it is my duty to hear nothing that it pleases not my lord I should hear. I will retire to my oratory,* and pray to the blessed Virgin to inspire you with her holy counsels, and to restore the heart of my gracious lord to its wonted peace and gentleness. Excellent woman! said the friar.—My lord, I attend your pleasure.

Manfred, accompanied by the friar, passed to his own apartment; where shutting the door, I perceive, father, said he, that Isabella has acquainted you with my purpose. Now hear my resolve, and obey. Reasons of state, most urgent reasons, my own and the safety of my people, demand that I should have a son. It is in vain to expect an heir from Hippolita. I have made choice of Isabella. You must bring her back; and you must do more. I know the influence you have with Hippolita: her conscience is in your hands. She is, I allow, a faultless woman: her soul is set on heaven, and scorns the little grandeur of this world: you can withdraw her from it entirely. Persuade her to consent to the dissolution of our marriage, and to retire into a monastery—she shall endow one if she will; and she shall have the means of being as liberal to your order as she or you can wish. Thus you will divert the calamities that are hanging over our heads, and have the merit of saving the principality of Otranto from destruction. You are a prudent man; and though the warmth of my temper betrayed me into some unbecoming expressions, I honour your virtue, and wish to be indebted to you for the repose of my life and the preservation of my family.

The will of heaven be done! said the friar. I am but its worthless instrument. It makes use of my tongue to tell thee, prince, of thy unwarrantable designs. The injuries of the virtuous Hippolita have mounted to the throne of pity. By me thou art reprimanded for thy adulterous intention of repudiating her: by me thou art warned not to pursue the incestuous design on thy contracted daughter. Heaven, that delivered her from thy fury, when the judgments so recently fallen on thy house ought to have inspired thee with other thoughts, will continue to watch over her. Even I, a poor and despised friar, am able to protect her from thy violence.—I, sinner as I am, and uncharitably reviled by your highness as an accomplice of I know not what amours, scorn the allurements with which it has pleased thee to tempt mine honesty. I love my order; I honour devout souls; I respect the piety of thy princess—but I will not betray the confidence she reposes* in me, nor serve even the cause of religion by foul and sinful compliances—But forsooth! the welfare of the state depends on your highness having a son. Heaven mocks the short-sighted views of man. But yester-morn, whose house was so great, so flourishing as Manfred's?—Where is young Conrad now?—My lord, I respect your tears—but I mean not to check them—Let them flow, prince! they will weigh more with heaven towards the welfare of thy subjects, than a marriage, which, founded on lust or policy, could never prosper. The sceptre, which passed from the race of Alfonso to thine, cannot be preserved by a match which the church will never allow. If it is the will of the Most High that Manfred's name must perish, resign yourself, my lord, to its decrees; and thus deserve a crown that can never pass away.*— Come, my lord, I like this sorrow—Let us return to the princess: she is not apprized of your cruel intentions; nor did I mean more than to alarm you. You saw with what gentle patience, with what efforts of love, she heard, she rejected hearing the extent of your guilt. I know she longs to fold you in her arms, and assure you of her unalterable affection. Father, said the prince, you mistake my compunction: true, I honour Hippolita's virtues; I think her a saint; and wish it were for my soul's health to tie faster the knot that has united us.—But alas! father, you know not the bitterest of my pangs! It is some time that I have had scruples on the legality of our union: Hippolita is related to me in the fourth degree*—It is true, we had a dispensation;* but I have been informed that she had also been contracted to another. This it is that sits heavy at my heart: to this state of unlawful wedlock I impute the visitation that has fallen on me in the death of Conrad!—Ease my conscience of this burden; dissolve our marriage, and accomplish the work of godliness which your divine exhortations have commenced in my soul.

How cutting was the anguish which the good man felt, when he perceived this turn in the wily prince! He trembled for Hippolita, whose ruin he saw was determined; and he feared, if Manfred had no hope of recovering Isabella, that his impatience for a son would direct him to some other object, who might not be equally proof against the temptation of Manfred's rank. For some time the holy man remained absorbed in thought. At length, conceiving some hope from delay, he thought the wisest conduct would be to prevent the prince from despairing of recovering Isabella. Her the friar knew he could dispose, from her affection to Hippolita, and from the aversion she had expressed to him for Manfred's addresses, to second his views, till the censures of the church could be fulminated* against a divorce. With this intention, as if struck with the prince's scruples, he at length said, My lord, I have been pondering on what your highness has said; and if in truth it is delicacy of conscience that is the real motive of your repugnance to your virtuous lady, far be it from me to endeavour to harden your heart! The church is an indulgent mother; unfold your griefs to her: she alone can administer comfort to your soul, either by satisfying your conscience, or, upon examination of your scruples, by setting you at liberty, and indulging you in the lawful means of continuing your lineage. In the latter case, if the lady Isabella can be brought to consent——Manfred, who concluded that he had either over-reached* the good man, or that his first warmth had been but a tribute paid to appearance, was overjoyed at this sudden turn, and repeated the most magnificent promises, if he should succeed by the friar's mediation. The well-meaning priest suffered him to deceive himself, fully determined to traverse his views,* instead of seconding them.

Since we now understand one another, resumed the prince, I expect, father, that you satisfy me in one point. Who is the youth that we found in the vault? He must have been privy to Isabella's flight: tell me truly; is he her lover? or is he an agent for another's passion? I have often suspected Isabella's indifference to my son: a thousand circumstances crowd on my mind that confirm that suspicion. She herself was so conscious of it, that, while I discoursed her in the gallery, she outran my suspicions, and endeavoured to justify herself from coolness to Conrad. The friar, who knew nothing of the youth but what he had learnt occasionally from the princess, ignorant what was become of him, and not sufficiently reflecting on the impetuosity of Manfred's temper, conceived that it might not be amiss to sow the seeds of jealousy in his mind: they might be turned to some use hereafter, either by prejudicing the prince against Isabella, if he persisted in that union; or, by diverting his attention to a wrong scent, and employing his thoughts on a visionary intrigue, prevent his engaging in any new pursuit. With this unhappy policy, he answered in a manner to confirm Manfred in the belief of some connection between Isabella and the youth. The prince, whose passions wanted little fuel to throw them into a blaze, fell into a rage at the idea of what the friar suggested. I will fathom to the bottom of this intrigue, cried he; and quitting Jerome abruptly, with a command to remain there till his return, he hastened to the great hall of the castle, and ordered the peasant to be brought before him.

Thou hardened young impostor! said the prince, as soon as he saw the youth; what becomes of thy boasted veracity now? It was Providence, was it, and the light of the moon, that discovered the lock of the trap-door to thee? Tell me, audacious boy, who thou art, and how long thou hast been acquainted with the princess—and take care to answer with less equivocation than thou didst last night, or tortures shall wring the truth from thee. The young man, perceiving that his share in the flight of the princess was discovered, and concluding that any thing he should say could no longer be of service or detriment to her, replied, I am no impostor, my lord; nor have I deserved opprobrious language. I answered to every question your highness put to me last night with the same veracity that I shall speak now: and that will not be from fear of your tortures, but because my soul abhors a falsehood. Please to repeat your questions, my lord; I am ready to give you all the satisfaction in my power. You know my questions, replied the prince, and only want time to prepare an evasion. Speak directly; who art thou? and how long hast thou been known to the princess? I am a labourer at the next village, said the peasant; my name is Theodore.* The princess found me in the vault last night: before that hour I never was in her presence.—I may believe as much or as little as I please of this, said Manfred; but I will hear thy own story, before I examine into the truth of it. Tell me, what reason did the princess give thee for making her escape? Thy life depends on thy answer. She told me, replied Theodore, that she was on the brink of destruction; and that, if she could not escape from the castle, she was in danger in a few moments of being made miserable for ever. And on this slight foundation, on a silly girl's report, said Manfred, thou didst hazard my displeasure? I fear no man's displeasure, said Theodore, when a woman in distress puts herself under my protection.—During this examination, Matilda was going to the apartment of Hippolita. At the upper end of the hall, where Manfred sat, was a boarded* gallery with latticed windows, through which Matilda and Bianca were to pass. Hearing her father's voice, and seeing the servants assembled round him, she stopped to learn the occasion. The prisoner soon drew her attention: the steady and composed manner in which he answered, and the gallantry of his last reply, which were the first words she heard distinctly, interested her in his favour. His person was noble, handsome and commanding, even in that situation: but his countenance soon engrossed her whole care. Heavens! Bianca, said the princess softly, do I dream? or is not that youth the exact resemblance of Alfonso's picture in the gallery? She could say no more, for her father's voice grew louder at every word. This bravado, said he, surpasses all thy former insolence. Thou shalt experience the wrath with which thou darest to trifle. Seize him, continued Manfred, and bind him—the first news the princess hears of her champion shall be, that he has lost his head for her sake. The injustice of which thou art guilty towards me, said Theodore, convinces me that I have done a good deed in delivering the princess from thy tyranny. May she be happy, whatever becomes of me!—This is a lover! cried Manfred in a rage: a peasant within sight of death is not animated by such sentiments. Tell me, tell me, rash boy, who thou art, or the rack shall force thy secret from thee. Thou hast threatened me with death already, said the youth, for the truth I have told thee: if that is all the encouragement I am to expect for sincerity, I am not tempted to indulge thy vain curiosity farther. Then thou wilt not speak? said Manfred. I will not, replied he. Bear him away into the court-yard, said Manfred; I will see his head this instant severed from his body.—Matilda fainted at hearing those words. Bianca shrieked, and cried, Help! help! the princess is dead! Manfred started at this ejaculation, and demanded what was the matter. The young peasant, who heard it too, was struck with horror, and asked eagerly the same question; but Manfred ordered him to be hurried into the court, and kept there for execution, till he had informed himself of the cause of Bianca's shrieks. When he learned the meaning, he treated it as a womanish panic; and ordering Matilda to be carried to her apartment, he rushed into the court, and, calling for one of his guards, bade Theodore kneel down and prepare to receive the fatal blow.

The undaunted youth received the bitter sentence with a resignation that touched every heart but Manfred's. He wished earnestly to know the meaning of the words he had heard relating to the princess; but, fearing to exasperate the tyrant more against her, he desisted. The only boon* he deigned to ask was, that he might be permitted to have a confessor, and make his peace with heaven. Manfred, who hoped by the confessor's means to come at the youth's history, readily granted his request: and being convinced that father Jerome was now in his interest, he ordered him to be called and shrieve* the prisoner. The holy man, who had little foreseen the catastrophe that his imprudence occasioned, fell on his knees to the prince, and adjured him in the most solemn manner not to shed innocent blood. He accused himself in the bitterest terms for his indiscretion, endeavoured to disculpate the youth, and left no method untried to soften the tyrant's rage. Manfred, more incensed than appeased by Jerome's intercession, whose retraction now made him suspect he had been imposed upon by both, commanded the friar to do his duty, telling him he would not allow the prisoner many minutes for confession. Nor do I ask many, my lord, said the unhappy young man. My sins, thank heaven! have not been numerous; nor exceed what might be expected at my years. Dry your tears, good father, and let us dispatch: this is a bad world; nor have I had cause to leave it with regret. Oh! wretched youth! said Jerome; how canst thou bear the sight of me with patience? I am thy murderer! It is I have brought this dismal hour upon thee!—I forgive thee from my soul, said the youth, as I hope heaven will pardon me. Hear my confession, father; and give me thy blessing. How can I prepare thee for thy passage, as I ought? said Jerome. Thou canst not be saved without pardoning thy foes—and canst thou forgive that impious man there? I can, said Theodore; I do.—And does not this touch thee, cruel prince? said the friar. I sent for thee to confess him, said Manfred sternly; not to plead for him. Thou didst first incense me against him—his blood be upon thy head!—It will! it will! said the good man in an agony of sorrow. Thou and I must never hope to go where this blessed youth is going.—Dispatch! said Manfred: I am no more to be moved by the whining of priests, than by the shrieks of women. What! said the youth, is it possible that my fate could have occasioned what I heard? Is the princess then again in thy power?—Thou dost but remember me of my wrath, said Manfred: prepare thee, for this moment is thy last. The youth, who felt his indignation rise, and who was touched with the sorrow which he saw he had infused into all the spectators, as well as into the friar, suppressed his emotions, and, putting off his doublet and unbuttoning his collar, knelt down to his prayers. As he stooped, his shirt flipped down below his shoulder, and discovered the mark of a bloody arrow.* Gracious heaven! cried the holy man starting, what do I see? It is my child! my Theodore!

The passions that ensued must be conceived; they cannot be painted. The tears of the assistants were suspended by wonder, rather than stopped by joy. They seemed to enquire in the eyes of their lord what they ought to feel. Surprise, doubt, tenderness, respect, succeeded each other in the countenance of the youth. He received with modest submission the effusion of the old man's tears and embraces: yet afraid of giving a loose to* hope, and suspecting from what had passed the inflexibility of Manfred's temper, he cast a glance towards the prince, as if to say, Canst thou be unmoved at such a scene as this?

Manfred's heart was capable of being touched.* He forgot his anger in his astonishment; yet his pride forbad his owning himself affected. He even doubted whether this discovery was not a contrivance of the friar to save the youth. What may this mean! said he. How can he be thy son? Is it consistent with thy profession or reputed sanctity to avow a peasant's offspring for the fruit of thy irregular amours?—Oh God! said the holy man, dost thou question his being mine? Could I feel the anguish I do, if I were not his father? Spare him! good prince, spare him! and revile me as thou pleasest.—Spare him! spare him! cried the attendants, for this good man's sake!—Peace! said Manfred sternly: I must know more, ere I am disposed to pardon. A saint's bastard may be no saint himself—Injurious lord! said Theodore: add not insult to cruelty. If I am this venerable man's son, though no prince as thou art, know, the blood that flows in my veins—Yes, said the friar, interrupting him, his blood is noble: nor is he that abject* thing, my lord, you speak* him. He is my lawful son; and Sicily can boast of few houses more ancient than that of Falconara—But alas! my lord, what is blood? what is nobility? We are all reptiles, miserable sinful creatures. It is piety alone that can distinguish us from the dust whence we sprung, and whither we must return.*— Truce to your sermon, said Manfred; you forget you are no longer friar Jerome, but the count of Falconara. Let me know your history; you will have time to moralize hereafter, if you should not happen to obtain the grace of that sturdy criminal there. Mother of God! said the friar, is it possible my lord can refuse a father the life of his only, his long lost child? Trample me, my lord, scorn, afflict me, accept my life for his, but spare my son!—Thou canst feel then, said Manfred, what it is to lose an only son? A little hour ago thou didst preach up resignation to me: *my* house, if fate so pleased, must perish—but the count of Falconara—Alas! my lord, said Jerome, I confess I have offended; but aggravate not an old man's sufferings. I boast not of my family, nor think of such vanities—it is nature that pleads for this boy; it is the memory of the dear woman that bore him—Is she, Theodore, is she dead?—Her soul has long been with the blessed, said Theodore. Oh how? cried Jerome, tell me—No—she is happy! Thou art all my care now!—Most dread lord! will you—will you grant me my poor boy's life? Return to thy convent, answered Manfred; conduct the princess hither; obey me in what else thou knowest; and I promise thee the life of thy son.——Oh! my lord, said Jerome, is honesty the price I must pay for this dear youth's safety?— For me! cried Theodore: let me die a thousand deaths, rather than stain thy conscience. What is it the tyrant would exact of thee? Is the princess safe from his power? Protect her, thou venerable old man! and let all his wrath fall on me. Jerome endeavoured to check the impetuosity of the youth; and ere Manfred

could reply, the trampling of horses was heard, and a brazen*
trumpet, which hung without the gate of the castle, was suddenly
sounded. At the same instant the sable plumes on the enchanted
helmet, which still remained at the other end of the court, were
tempestuously agitated, and nodded thrice, as if bowed by some
invisible wearer.

CHAPTER III

MANFRED'S heart misgave him when he beheld the plumage on the miraculous casque shaken in concert with the sounding of the brazen trumpet. Father! said he to Jerome, whom he now ceased to treat as count of Falconara, what mean these portents? If I have offended—[the plumes were shaken with greater violence than before] Unhappy prince that I am! cried Manfred—Holy Father! will you not assist me with your prayers?—My lord, replied Jerome, heaven is no doubt displeased with your mockery of its servants. Submit yourself to the church; and cease to persecute her ministers. Dismiss this innocent youth; and learn to respect the holy character I wear: heaven will not be trifled with: you see——[the trumpet sounded again] I acknowledge I have been too hasty, said Manfred. Father, do you go to the wicket,* and demand who is at the gate. Do you grant me the life of Theodore? replied the friar. I do, said Manfred; but enquire who is without.

Jerome, falling on the neck of his son, discharged a flood of tears, that spoke the fulness of his soul. You promised to go to the gate, said Manfred. I thought, replied the friar, your highness would excuse my thanking you first in this tribute of my heart. Go, dearest sir, said Theodore, obey the prince; I do not deserve that you should delay his satisfaction for me.

Jerome, enquiring who was without, was answered, A herald.* From whom? said he. From the knight of the gigantic sabre, said the herald: and I must speak with the usurper of Otranto. Jerome returned to the prince, and did not fail to repeat the message in the very words it had been uttered. The first sounds struck Manfred with terror; but when he heard himself styled usurper, his rage rekindled, and all his courage revived. Usurper!—Insolent villain! cried he, who dares to question my title? Retire, father; this is no business for monks: I will meet this presumptuous man myself. Go to your convent, and prepare the princess's return: your son shall be a hostage for your fidelity: his life depends on your obedience.—Good heaven! my lord, cried Jerome, your highness did but this instant freely pardon my child—have you so soon forgot the interposition* of heaven?—Heaven, replied Manfred, does not send heralds to question the title of a lawful prince—I doubt whether it even notifies its will through friars—but that is your affair, not mine. At present you know my pleasure; and it is not a saucy* herald that shall save your son, if you do not return with the princess.

It was in vain for the holy man to reply. Manfred commanded him to be conducted to the postern-gate, and shut out from the castle: and he ordered some of his attendants to carry Theodore to the top of the black tower, and guard him strictly; scarce permitting the father and son to exchange a hasty embrace at parting. He then withdrew to the hall, and, seating himself in princely state, ordered the herald to be admitted to his presence.

Well, thou insolent! said the prince, what wouldst thou with me? I come, replied he, to thee, Manfred, usurper of the principality of Otranto, from the renowned and invincible knight, the knight of the gigantic sabre: in the name of his lord, Frederic marquis of Vicenza,* he demands the lady Isabella, daughter of that prince, whom thou hast basely and traitorously got into thy power, by bribing her false guardians during his absence; and he requires thee to resign the principality of Otranto, which thou hast usurped from the said lord Frederic, the nearest of blood to the last rightful lord Alfonso the Good. If thou dost not instantly comply with these just demands, he defies* thee to single combat to the last extremity. And so saying, the herald cast down his warder.*

And where is this braggart, who sends thee? said Manfred. At the distance of a league,* said the herald: he comes to make good his lord's claim against thee, as he is a true knight, and thou an usurper and ravisher.

Injurious as this challenge was, Manfred reflected that it was not his interest to provoke the marquis. He knew how well-founded the claim of Frederic was; nor was this the first time he had heard of it. Frederic's ancestors had assumed the style of princes of Otranto, from the death of Alfonso the Good without issue:*

but Manfred, his father, and grandfather, had been too powerful for the house of Vicenza to dispossess them. Frederic, a martial and amorous young prince, had married a beautiful young lady, of whom he was enamoured, and who had died in childbed of Isabella. Her death affected him so much, that he had taken the cross and gone to the Holy Land,* where he was wounded in an engagement against the infidels, made prisoner, and reported to be dead. When the news reached Manfred's ears, he bribed the guardians of the lady Isabella to deliver her up to him as a bride for his son Conrad; by which alliance he had purposed to unite the claims of the two houses. This motive, on Conrad's death, had co-operated to make him so suddenly resolve on espousing her himself;* and the same reflection determined him now to endeavour at obtaining the consent of Frederic to this marriage. A like policy inspired him with the thought of inviting Frederic's champion into his castle, lest he should be informed of Isabella's flight, which he strictly enjoined his domestics not to disclose to any of the knight's retinue.

Herald, said Manfred, as soon as he had digested these reflections, return to thy master, and tell him, ere we liquidate our differences by the sword, Manfred would hold some converse with him. Bid him welcome to my castle, where, by my faith, as I am a true knight, he shall have courteous reception, and full security for himself and followers. If we cannot adjust* our quarrel by amicable means, I swear he shall depart in safety, and shall have full satisfaction according to the law of arms: so help me God and his holy Trinity!—The herald made three obeisances, and retired.

During this interview Jerome's mind was agitated by a thousand contrary passions. He trembled for the life of his son, and his first idea was to persuade Isabella to return to the castle. Yet he was scarce less alarmed at the thought of her union with Manfred. He dreaded Hippolita's unbounded submission to the will of her lord: and though he did not doubt but he could alarm her piety not to consent to a divorce, if he could get access to her; yet should Manfred discover that the obstruction came from him, it might be equally fatal to Theodore. He was impatient to know whence came the herald, who with so little management* had questioned the title of Manfred: yet he did not dare absent himself from the convent, lest Isabella should leave it, and her flight be imputed to him. He returned disconsolately to the monastery, uncertain on what conduct to resolve. A monk, who met him in the porch and observed his melancholy air, said, Alas! brother, is it then true that we have lost our excellent princess Hippolita? The holy man started, and cried, What meanest thou, brother? I come this instant from the castle, and left her in perfect health. Martelli, replied the other friar, passed by the convent but a quarter of an hour ago on his way from the castle, and reported that her highness was dead. All our brethren are gone to the chapel to pray for her happy transit to a better life, and willed me to wait thy arrival. They know thy holy attachment to that good lady, and are anxious for the affliction it will cause in thee—Indeed we have all reason to weep; she was a mother to our house—But this life is but a pilgrimage; we must not murmur—we shall all follow her; may our end be like hers!—Good brother, thou dreamest, said Jerome: I tell thee I come from the castle, and left the princess well—Where is the lady Isabella?—Poor gentle-woman! replied the friar; I told her the sad news, and offered her spiritual comfort; I reminded her of the transitory condition of mortality, and advised her to take the veil: I quoted the example of the holy princess Sanchia of Arragon.*—Thy zeal was laudable, said Jerome impatiently; but at present it was unnecessary: Hippolita is well—at least I trust in the Lord she is; I heard nothing to the contrary—Yet methinks the prince's earnestness—Well, brother, but where is the lady Isabella?—I know not, said the friar: she wept much, and said she would retire to her chamber. Jerome left his comrade abruptly, and hasted* to the princess, but she was not in her chamber. He enquired of the domestics of the convent, but could learn no news of her. He searched in vain throughout the monastery and the church, and dispatched messengers round the neighbourhood, to get intelligence if she had been seen; but to no purpose. Nothing could equal the good man's perplexity. He judged that Isabella, suspecting Manfred of having precipitated his wife's death, had taken the alarm, and withdrawn herself to some more secret place of concealment. This new flight would probably carry the prince's fury to the height. The report of Hippolita's death, though it seemed almost incredible, increased his consternation; and though Isabella's escape bespoke her aversion of Manfred for a husband, Jerome could feel no comfort from it, while it endangered the life of his son. He determined to return to the castle, and made several of his brethren accompany him, to attest his innocence to Manfred, and, if necessary, join their intercession with his for Theodore.

The prince, in the mean time, had passed into the court, and ordered the gates of the castle to be flung open for the reception of the stranger knight and his train. In a few minutes the cavalcade arrived.* First came two harbingers* with wands.* Next a herald, followed by two pages and two trumpets. Then an hundred foot-guards. These were attended by as many horse. After them fifty footmen, clothed in scarlet and black, the colours of the knight. Then a led horse.* Two heralds on each side of a gentleman on horseback bearing a banner with the arms of Vicenza and Otranto quarterly*—a circumstance that much offended Manfred—but he stifled his resentment. Two more pages. The knight's confessor telling his beads.* Fifty more footmen, clad as before. Two knights habited in complete armour, their beavers* down, comrades to the principal knight. The 'squires of the two knights, carrying their shields and devices. The knight's own 'squire. An hundred gentle-men bearing an enormous sword, and seeming to faint under the weight of it. The knight himself on a chestnut steed, in complete armour, his lance in the rest, his face entirely concealed by his vizor, which was surmounted by a large plume of scarlet and black feathers. Fifty foot-guards with drums and trumpets closed the procession, which wheeled off to the right and left to make room for the principal knight.

As soon as he approached the gate, he stopped; and the herald advancing, read again the words of the challenge. Manfred's eyes were fixed on the gigantic sword, and he scarce seemed to attend to the cartel:* but his attention was soon diverted by a tempest of wind that rose behind him. He turned, and beheld the plumes of the enchanted helmet agitated in the same extraordinary manner as before. It required intrepidity like Manfred's not to sink under a concurrence of circumstances that seemed to announce his fate. Yet scorning in the presence of strangers to betray the courage he had always manifested, he said boldly, Sir knight, whoever thou art, I bid thee welcome. If thou art of mortal mould, thy valour shall meet its equal: and if thou art a true knight, thou wilt scorn to employ sorcery to carry thy point. Be these omens from heaven or hell, Manfred trusts to the righteousness of his cause and to the aid of saint Nicholas, who has ever protected his house. Alight, sir knight, and repose thyself. To-morrow thou shalt have a fair field; and heaven befriend the juster side!

The knight made no reply, but, dismounting, was conducted by Manfred to the great hall of the castle. As they traversed the court, the knight stopped to gaze at the miraculous casque; and, kneeling down, seemed to pray inwardly for some minutes. Rising, he made a sign to the prince to lead on. As soon as they entered the hall, Manfred proposed to the stranger to disarm; but the knight shook his head in token of refusal. Sir knight, said Manfred, this is not courteous; but by my good faith I will not cross thee! nor shalt thou have cause to complain of the prince of Otranto. No treachery is designed on my part: I hope none is intended on thine. Here take my gage:* [giving him his ring] your friends and you shall enjoy the laws of hospitality. Rest here until refreshments are brought: I will but give orders for the accommodation of your train, and return to you. The three knights bowed, as accepting his courtesy. Manfred directed the stranger's retinue to be conducted to an adjacent hospital,* founded by the princess Hippolita for the reception of pilgrims. As they made the circuit of the court to return towards the gate, the gigantic sword burst from the supporters, and, falling to the ground opposite to the helmet, remained immoveable. Manfred, almost hardened to preternatural* appearances, surmounted the shock of this new prodigy; and returning to the hall, where by this time the feast was ready, he invited his silent guests to take their places. Manfred, however ill his heart was at ease, endeavoured to inspire the company with mirth. He put several questions to them, but was answered only by signs. They raised their vizors but sufficiently to feed themselves, and that sparingly. Sirs, said the prince, ye are the first guests I ever treated within these walls, who scorned to hold any intercourse with me: nor has it oft been customary, I ween,* for princes to hazard their state and dignity against strangers and mutes. You say you come in the name of Frederic of Vicenza: I have ever heard that he was a gallant and courteous knight; nor would he, I am bold to say, think it beneath him to mix in social converse with a prince that is his equal, and not unknown by deeds in arms.—Still ye are silent—Well! be it as it may—by the laws of hospitality and chivalry ye are masters under this roof: ye shall do your pleasure—but come, give me a goblet of wine; ye will not refuse to pledge me to the healths of your fair mistresses. The principal knight sighed and crossed himself, and was rising from the board—Sir knight, said Manfred, what I said was but in sport: I shall constrain you in nothing; use your good liking. Since mirth is not your mood, let us be sad. Business may hit your fancies better: let us withdraw; and hear if what I have to unfold may be better relished than the vain efforts I have made for your pastime.

Manfred, then, conducting the three knights into an inner chamber, shut the door, and, inviting them to be seated, began thus, addressing himself to the chief personage:

You come, sir knight, as I understand, in the name of the marquis of Vicenza, to re-demand* the lady Isabella his daughter, who has been contracted in the face of holy church to my son, by the consent of her legal guardians; and to require me to resign my dominions to your lord, who gives himself for the nearest of blood to prince Alfonso, whose soul God rest! I shall speak to the latter article of your demands first. You must know, your lord knows, that I enjoy the principality of Otranto from my father Don Manuel, as he received it from his father Don Ricardo. Alfonso, their predecessor, dying childless in the Holy Land, bequeathed his estates to my grandfather Don Ricardo, in consideration of his faithful services—[The stranger shook his head]—Sir knight, said Manfred warmly, Ricardo was a valiant and upright man; he was a pious man; witness his munificent foundation of the adjoining church and two convents. He was peculiarly patronized by saint Nicholas—My grandfather was incapable—I say, sir, Don Ricardo was incapable—Excuse me, your interruption has disordered me—I venerate the memory of my grandfather—Well, sirs! he held this estate; he held it by his good sword, and by the favour of saint Nicholas—so did my father; and so, sirs, will I, come what will.—But Frederic, your lord, is nearest in blood—I have consented to put my title to the issue of the sword—does that imply a vitious* title? I might have asked, where is Frederic, your lord? Report speaks him dead in captivity. You say, your actions say, he lives—I question it not—I might, sirs, I might—but I do not. Other princes would bid Frederic take his inheritance by force, if he can: they would not stake their dignity on a single combat: they would not submit it to the decision of unknown mutes!* Pardon me, gentlemen, I am too warm: but suppose yourselves in my situation: as ye are stout knights, would it not move your choler* to have your own and the honour of your ancestors called in question?—But to the point. Ye require me to deliver up the lady Isabella—Sirs, I must ask if ye are authorized to receive her? [The knight nodded.] Receive her—continued Manfred: Well! you are authorized to receive her—But, gentle knight, may I ask if you have full powers? [The knight nodded.] 'Tis well, said Manfred: then hear what I have to offer—Ye see, gentlemen, before you the most unhappy of men! [he began to weep] afford me your compassion; I am entitled to it; indeed I am. Know, I have lost my only hope, my joy, the support of my house—Conrad died yester-morning. [The knights discovered signs of surprise.] Yes, sirs, fate has disposed of my son. Isabella is at liberty.—Do you then restore her, cried the chief knight, breaking silence. Afford me your patience, said Manfred. I rejoice to find, by this testimony of your good-will, that this matter may be adjusted without blood. It is no interest of mine dictates what little I have farther to say. Ye behold in me a man disgusted with the world:* the loss of my son has weaned me from earthly cares. Power and greatness have no longer any charms in my eyes. I wished to transmit the sceptre I had received from my ancestors with honour to my son—but that is over! Life itself is so indifferent to me, that I accepted your defiance with joy: a good knight cannot go to the grave with more satisfaction than when falling in his vocation. Whatever is the will of heaven, I submit; for, alas! sirs, I am a man of many sorrows.* Manfred is no object of envy—but no doubt you are acquainted with my story. [The knight made signs of ignorance, and seemed curious to have Manfred proceed.] Is it possible, sirs, continued the prince, that my story should be a secret to you? Have you heard nothing relating to me and the princess Hippolita? [They shook their heads]—No! Thus then, sirs, it is. You think me ambitious: ambition, alas, is composed of more rugged materials.* If I were ambitious, I should not for so many years have been a prey to the hell of conscientious scruples—But I weary your patience: I will be brief. Know then, that I have long been troubled in mind on my union with the princess Hippolita.—Oh! sirs, if ye were acquainted with that excellent woman! if ye knew that I adore her like a mistress, and cherish her as a friend—But man was not born for perfect happiness! She shares my scruples, and with her consent I have brought this matter before the church, for we are related within the forbidden degrees. I expect every hour the definitive sentence that must separate us forever. I am sure you feel for me—I see you do—Pardon these tears! [The knights gazed on each other, wondering where this would end.] Manfred continued: The death of my son betiding while my soul was under this anxiety, I thought of nothing but resigning my dominions, and retiring forever from the sight of mankind. My only difficulty was to fix on a successor, who would be tender of my people, and to dispose of the lady Isabella, who is dear to me as my own blood. I was willing to restore the line of Alfonso, even in his most distant kindred: and though, pardon me, I am satisfied it was his will that Ricardo's lineage should take place of his own relations; yet, where was I to search for those relations? I knew of none but Frederic, your lord: he was a captive to the infidels, or dead; and were he living, and at home, would he quit the flourishing state of Vicenza for the inconsiderable principality of Otranto? If he would not, could I bear the thought of seeing a hard unfeeling viceroy* set over my poor faithful people?—for, sirs, I love my people, and thank heaven am beloved by them.—But ye will ask, Whither tends this long discourse? Briefly then, thus, sirs. Heaven in your arrival seems to point out a remedy for these difficulties and my misfortunes. The lady Isabella is at liberty: I shall soon be so. I would submit to any thing for the good of my people—Were it not the best, the only way to extinguish the feuds between our families, if I were to take the lady Isabella to wife?—You start—But though Hippolita's virtues will ever be dear to me, a prince must not consider himself; he is born for his people.—A servant at that instant entering the chamber, apprized Manfred that Jerome and several of his brethren demanded immediate access to him.

The prince, provoked at this interruption, and fearing that the friar would discover to the strangers that Isabella had taken sanctuary, was going to forbid Jerome's entrance. But recollecting that he was certainly arrived to notify the princess's return, Manfred began to excuse himself to the knights for leaving them for a few moments, but was prevented by the arrival of the friars. Manfred angrily reprimanded them for their intrusion, and would have forced them back from the chamber; but Jerome was too much agitated to be repulsed. He declared aloud the flight of Isabella, with protestations of his own innocence. Manfred, distracted at the news, and not less at its coming to the knowledge of the strangers, uttered nothing but incoherent sentences, now upbraiding the friar, now apologizing to the knights, earnest to know what was become of Isabella, yet equally afraid of their knowing, impatient to pursue her, yet dreading to have them join in the pursuit. He offered to dispatch messengers in quest of her:—but the chief knight, no longer keeping silence, reproached Manfred in bitter terms for his dark and ambiguous dealing, and demanded the cause of Isabella's first absence from the castle. Manfred, casting a stern look at Jerome, implying a command of silence, pretended that on Conrad's death he had placed her in sanctuary until he could determine how to dispose of her. Jerome, who trembled for his son's life, did not dare contradict this falsehood; but one of his brethren, not under the same anxiety, declared frankly that she had fled to their church in the preceding night. The prince in vain endeavoured to stop this discovery, which overwhelmed him with shame and confusion. The principal stranger, amazed at the contradictions he heard, and more than half persuaded that Manfred had secreted the princess, notwithstanding the concern he expressed at her flight, rushing to the door, said, Thou traitor-prince! Isabella shall be found. Manfred endeavoured to hold him; but the other knights assisting their comrade, he broke from the prince, and hastened into the court, demanding his attendants. Manfred, finding it in vain to divert him from the pursuit, offered to accompany him; and summoning his attendants, and taking Jerome and some of the friars to guide them, they issued from the castle; Manfred privately giving orders to have the knight's company secured, while to the knight he affected to dispatch a messenger to require their assistance.

The company had no sooner quitted the castle, than Matilda, who felt herself deeply interested for the young peasant, since she had seen him condemned to death in the hall, and whose thoughts had been taken up with concerting measures to save him, was informed by some of the female attendants that Manfred had dispatched all his men various ways in pursuit of Isabella. He had in his hurry given this order in general terms, not meaning to extend it to the guard he had set upon Theodore, but forgetting it. The domestics, officious to obey so peremptory a prince, and urged by their own curiosity and love of novelty to join in any precipitate chace, had to a man left the castle. Matilda disengaged herself from her women, stole up to the black tower, and, unbolting the door, presented herself to the astonished Theodore. Young man, said she, though filial duty and womanly modesty condemn the step I am taking, yet holy charity, surmounting all other ties, justifies this act. Fly; the doors of thy prison are open: my father and his domestics are absent; but they may soon return: begone in safety; and may the angels of heaven direct thy course!—Thou art surely one of those angels! said the enraptured Theodore: none but a blessed saint could speak, could act, could look like thee!— May I not know the name of my divine protectress? Methought thou namedst thy father: is it possible? can Manfred's blood feel holy pity?—Lovely lady, thou answerest not—But how art thou here thyself? Why dost thou neglect thy own safety, and waste a thought on a wretch like Theodore? Let us fly together: the life thou bestowest shall be dedicated to thy defence. Alas! thou mistakest, said Matilda sighing: I am Manfred's daughter, but no dangers await me. Amazement! said Theodore: but last night I blessed myself for yielding thee the service thy gracious compassion so charitably returns me now. Still thou art in an error, said the princess; but this is no time for explanation. Fly, virtuous youth, while it is in my power to save thee: should my father return, thou and I both should indeed have cause to tremble. How? said Theodore: thinkest thou, charming maid, that I will accept of life at the hazard of aught calamitous to thee? Better I endured a thousand deaths——I run no risk, said Matilda, but by thy delay. Depart: it cannot be known that I assisted thy flight. Swear by the saints above, said Theodore, that thou canst not be suspected; else here I vow to await whatever can befall me. Oh! thou art too generous, said Matilda; but rest assured that no suspicion can alight on me. Give me thy beauteous hand in token that thou dost not deceive me, said Theodore; and let me bathe it with the warm tears of gratitude.—Forbear, said the princess: this must not be.—Alas! said Theodore, I have never known but calamity until this hour—perhaps shall never know other fortune again: suffer the chaste raptures of holy gratitude: 'tis my soul would print its effusions on thy hand.—Forbear, and begone, said Matilda: how would Isabella approve of seeing thee at my feet? Who is Isabella? said the young man with surprise. Ah me! I fear, said the princess, I am serving a deceitful one! Hast thou forgot thy curiosity this morning?—Thy looks, thy actions, all thy beauteous self seems an emanation of divinity, said Theodore, but thy words are dark and mysterious——Speak, lady, speak to thy servant's comprehension.—Thou understandest but too well, said Matilda: but once more I command thee to be gone: thy blood, which I may preserve, will be on my head, if I waste the time in vain discourse. I go, lady, said Theodore, because it is thy will, and because

I would not bring the grey hairs of my father with sorrow to the grave. Say but, adored lady, that I have thy gentle pity.—Stay, said Matilda; I will conduct thee to the subterraneous vault by which Isabella escaped; it will lead thee to the church of saint Nicholas, where thou mayst take sanctuary.—What! said Theodore, was it another, and not thy lovely self, that I assisted to find the subterraneous passage? It was, said Matilda: but ask no more; I tremble to see thee still abide here: fly to the sanctuary.—To sanctuary! said Theodore: No princess; sanctuaries are for helpless damsels, or for criminals. Theodore's soul is free from guilt, nor will wear the appearance of it. Give me a sword, lady, and thy father shall learn that Theodore scorns an ignominious flight. Rash youth! said Matilda, thou wouldst not dare to lift thy presumptuous arm against the prince of Otranto? Not against *thy* father; indeed I dare not, said Theodore: excuse me, lady; I had forgotten—but could I gaze on thee, and remember thou art sprung from the tyrant Manfred?—But he is thy father, and from this moment my injuries are buried in oblivion. A deep and hollow groan, which seemed to come from above, startled the princess and Theodore. Good heaven! we are overheard! said the princess. They listened; but perceiving no farther noise, they both concluded it the effect of pent-up vapours:* and the princess, preceding Theodore softly, carried him to her father's armoury; where equipping him with a complete suit,* he was conducted by Matilda to the postern-gate. Avoid the town, said the princess, and all the western side of the castle: 'tis there the search must be making by Manfred and the strangers: but hie thee to the opposite quarter. Yonder, behind that forest to the east is a chain of rocks, hollowed into a labyrinth of caverns that reach to the sea-coast. There thou mayst lie concealed, till thou canst make signs to some vessel to put on shore and take thee off. Go! heaven be thy guide!—and sometimes in thy prayers remember—Matilda!—Theodore flung himself at her feet, and seizing her lily hand, which with struggles she suffered him to kiss, he vowed on the earliest opportunity to get himself knighted, and fervently entreated her permission to swear himself eternally her knight.*—Ere the princess could reply, a clap of thunder was suddenly heard, that shook the battlements. Theodore, regardless* of the tempest, would have urged his suit; but the princess, dismayed, retreated hastily into the castle, and commanded the youth to be gone, with an air that would not be disobeyed. He sighed, and retired, but with eyes fixed on the gate, until Matilda closing it put an end to an interview, in which the hearts of both had drunk so deeply of a passion which both now tasted for the first time.

Theodore went pensively to the convent, to acquaint his father with his deliverance. There he learned the absence of Jerome, and the pursuit that was making after the lady Isabella, with some particulars of whose story he now first became acquainted. The generous gallantry of his nature prompted him to wish to assist her; but the monks could lend him no lights to guess at the route she had taken. He was not tempted to wander far in search of her; for the idea of Matilda had imprinted itself so strongly on his heart, that he could not bear to absent himself at much distance from her abode. The tenderness Jerome had expressed for him concurred to confirm this reluctance; and he even persuaded himself that filial affection was the chief cause of his hovering between the castle and monastery. Until Jerome should return at night, Theodore at length determined to repair* to the forest that Matilda had pointed out to him. Arriving there, he sought the gloomiest shades,* as best suited to the pleasing melancholy* that reigned in his mind. In this mood he roved insensibly to the caves* which had formerly served as a retreat to hermits, and were now reported round the country to be haunted by evil spirits. He recollected to have heard this tradition; and being of a brave and adventurous disposition, he willingly indulged his curiosity in exploring the secret recesses of this labyrinth. He had not penetrated far before he thought he heard the steps of some person who seemed to retreat before him. Theodore, though firmly grounded in all our holy faith enjoins to be believed, had no apprehension that good men were abandoned without cause to the malice of the powers of darkness. He thought the place more likely to be infested by robbers, than by those infernal agents who are reported to molest

and bewilder travellers. He had long burned with impatience
to approve* his valour. Drawing his sabre, he marched sedately
onwards, still directing his steps as the imperfect rustling sound
before him led the way. The armour he wore was a like indication
to the person who avoided him. Theodore, now convinced that he
was not mistaken, redoubled his pace, and evidently gained on the
person that fled; whose haste increasing, Theodore came up just
as a woman fell breathless before him. He hasted to raise her; but
her terror was so great, that he apprehended she would faint in his
arms. He used every gentle word to dispel her alarms, and assured
her that, far from injuring, he would defend her at the peril of his
life. The lady recovering her spirits from his courteous demean-
our, and gazing on her protector, said, Sure I have heard that
voice before?—Not to my knowledge, replied Theodore, unless,
as I conjecture, thou art the lady Isabella.—Merciful heaven!
cried she, thou art not sent in quest of me, art thou? And saying
those words she threw herself at his feet, and besought him not
to deliver her up to Manfred. To Manfred! cried Theodore—No,
lady: I have once already delivered thee from his tyranny, and it
shall fare hard with me now, but I will place thee out of the reach
of his daring. Is it possible, said she, that thou shouldst be the
generous unknown I met last night in the vault of the castle? Sure
thou art not a mortal, but my guardian angel: on my knees let me
thank—Hold, gentle princess, said Theodore, nor demean thyself
before a poor and friendless young man. If heaven has selected
me for thy deliverer, it will accomplish its work, and strengthen
my arm in thy cause. But come, lady, we are too near the mouth
of the cavern; let us seek its inmost recesses: I can have no tran-
quillity till I have placed thee beyond the reach of danger.—Alas!
what mean you, sir? said she. Though all your actions are noble,
though your sentiments speak the purity of your soul, is it fitting
that I should accompany you alone into these perplexed retreats?
Should we be found together, what would a censorious world think
of my conduct?*—I respect your virtuous delicacy, said Theodore;
nor do you harbour a suspicion that wounds my honour. I meant
to conduct you into the most private cavity of these rocks; and

then, at the hazard of my life, to guard their entrance against every living thing. Besides, lady, continued he, drawing a deep sigh, beauteous and all perfect as your form is, and though my wishes are not guiltless of aspiring, know, my soul is dedicated to another; and although——A sudden noise prevented Theodore from proceeding. They soon distinguished these sounds, Isabella! What ho! Isabella!—The trembling princess relapsed into her former agony of fear. Theodore endeavoured to encourage her, but in vain. He assured her he would die rather than suffer her to return under Manfred's power; and begging her to remain concealed, he went forth to prevent the person in search of her from approaching.

At the mouth of the cavern he found an armed knight discoursing with a peasant, who assured him he had seen a lady enter the passes of the rock. The knight was preparing to seek her, when Theodore, placing himself in his way, with his sword drawn, sternly forbad him at his peril to advance. And who are thou who darest to cross my way? said the knight haughtily. One who does not dare more than he will perform, said Theodore. I seek the lady Isabella, said the knight; and understand she has taken refuge among these rocks. Impede me not, or thou wilt repent having provoked my resentment.—Thy purpose is as odious as thy resentment is contemptible, said Theodore. Return whence thou camest, or we shall soon know whose resentment is most terrible.—The stranger, who was the principal knight that had arrived from the marquis of Vicenza, had galloped from Manfred as he was busied in getting information of the princess, and giving various orders to prevent her falling into the power of the three knights. Their chief had suspected Manfred of being privy to the princess's absconding; and this insult from a man who he concluded was stationed by that prince to secrete her, confirming his suspicions, he made no reply, but, discharging a blow with his sabre at Theodore, would soon have removed all obstruction, if Theodore, who took him for one of Manfred's captains, and who had no sooner given the provocation than prepared to support it, had not received the stroke on his shield. The valour that had so long been smothered in his breast, broke forth at once: he rushed impetuously on the knight, whose pride and wrath were not less powerful incentives to hardy deeds. The combat was furious, but not long. Theodore wounded the knight in three several places, and at last disarmed him as he fainted by the loss of blood. The peasant, who had fled on the first onset, had given the alarm to some of Manfred's domestics, who by his orders were dispersed through the forest in pursuit of Isabella. They came up as the knight fell, whom they soon discovered to be the noble stranger. Theodore, notwithstanding his hatred to Manfred, could not behold the victory he had gained without emotions of pity and generosity: but he was more touched, when he learned the quality of his adversary, and was informed that he was no retainer, but an enemy of Manfred. He assisted the servants of the latter in disarming the knight, and in endeavouring to staunch the blood that flowed from his wounds. The knight, recovering his speech, said in a faint and faltering voice, Generous foe, we have both been in an error: I took thee for an instrument of the tyrant; I perceive thou hast made the like mistake—It is too late for excuses—I faint.—If Isabella is at hand, call her—I have important secrets to—He is dying! said one of the attendants; has nobody a crucifix about them? Andrea, do thou pray over him.—Fetch some water, said Theodore, and pour it down his throat, while I hasten to the princess. Saying this, he flew to Isabella; and in a few words told her modestly, that he had been so unfortunate by mistake as to wound a gentleman from her father's court, who wished ere he died to impart something of consequence to her. The princess, who had been transported at hearing the voice of Theodore as he called her to come forth, was astonished at what she heard. Suffering herself to be conducted by Theodore, the new proof of whose valour recalled her dispersed spirits, she came where the bleeding knight lay speechless on the ground—but her fears returned when she beheld the domestics of Manfred. She would again have fled, if Theodore had not made her observe that they were unarmed, and had not threatened them with instant death, if they should dare to seize the princess. The stranger, opening his eyes, and beholding a woman, said, Art thou—pray tell me truly—art thou Isabella of Vicenza? I am, said

she; good heaven restore thee!—Then thou—then thou—said the
knight, struggling for utterance—seest—thy father!—Give me
one——Oh! amazement! horror! what do I hear? what do I see?
cried Isabella. My father! You my father! How come you here, sir?
For heaven's sake speak!—Oh! run for help, or he will expire!—
'Tis most true, said the wounded knight, exerting all his force;
I am Frederic thy father—Yes, I came to deliver thee—It will not
be—Give me a parting kiss, and take——Sir, said Theodore, do
not exhaust yourself: suffer us to convey you to the castle.—To the
castle! said Isabella: Is there no help nearer than the castle? Would
you expose my father to the tyrant? If he goes thither, I dare not
accompany him.—And yet, can I leave him?—My child, said
Frederic, it matters not for me whither I am carried: a few minutes
will place me beyond danger: but while I have eyes to dote on
thee, forsake me not, dear Isabella! This brave knight—I know not
who he is—will protect thy innocence. Sir, you will not abandon
my child, will you?—Theodore, shedding tears over his victim,
and vowing to guard the princess at the expence of his life, persuaded Frederic to suffer himself to be conducted to the castle.
They placed him on a horse belonging to one of the domestics,
after binding up his wounds as well as they were able. Theodore
marched by his side; and the afflicted Isabella, who could not bear
to quit him, followed mournfully behind.

CHAPTER IV

THE sorrowful troop no sooner arrived at the castle, than they were met by Hippolita and Matilda, whom Isabella had sent one of the domestics before to advertise of their approach. The ladies, causing Frederic to be conveyed into the nearest chamber, retired, while the surgeons examined his wounds. Matilda blushed at seeing Theodore and Isabella together; but endeavoured to conceal it by embracing the latter, and condoling with her on her father's mischance. The surgeons soon came to acquaint Hippolita that none of the marquis's wounds were dangerous; and that he was desirous of seeing his daughter and the princesses. Theodore, under pretence of expressing his joy at being freed from his apprehensions of the combat being fatal to Frederic, could not resist the impulse of following Matilda. Her eyes were so often cast down on meeting his, that Isabella, who regarded Theodore as attentively as he gazed on Matilda, soon divined who the object was that he had told her in the cave engaged his affections. While this mute scene passed, Hippolita demanded of Frederic the cause of his having taken that mysterious course for reclaiming his daughter; and threw in various apologies to excuse her lord for the match contracted between their children. Frederic, however incensed against Manfred, was not insensible to the courtesy and benevolence of Hippolita: but he was still more struck with the lovely form of Matilda. Wishing to detain them by his bed-side, he informed Hippolita of his story. He told her, that, while prisoner to the infidels, he had dreamed* that his daughter, of whom he had learned no news since his captivity, was detained in a castle, where she was in danger of the most dreadful misfortunes; and that if he obtained his liberty, and repaired to a wood near Joppa,* he would learn more. Alarmed at this dream, and incapable of obeying the direction given by it, his chains became more grievous than ever. But while his thoughts were occupied on the means of obtaining his liberty, he received the agreeable news that the confederate princes, who were warring in Palestine, had paid his ransom. He instantly set out for the wood that had been marked in his dream. For three days he and his attendants had wandered in the forest without seeing a human form: but on the evening of the third they came to a cell, in which they found a venerable hermit in the agonies of death. Applying rich cordials, they brought the saint-like man to his speech. My sons, said he, I am bounden to your charity—but it is in vain—I am going to my eternal rest—yet I die with the satisfaction of performing the will of heaven. When first I repaired to this solitude, after seeing my country become a prey to unbelievers [it is, alas! above fifty years since I was witness to that dreadful scene!] saint Nicholas appeared to me, and revealed a secret, which he bade me never disclose to mortal man, but on my death-bed. This is that tremendous hour, and ye are no doubt the chosen warriors to whom I was ordered to reveal my trust. As soon as ye have done the last offices to this wretched corse,* dig under the seventh tree on the left hand of this poor cave, and your pains will—Oh! good heaven receive my soul! With those words the devout man breathed his last. By break of day, continued Frederic, when we had committed the holy relics to earth, we dug according to direction—But what was our astonishment, when about the depth of six feet we discovered an enormous sabre*—the very weapon yonder in the court! On the blade, which was then partly out of the scabbard, though since closed by our efforts in removing it, were written the following lines——No; excuse me, madam, added the marquis, turning to Hippolita, if I forbear to repeat them: I respect your sex and rank, and would not be guilty of offending your ear with sounds injurious to aught that is dear to you.—He paused. Hippolita trembled. She did not doubt but Frederic was destined by heaven to accomplish the fate that seemed to threaten her house. Looking with anxious fondness at Matilda, a silent tear stole down her cheek; but recollecting herself, she said, Proceed, my lord; heaven does nothing in vain: mortals must receive its divine behests with lowliness and submission. It is our part to deprecate its wrath, or bow to its decrees. Repeat the sentence, my lord: we listen resigned.—Frederic was grieved that he had proceeded so far. The dignity and patient firmness of Hippolita penetrated him with respect, and the tender silent affection, with which the princess and her daughter regarded each other, melted him almost to tears. Yet apprehensive that his forbearance to obey would be more alarming, he repeated in a faltering and low voice the following lines:

> Where'er a casque that suits this sword is found,
> With perils is thy daughter compass'd round:
> Alfonso's blood alone can save the maid,
> And quiet a long-restless prince's shade.

What is there in these lines, said Theodore impatiently, that affects these princesses? Why were they to be shocked by a mysterious delicacy, that has so little foundation? Your words are rude, young man, said the marquis; and though fortune has favoured you once—My honoured lord, said Isabella, who resented Theodore's warmth, which she perceived was dictated by his sentiments for Matilda, discompose not yourself for the glosing* of a peasant's son: he forgets the reverence he owes you; but he is not accustomed—Hippolita, concerned at the heat that had arisen, checked Theodore for his boldness, but with an air acknowledging his zeal; and, changing the conversation, demanded of Frederic where he had left her lord? As the marquis was going to reply, they heard a noise without; and rising to enquire the cause, Manfred, Jerome, and part of the troop, who had met an imperfect rumour of what had happened, entered the chamber. Manfred advanced hastily towards Frederic's bed to condole with him on his misfortune, and to learn the circumstances of the combat; when starting in an agony of terror and amazement, he cried. Ha! what art thou, thou dreadful spectre! Is my hour come?—My dearest, gracious lord, cried Hippolita, clasping him in her arms, what is it you see? Why do you fix your eye-balls thus?*—What! cried Manfred breathless—dost thou see nothing; Hippolita? Is this ghastly phantom sent to me alone—to me, who did not——For mercy's sweetest self, my lord, said Hippolita, resume your soul, command your reason. There is none here but we, your friends.—What, is not that Alfonso? cried Manfred: dost thou not see him? Can it be my brain's delirium?—This! my lord, said Hippolita: this is Theodore, the youth who has been so unfortunate—Theodore! said Manfred mournfully, and striking his forehead—Theodore, or a phantom, he has unhinged the soul of Manfred.—But how comes he here? and how comes he in armour? I believe he went in search of Isabella, said Hippolita. Of Isabella? said Manfred, relapsing into rage—Yes, yes, that is not doubtful—But how did he escape from durance in which I left him? Was it Isabella, or this hypocritical old friar, that procured his enlargement?—And would a parent be criminal, my lord, said Theodore, if he meditated the deliverance of his child? Jerome, amazed to hear himself in a manner accused by his son, and without foundation, knew not what to think. He could not comprehend how Theodore had escaped, how he came to be armed, and to encounter Frederic. Still he would not venture to ask any questions that might tend to inflame Manfred's wrath against his son. Jerome's silence convinced Manfred that he had contrived Theodore's release.—And is it thus, thou ungrateful old man, said the prince, addressing himself to the friar, that thou repayest mine and Hippolita's bounties? And not content with traversing my heart's nearest wishes, thou armest thy bastard, and bringest him into my own castle to insult me!—My lord, said Theodore, you wrong my father: nor he nor I is capable of harbouring a thought against your peace. Is it insolence thus to surrender myself to your highness's pleasure? added he, laying his sword respectfully at Manfred's feet. Behold my bosom; strike, my lord, if you suspect that a disloyal thought is lodged there. There is not a sentiment engraven on my heart, that does not venerate you and yours. The grace and fervour with which Theodore uttered these words, interested every person present in his favour. Even Manfred was touched—yet still possessed with his resemblance to Alfonso, his admiration was dashed with secret horror. Rise, said he; thy life is not my present purpose.— But tell me thy history, and how thou camest connected with this old traitor here. My lord! said Jerome eagerly.—Peace, impostor! said Manfred; I will not have him prompted. My lord, said

Theodore, I want no assistance; my story is very brief. I was carried at five years of age to Algiers with my mother, who had been
taken by corsairs* from the coast of Sicily. She died of grief in less
than a twelvemonth.—The tears gushed from Jerome's eyes, on
whose countenance a thousand anxious passions stood expressed.
Before she died, continued Theodore, she bound a writing about
my arm under my garments, which told me I was the son of the
count Falconara.—It is most true, said Jerome; I am that wretched
father.—Again I enjoin thee silence, said Manfred: proceed.
I remained in slavery, said Theodore, until within these two years,
when attending on my master in his cruizes, I was delivered by
a christian vessel, which overpowered the pirate; and discovering
myself to the captain, he generously put me on shore in Sicily. But
alas! instead of finding a father, I learned that his estate, which was
situated on the coast, had during his absence been laid waste by
the rover* who had carried my mother and me into captivity: that
his castle had been burnt to the ground: and that my father on
his return had sold what remained, and was retired into religion
in the kingdom of Naples, but where, no man could inform me.
Destitute and friendless, hopeless almost of attaining the transport of a parent's embrace, I took the first opportunity of setting
sail for Naples; from whence within these six days I wandered into
this province, still supporting myself by the labour of my hands;
nor till yester-morn did I believe that heaven had reserved any
lot for me but peace of mind and contented poverty. This, my
lord, is Theodore's story. I am blessed beyond my hope in finding
a father; I am unfortunate beyond my desert* in having incurred
your highness's displeasure. He ceased. A murmur of approbation
gently arose from the audience. This is not all, said Frederic; I am
bound in honour to add what he suppresses. Though he is modest,
I must be generous—he is one of the bravest youths on christian
ground. He is warm* too; and from the short knowledge I have
of him, I will pledge myself for his veracity: if what he reports of
himself were not true, he would not utter it—and for me, youth,
I honour a frankness which becomes thy birth. But now, and thou
didst offend me; yet the noble blood which flows in thy veins may

well be allowed to boil out, when it has so recently traced itself to its source. Come, my lord, [turning to Manfred] if I can pardon him, surely you may: it is not the youth's fault, if you took him for a spectre. This bitter taunt galled the soul of Manfred. If beings from another world, replied he haughtily, have power to impress my mind with awe, it is more than living man can do; nor could a stripling's arm——My lord, interrupted Hippolita, your guest has occasion for repose; shall we not leave him to his rest? Saying this, and taking Manfred by the hand, she took leave of Frederic, and led the company forth. The prince, not sorry to quit a conversation which recalled to mind the discovery he had made of his most secret sensations, suffered himself to be conducted to his own apartment, after permitting Theodore, though under engagement to return to the castle on the morrow, [a condition the young man gladly accepted] to retire with his father to the convent. Matilda and Isabella were too much occupied with their own reflections, and too little content with each other, to wish for farther converse that night. They separated each to her chamber, with more expressions of ceremony, and fewer of affection, than had passed between them since their childhood.

If they parted with small cordiality, they did but meet with greater impatience as soon as the sun was risen. Their minds were in a situation that excluded sleep, and each recollected a thousand questions which she wished she had put to the other overnight. Matilda reflected that Isabella had been twice delivered by Theodore in very critical situations, which she could not believe accidental. His eyes, it was true, had been fixed on her in Frederic's chamber; but that might have been to disguise his passion for Isabella from the fathers of both. It were better to clear this up. She wished to know the truth, lest she should wrong her friend by entertaining a passion for Isabella's lover. Thus jealousy prompted, and at the same time borrowed an excuse from friendship to justify its curiosity.

Isabella, not less restless, had better foundation for her suspicions. Both Theodore's tongue and eyes had told her his heart was engaged, it was true—yet perhaps Matilda might not correspond to his passion—She had ever appeared insensible to love; all her thoughts were set on heaven—Why did I dissuade her? said Isabella to herself; I am punished for my generosity— But when did they meet? where?—It cannot be; I have deceived myself—Perhaps last night was the first time they ever beheld each other—it must be some other object that has prepossessed his affections—If it is, I am not so unhappy as I thought; if it is not my friend Matilda—How! can I stoop to wish for the affection of a man, who rudely and unnecessarily acquainted me with his indifference? and that at the very moment in which common courtesy demanded at least expressions of civility. I will go to my dear Matilda, who will confirm me in this becoming pride— Man is false—I will advise with her on taking the veil: she will rejoice to find me in this disposition; and I will acquaint her that I no longer oppose her inclination for the cloister. In this frame of mind, and determined to open her heart entirely to Matilda, she went to that princess's chamber, whom she found already dressed, and leaning pensively on her arm. This attitude,* so correspondent to what she felt herself, revived Isabella's suspicions, and destroyed the confidence she had purposed to place in her friend. They blushed at meeting, and were too much novices to disguise their sensations with address. After some unmeaning questions and replies, Matilda demanded of Isabella the cause of her flight. The latter, who had almost forgotten Manfred's passion, so entirely was she occupied by her own, concluding that Matilda referred to her last escape from the convent, which had occasioned the events of the preceding evening, replied, Martelli brought word to the convent that your mother was dead.—Oh! said Matilda interrupting her, Bianca has explained that mistake to me: on seeing me faint, she cried out, The princess is dead! and Martelli, who had come for the usual dole* to the castle——And what made you faint? said Isabella, indifferent to the rest. Matilda blushed, and stammered—My father—he was sitting in judgment on a criminal.—What criminal? said Isabella eagerly.—— A young man, said Matilda—I believe—I think it was that young man that—What, Theodore? said Isabella. Yes, answered she;

I never saw him before; I do not know how he had offended my father—but, as he has been of service to you, I am glad my lord has pardoned him. Served me? replied Isabella: do you term it serving me, to wound my father, and almost occasion his death? Though it is but since yesterday that I am blessed with knowing a parent, I hope Matilda does not think I am such a stranger to filial* tenderness as not to resent the boldness of that audacious youth, and that it is impossible for me ever to feel any affection for one who dared to lift his arm against the author of my being. No, Matilda, my heart abhors him; and if you still retain the friendship for me that you have vowed from your infancy, you will detest a man who has been on the point of making me miserable for ever. Matilda held down her head, and replied, I hope my dearest Isabella does not doubt her Matilda's friendship: I never beheld that youth until yesterday; he is almost a stranger to me: but as the surgeons have pronounced your father out of danger, you ought not to harbour uncharitable resentment against one who I am persuaded did not know the marquis was related to you. You plead his cause very pathetically, said Isabella, considering he is so much a stranger to you! I am mistaken, or he returns your charity. What mean you? said Matilda. Nothing, said Isabella; repenting that she had given Matilda a hint of Theodore's inclination for her. Then changing the discourse, she asked Matilda what occasioned Manfred to take Theodore for a spectre? Bless me, said Matilda, did not you observe his extreme resemblance to the portrait of Alfonso in the gallery? I took notice of it to Bianca even before I saw him in armour; but with the helmet on, he is the very image of that picture. I do not much observe pictures, said Isabella; much less have I examined this young man so attentively as you seem to have done.——Ah! Matilda, your heart is in danger—but let me warn you as a friend—He has owned to me that he is in love: it cannot be with you, for yesterday was the first time you ever met—was it not? Certainly, replied Matilda. But why does my dearest Isabella conclude from any thing I have said, that—She paused—then continuing, He saw you first, and I am far from having the vanity to think that my little portion of charms could engage a heart devoted to you. May you be happy, Isabella, whatever is the fate of Matilda!—My lovely friend, said Isabella, whose heart was too honest to resist a kind expression, it is you that Theodore admires; I saw it; I am persuaded of it; nor shall a thought of my own happiness suffer me to interfere with yours. This frankness drew tears from the gentle Matilda; and jealousy, that for a moment had raised a coolness between these amiable maidens, soon gave way to the natural sincerity and candour of their souls. Each confessed to the other the impression that Theodore had made on her; and this confidence was followed by a struggle of generosity, each insisting on yielding her claim to her friend. At length, the dignity of Isabella's virtue reminding her of the preference which Theodore had almost declared for her rival, made her determine to conquer her passion, and cede the beloved object to her friend.

During this contest of amity, Hippolita entered her daughter's chamber. Madam, said she to Isabella, you have so much tenderness for Matilda, and interest yourself so kindly in whatever affects our wretched house, that I can have no secrets with my child, which are not proper for you to hear. The princesses were all attention and anxiety. Know then, madam, continued Hippolita, and you, my dearest Matilda, that being convinced by all the events of these two last ominous days, that heaven purposes* the sceptre of Otranto should pass from Manfred's hands into those of the marquis Frederic, I have been perhaps inspired with the thought of averting our total destruction by the union of our rival houses. With this view I have been proposing to Manfred my lord to tender this dear dear child to Frederic your father——Me to lord Frederic! cried Matilda—Good heavens! my gracious mother—and have you named it to my father? I have, said Hippolita: he listened benignly to my proposal, and is gone to break it to the marquis. Ah! wretched princess! cried Isabella, what hast thou done? What ruin has thy inadvertent goodness been preparing for thyself, for me, and for Matilda! Ruin from me to you and to my child! said Hippolita: What can this mean? Alas! said Isabella, the purity of your own heart prevents your seeing the depravity of others. Manfred, your lord, that impious man——Hold, said Hippolita; you must not in my presence, young lady, mention Manfred with disrespect: he is my lord and husband, and—Will not be long so, said Isabella, if his wicked purposes can be carried into execution. This language amazes me, said Hippolita. Your feeling, Isabella, is warm; but until this hour I never knew it betray you into intemperance. What deed of Manfred authorizes you to treat him as a murderer, an assassin?* Thou virtuous and too credulous princess! replied Isabella; it is not thy life he aims at—it is to separate himself from thee! to divorce thee! To—to divorce me! To divorce my mother! cried Hippolita and Matilda at once.—Yes, said Isabella; and to complete his crime, he meditates—I cannot speak it! What can surpass what thou hast already uttered? said Matilda. Hippolita was silent. Grief choked her speech: and the recollection of Manfred's late ambiguous discourses confirmed what she heard. Excellent, dear lady! madam! mother! cried Isabella, flinging herself at Hippolita's feet in a transport of passion; trust me, believe me, I will die a thousand deaths sooner than consent to injure you, than yield to so odious—oh!— This is too much! cried Hippolita: what crimes does one crime suggest! Rise, dear Isabella; I do not doubt your virtue. Oh! Matilda, this stroke is too heavy for thee! Weep not, my child; and not a murmur, I charge thee. Remember, he is *thy* father still.—But you are my mother too, said Matilda fervently; and *you* are virtuous, *you* are guiltless!——Oh! must not I, must not I complain? You must not, said Hippolita—Come, all will yet be well. Manfred, in the agony for the loss of thy brother, knew not what he said: perhaps Isabella misunderstood him: his heart is good—and, my child, thou knowest not all. There is a destiny hangs over us; the hand of Providence is stretched out—Oh! could I but save thee from the wreck!—Yes, continued she in a firmer tone, perhaps the sacrifice of myself may atone for all——I will go and offer myself to this divorce—it boots not what becomes of me. I will withdraw into the neighbouring monastery, and waste the remainder of life in prayers and tears for my child and—the prince! Thou art as much too good for this world, said Isabella, as Manfred is execrable—But think not, lady, that thy weakness shall determine for me. I swear—hear me, all ye angels—— Stop, I adjure thee, cried Hippolita; remember, thou dost not depend on thyself; thou hast a father.——My father is too pious, too noble, interrupted Isabella, to command an impious deed. But should he command it, can a father enjoin a cursed act? I was contracted to the son; can I wed the father?——No, madam, no; force should not drag me to Manfred's hated bed. I loathe him, I abhor him: divine and human laws forbid.——And my friend, my dearest Matilda! would I wound her tender soul by injuring her adored mother? my own mother——I never have known another.——Oh! she is the mother of both! cried Matilda. Can we, can we, Isabella, adore her too much? My lovely children, said the touched Hippolita, your tenderness overpowers me——but I must not give way to it. It is not ours to make election for ourselves; heaven, our fathers, and our husbands, must decide for us. Have patience until you hear what Manfred and Frederic have determined. If the marquis accepts Matilda's hand, I know she will readily obey. Heaven may interpose and prevent the rest. What means my child? continued she, seeing Matilda fall at her feet with a flood of speechless tears——But no; answer me not, my daughter; I must not hear a word against the pleasure of thy father. Oh! doubt not my obedience, my dreadful obedience to him and to you! said Matilda. But can I, most respected of women, can I experience all this tenderness, this world of goodness, and conceal a thought from the best of mothers? What art thou going to utter? said Isabella trembling. Recollect thyself, Matilda. No, Isabella, said the princess, I should not deserve this incomparable parent, if the inmost recesses of my soul harboured a thought without her permission——Nay, I have offended her; I have suffered a passion to enter my heart without her avowal——But here I disclaim it; here I vow to heaven and her——My child! my child! said Hippolita, what words are these? What new calamities has fate in store for us? Thou, a passion! thou, in this hour of destruction——Oh! I see all my guilt! said Matilda. I abhor myself, if I cost my mother a pang. She is the dearest thing I have on earth——Oh! I will never, never behold him more!* Isabella, said Hippolita, thou art conscious to this unhappy secret, whatever it is. Speak——What! cried Matilda, have I so forfeited my mother's love that she will not permit me even to speak my own guilt? Oh! wretched, wretched

Matilda!—Thou art too cruel, said Isabella to Hippolita: canst thou behold this anguish of a virtuous mind, and not commiserate it? Not pity my child! said Hippolita, catching Matilda in her arms—Oh! I know she is good, she is all virtue, all tenderness, and duty. I do forgive thee, my excellent, my only hope! The princesses then revealed to Hippolita their mutual inclination for Theodore, and the purpose of Isabella to resign him to Matilda. Hippolita blamed their imprudence, and shewed them the improbability that either father would consent to bestow his heiress on so poor a man, though nobly born. Some comfort it gave her to find their passion of so recent a date, and that Theodore had but little cause to suspect it in either. She strictly enjoined them to avoid all correspondence with him. This Matilda fervently promised: but Isabella, who flattered herself that she meant no more than to promote his union with her friend, could not determine to avoid him; and made no reply. I will go to the convent, said Hippolita, and order new masses to be said for a deliverance from these calamities.—Oh! my mother, said Matilda, you mean to quit us: you mean to take sanctuary, and to give my father an opportunity of pursuing his fatal intention. Alas! on my knees I supplicate you to forbear—Will you leave me a prey to Frederic? I will follow you to the convent.—Be at peace, my child, said Hippolita: I will return instantly. I will never abandon thee, until I know it is the will of heaven, and for thy benefit. Do not deceive me, said Matilda. I will not marry Frederic until thou commandest it. Alas! what will become of me!—Why that exclamation! said Hippolita. I have promised thee to return.—Ah! my mother, replied Matilda, stay and save me from myself. A frown from thee can do more than all my father's severity. I have given away my heart, and you alone can make me recall it. No more, said Hippolita: thou must not relapse, Matilda. I can quit Theodore, said she, but must I wed another? Let me attend thee to the altar, and shut myself from the world forever. Thy fate depends on thy father, said Hippolita: I have ill bestowed my tenderness, if it has taught thee to revere aught beyond him. Adieu, my child! I go to pray for thee.

Hippolita's real purpose was to demand of Jerome, whether in conscience she might not consent to the divorce. She had oft urged Manfred to resign the principality, which the delicacy of her conscience rendered an hourly burthen* to her. These scruples concurred to make the separation from her husband appear less dreadful to her than it would have seemed in any other situation.

Jerome, at quitting the castle overnight, had questioned Theodore severely why he had accused him to Manfred of being privy to his escape. Theodore owned it had been with design to prevent Manfred's suspicion from alighting on Matilda; and added, the holiness of Jerome's life and character secured him from the tyrant's wrath. Jerome was heartily grieved to discover his son's inclination for that princess; and, leaving him to his rest, promised in the morning to acquaint him with important reasons for conquering his passion. Theodore, like Isabella, was too recently acquainted with parental authority to submit to its decisions against the impulse of his heart. He had little curiosity to learn the friar's reasons, and less disposition to obey them. The lovely Matilda had made stronger impressions on him than filial affection. All night he pleased himself with visions of love; and it was not till late after the morning office,* that he recollected the friar's commands to attend him at Alfonso's tomb.

Young man, said Jerome, when he saw him, this tardiness does not please me. Have a father's commands already so little weight? Theodore made awkward excuses, and attributed his delay to having overslept himself. And on whom were thy dreams employed? said the friar sternly. His son blushed. Come, come, resumed the friar, inconsiderate youth, this must not be; eradicate this guilty passion from thy breast.—Guilty passion! cried Theodore: can guilt dwell with innocent beauty and virtuous modesty? It is sinful, replied the friar, to cherish those whom heaven has doomed to destruction. A tyrant's race must be swept from the earth to the third and fourth generation. Will heaven visit the innocent for the crimes of the guilty?* said Theodore. The fair Matilda has virtues enough—To undo thee, interrupted Jerome. Hast thou so soon forgotten that twice the savage Manfred has pronounced thy sentence? Nor have I forgotten, sir, said Theodore, that the charity of his daughter delivered me from his power. I can forget injuries, but never benefits. The injuries thou hast received from Manfred's race, said the friar, are beyond what thou canst conceive.—Reply not, but view this holy image! Beneath this marble monument rest the ashes of the good Alfonso; a prince adorned with every virtue: the father of his people! the delight of mankind! Kneel, head-strong boy, and list, while a father unfolds a tale of horror, that will expel every sentiment from thy soul, but sensations of sacred vengeance.*—Alfonso! much-injured prince! let thy unsatisfied shade* sit awful on the troubled air, while these trembling lips—Ha! who comes there?—The most wretched of women, said Hippolita, entering the choir. Good father, art thou at leisure?—But why this kneeling youth? what means the horror imprinted on each countenance? why at this venerable tomb— Alas! hast thou seen aught? We were pouring forth our orisons to heaven, replied the friar with some confusion, to put an end to the woes of this deplorable province. Join with us, lady! thy spotless soul may obtain an exemption from the judgments which the portents of these days but too speakingly denounce against thy house. I pray fervently to heaven to divert them, said the pious princess. Thou knowest it has been the occupation of my life to wrest a blessing for my lord and my harmless children—One, alas! is taken from me! Would heaven but hear me for my poor Matilda! Father, intercede for her!—Every heart will bless her, cried Theodore with rapture.—Be dumb, rash youth! said Jerome. And thou, fond princess, contend not with the powers above! The Lord giveth, and the Lord taketh away:* bless his holy name, and submit to his decrees. I do most devoutly, said Hippolita: but will he not spare my only comfort? must Matilda perish too?—Ah! father, I came—But dismiss thy son. No ear but thine must hear what I have to utter. May heaven grant thy every wish, most excellent princess! said Theodore retiring. Jerome frowned.

Hippolita then acquainted the friar with the proposal she had suggested to Manfred, his approbation of it, and the tender of Matilda that he was gone to make to Frederic. Jerome could not conceal his dislike of the motion, which he covered under pretence of the improbability that Frederic, the nearest of blood to Alfonso, and who was come to claim his succession, would yield to an alliance with the usurper of his right. But nothing could equal the perplexity of the friar, when Hippolita confessed her readiness not to oppose the separation, and demanded his opinion on the legality of her acquiescence. The friar catched eagerly at her request of his advice; and without explaining his aversion to the proposed marriage of Manfred and Isabella, he painted to Hippolita in the most alarming colours the sinfulness of her consent, denounced judgments against her if she complied, and enjoined her in the severest terms to treat any such proposition with every mark of indignation and refusal.

Manfred, in the mean time, had broken his purpose to Frederic, and proposed the double marriage. That weak prince, who had been struck with the charms of Matilda, listened but too eagerly to the offer. He forgot his enmity to Manfred, whom he saw but little hope of dispossessing by force; and flattering himself that no issue might succeed from the union of his daughter with the tyrant, he looked upon his own succession to the principality as facilitated by wedding Matilda. He made faint opposition to the proposal; affecting, for form only, not to acquiesce unless Hippolita should consent to the divorce. Manfred took that upon himself. Transported with his success, and impatient to see himself in a situation to expect sons, he hastened to his wife's apartment, determined to extort her compliance. He learned with indignation that she was absent at the convent. His guilt suggested to him that she had probably been informed by Isabella of his purpose. He doubted whether her retirement to the convent did not import an intention of remaining there, until she could raise obstacles to their divorce; and the suspicions he had already entertained of Jerome, made him apprehend that the friar would not only traverse his views, but might have inspired Hippolita with the resolution of taking sanctuary. Impatient to unravel this clue, and to defeat its success, Manfred hastened to the convent, and arrived there as the friar was earnestly exhorting the princess never to yield to the divorce.

Madam, said Manfred, what business drew you hither? Why did not you await my return from the marquis? I came to implore a blessing on your councils, replied Hippolita. My councils do not need a friar's intervention, said Manfred—and of all men living is that hoary traitor the only one whom you delight to confer with? Profane prince! said Jerome: is it at the altar that thou choosest to insult the servants of the altar?—But, Manfred, thy impious schemes are known. Heaven and this virtuous lady know them. Nay, frown not, prince. The church despises thy menaces. Her thunders will be heard above thy wrath. Dare to proceed in thy curst purpose of a divorce, until her sentence be known, and here I lance her anathema* at thy head. Audacious rebel! said Manfred, endeavouring to conceal the awe with which the friar's words inspired him; dost thou presume to threaten thy lawful prince? Thou art no lawful prince, said Jerome; thou art no prince—Go, discuss thy claim with Frederic; and when that is done—It is done, replied Manfred: Frederic accepts Matilda's hand, and is content to wave his claim, unless I have no male issue.—As he spoke those words three drops of blood fell from the nose of Alfonso's statue.* Manfred turned pale, and the princess sunk on her knees. Behold! said the friar: mark this miraculous indication that the blood of Alfonso will never mix with that of Manfred! My gracious lord, said Hippolita, let us submit ourselves to heaven. Think not thy ever obedient wife rebels against thy authority. I have no will but that of my lord and the church. To that revered tribunal let us appeal. It does not depend on us to burst the bonds that unite us. If the church shall approve the dissolution of our marriage, be it so—I have but few years, and those of sorrow, to pass. Where can they be worn away so well as at the foot of this altar, in prayers for thine and Matilda's safety?—But thou shalt not remain here until then, said Manfred. Repair with me to the castle, and there I will advise on the proper measures for a divorce.—But this meddling friar* comes not thither; my hospitable roof shall never more harbour a traitor—and for thy reverence's offspring, continued he, I banish him from my dominions. He, I ween, is no sacred personage, nor under the protection of the church. Whoever weds Isabella, it shall not be father Falconara's started-up son. They start up, said the friar, who are suddenly beheld in the seat of lawful princes; but they wither away like the grass, and their place knows them no more.* Manfred, casting a look of scorn at the friar, led Hippolita forth; but at the door of the church whispered one of his attendants to remain concealed about the convent, and bring him instant notice, if any one from the castle should repair thither.

CHAPTER V

EVERY reflection which Manfred made on the friar's behaviour, conspired to persuade him that Jerome was privy to an amour between Isabella and Theodore. But Jerome's new presumption, so dissonant from his former meekness, suggested still deeper apprehensions. The prince even suspected that the friar depended on some secret support from Frederic, whose arrival coinciding with the novel appearance of Theodore seemed to bespeak a correspondence. Still more was he troubled with the resemblance of Theodore to Alfonso's portrait. The latter he knew had unquestionably died without issue. Frederic had consented to bestow Isabella on him. These contradictions agitated his mind with numberless pangs. He saw but two methods of extricating himself from his difficulties. The one was to resign his dominions to the marquis.—Pride, ambition, and his reliance on ancient prophecies,* which had pointed out a possibility of his preserving them to his posterity, combated that thought. The other was to press his marriage with Isabella. After long ruminating on these anxious thoughts, as he marched silently with Hippolita to the castle, he at last discoursed with that princess on the subject of his disquiet, and used every insinuating and plausible argument to extract her consent to, even her promise of promoting, the divorce. Hippolita needed little persuasion to bend her to his pleasure. She endeavoured to win him over to the measure of resigning his dominions; but finding her exhortations fruitless, she assured him, that as far as her conscience would allow, she would raise no opposition to a separation, though, without better founded scruples than what he yet alleged, she would not engage to be active in demanding it.

This compliance, though inadequate, was sufficient to raise Manfred's hopes. He trusted that his power and wealth would easily advance his suit at the court of Rome, whither he resolved to engage Frederic to take a journey on purpose. That prince had discovered so much passion for Matilda, that Manfred hoped to obtain all he wished by holding out or withdrawing his daughter's charms, according as the marquis should appear more or less disposed to co-operate in his views. Even the absence of Frederic would be a material point gained, until he could take farther measures for his security.

Dismissing Hippolita to her apartment, he repaired to that of the marquis; but crossing the great hall through which he was to pass, he met Bianca. That damsel he knew was in the confidence of both the young ladies. It immediately occurred to him to sift her on the subject of Isabella and Theodore. Calling her aside into the recess of the oriel window* of the hall, and soothing her with many fair words and promises, he demanded of her whether she knew aught of the state of Isabella's affections. I! my lord? No, my lord—Yes, my lord—Poor lady! she is wonderfully alarmed about her father's wounds; but I tell her he will do well; don't your highness think so? I do not ask you, replied Manfred, what she thinks about her father: but you are in her secrets: come, be a good girl and tell me, is there any young man—ha?—you understand me. Lord bless me! understand your highness? No, not I: I told her a few vulnerary herbs* and repose——I am not talking, replied the prince impatiently, about her father: I know he will do well. Bless me, I rejoice to hear your highness say so; for though I thought it right not to let my young lady despond, methought his greatness had a wan look, and a something—I remember when young Ferdinand was wounded by the Venetian. Thou answerest from the point, interrupted Manfred; but here, take this jewel, perhaps that may fix thy attention—Nay, no reverences; my favour shall not stop here—Come, tell me truly; how stands Isabella's heart? Well, your highness has such a way, said Bianca—to be sure—but can your highness keep a secret? If it should ever come out of your lips——It shall not, it shall not, cried Manfred. Nay, but swear, your highness—by my halidame,* if it should ever be known that I said it—Why, truth is truth, I do not think my lady Isabella ever much affectioned* my young lord, your son: yet he was a sweet youth as one should see. I am sure if I had been a princess—But bless me! I must attend my lady Matilda; she will marvel what is become of me.—Stay, cried Manfred, thou hast not satisfied my question. Hast thou ever carried any message, any letter?—I! Good gracious! cried Bianca: I carry a letter? I would not to be a queen. I hope your highness thinks, though I am poor, I am honest.* Did your highness never hear what count Marsigli offered me, when he came a-wooing to my lady Matilda?—I have not leisure, said Manfred, to listen to thy tales. I do not question thy honesty; but it is thy duty to conceal nothing from me. How long has Isabella been acquainted with Theodore?—Nay, there is nothing can escape your highness, said Bianca—not that I know any thing of the matter. Theodore, to be sure, is a proper young man, and, as my lady Matilda says, the very image of good Alfonso: Has not your highness remarked it? Yes, yes—No—thou torturest me, said Manfred: Where did they meet? when?—Who, my lady Matilda? said Bianca. No, no, not Matilda; Isabella: When did Isabella first become acquainted with this Theodore?—Virgin Mary! said Bianca, how should I know? Thou dost know, said Manfred; and I must know; I will.—Lord! your highness is not jealous of young Theodore? said Bianca.—Jealous! No, no: why should I be jealous?—Perhaps I mean to unite them—if I was sure Isabella would have no repugnance.—Repugnance! No, I'll warrant her, said Bianca. he is as comely a youth as ever trod on christian ground: we are all in love with him: there is not a soul in the castle but would be rejoiced to have him for our prince—I mean, when it shall please heaven to call your highness to itself.—Indeed! said Manfred: has it gone so far? Oh! this cursed friar!—But I must not lose time—Go, Bianca, attend Isabella; but I charge thee, not a word of what has passed. Find out how she is affected towards Theodore; bring me good news, and that ring has a companion. Wait at the foot of the winding staircase: I am going to visit the marquis, and will talk farther with thee at my return.

Manfred, after some general conversation, desired Frederic to dismiss the two knights his companions, having to talk with him on urgent affairs. As soon as they were alone, he began in artful guise to sound the marquis on the subject of Matilda; and finding him disposed to his wish, he let drop hints on the difficulties that

would attend the celebration of their marriage, unless——At that
instant Bianca burst into the room, with a wildness in her look and
gestures that spoke the utmost terror. Oh! my lord, my lord! cried
she, we are all undone! It is come again! it is come again!——What
is come again? cried Manfred amazed.——Oh! the hand! the giant!
the hand!——Support me! I am terrified out of my senses, cried
Bianca: I will not sleep in the castle to-night. Where shall I go? My
things may come after me to-morrow.——Would I had been content
to wed Francesco!* This comes of ambition!——What has terrified
thee thus, young woman? said the marquis: thou art safe here; be
not alarmed. Oh! your greatness is wonderfully good, said Bianca,
but I dare not——No, pray let me go——I had rather leave every thing
behind me, than stay another hour under this roof. Go to, thou
hast lost thy senses, said Manfred. Interrupt us not; we were com-
muning on important matters.——My lord, this wench is subject to
fits——Come with me, Bianca.——Oh! the saints! No, said Bianca——
for certain it comes to warn your highness; why should it appear to
me else! I say my prayers morning and evening——Oh! if your highness had believed Diego! 'Tis the same hand that he saw the foot
to in the gallery-chamber——Father Jerome has often told us the
prophecy would be out one of these days——Bianca, said he, mark
my words.——Thou ravest, said Manfred in a rage: Begone, and
keep these fooleries to frighten thy companions.——What! my lord,
cried Bianca, do you think I have seen nothing? Go to the foot of
the great stairs yourself——As I live I saw it. Saw what? Tell us fair
maid, what thou hast seen, said Frederic. Can your highness listen, said Manfred, to the delirium of a silly wench, who has heard
stories of apparitions until she believes them? This is more than
fancy, said the marquis; her terror is too natural and too strongly
impressed to be the work of imagination. Tell us, fair maiden, what
it is has moved thee thus. Yes, my lord, thank your greatness, said
Bianca——I believe I look very pale; I shall be better when I have
recovered myself.——I was going to my lady Isabella's chamber by
his highness's order——We do not want the circumstances, interrupted Manfred: since his highness will have it so, proceed; but be
brief.——Lord, your highness thwarts one so! replied Bianca——I fear

my hair*—I am sure I never in my life—Well! as I was telling your
greatness, I was going by his highness's order to my lady Isabella's
chamber: she lies in the watchet-coloured* chamber, on the right
hand, one pair of stairs: so when I came to the great stairs—I was
looking on his highness's present here. Grant me patience! said
Manfred, will this wench never come to the point? What imports it
to the marquis, that I gave thee a bawble for thy faithful attendance
on my daughter? We want to know what thou sawest. I was going
to tell your highness, said Bianca, if you would permit me.—So, as
I was rubbing the ring*—I am sure I had not gone up three steps,
but I heard the rattling of armour; for all the world such a clatter,
as Diego says he heard when the giant turned him about in the
gallery-chamber.—What does she mean, my lord? said the marquis.
Is your castle haunted by giants and goblins?—Lord, what, has not
your greatness heard the story of the giant in the gallery-chamber?
cried Bianca. I marvel his highness has not told you—mayhap
you do not know there is a prophecy—This trifling is intolerable,
interrupted Manfred. Let us dismiss this silly wench, my lord:
we have more important affairs to discuss. By your favour, said
Frederic, these are no trifles: the enormous sabre I was directed to
in the wood; yon casque, its fellow—are these visions of this poor
maiden's brain?—So Jaquez thinks, may it please your greatness,
said Bianca. He says this moon will not be out without our seeing
some strange revolution. For my part, I should not be surprised if
it was to happen to-morrow; for, as I was saying, when I heard the
clattering of armour, I was all in a cold sweat—I looked up, and,
if your greatness will believe me, I saw upon the uppermost banister of the great stairs a hand in armour as big, as big—I thought
I should have swooned—I never stopped until I came hither—
Would I were well out of this castle! My lady Matilda told me but
yester-morning that her highness Hippolita knows something—
Thou art an insolent! cried Manfred—Lord marquis, it much
misgives me that this scene is concerted to affront me. Are my
own domestics suborned* to spread tales injurious to my honour?
Pursue your claim by manly daring; or let us bury our feuds, as
was proposed, by the intermarriage of our children: but trust me,

it ill becomes a prince of your bearing to practise on mercenary wenches.—I scorn your imputation, said Frederic; until this hour I never set eyes on this damsel: I have given her no jewel!—My lord, my lord, your conscience, your guilt accuses you, and would throw the suspicion on me—But keep your daughter, and think no more of Isabella: the judgments already fallen on your house forbid me matching into it.

Manfred, alarmed at the resolute tone in which Frederic delivered these words, endeavoured to pacify him. Dismissing Bianca, he made such submissions to the marquis, and threw in such artful encomiums on Matilda, that Frederic was once more staggered.* However, as his passion was of so recent a date, it could not at once surmount the scruples he had conceived. He had gathered enough from Bianca's discourse to persuade him that heaven declared itself against Manfred. The proposed marriages too removed his claim to a distance: and the principality of Otranto was a stronger temptation, than the contingent reversion of it with Matilda.* Still he would not absolutely recede from his engagements; but purposing to gain time, he demanded of Manfred if it was true in fact that Hippolita consented to the divorce. The prince, transported to find no other obstacle, and depending on his influence over his wife, assured the marquis it was so, and that he might satisfy himself of the truth from her own mouth.

As they were thus discoursing, word was brought that the banquet was prepared. Manfred conducted Frederic to the great hall, where they were received by Hippolita and the young princesses. Manfred placed the marquis next to Matilda, and seated himself between his wife and Isabella. Hippolita comported herself with an easy gravity; but the young ladies were silent and melancholy. Manfred, who was determined to pursue his point with the marquis in the remainder of the evening, pushed on the feast until it waxed late; affecting unrestrained gaiety, and plying Frederic with repeated goblets of wine. The latter, more upon his guard than Manfred wished, declined his frequent challenges, on pretence of his late loss of blood; while the prince, to raise his own disordered spirits, and to counterfeit unconcern, indulged himself in plentiful draughts, though not to the intoxication of his senses.

The evening being far advanced, the banquet concluded. Manfred would have withdrawn with Frederic; but the latter, pleading weakness and want of repose, retired to his chamber, gallantly telling the prince, that his daughter should amuse his highness until himself could attend him. Manfred accepted the party; and, to the no small grief of Isabella, accompanied her to her apartment. Matilda waited on her mother, to enjoy the freshness of the evening on the ramparts of the castle.

Soon as the company was dispersed their several ways, Frederic, quitting his chamber, enquired if Hippolita was alone; and was told by one of her attendants, who had not noticed her going forth, that at that hour she generally withdrew to her oratory, where he probably would find her. The marquis during the repast had beheld Matilda with increase of passion. He now wished to find Hippolita in the disposition her lord had promised. The portents that had alarmed him were forgotten in his desires. Stealing softly and unobserved to the apartment of Hippolita, he entered it with a resolution to encourage her acquiescence to the divorce, having perceived that Manfred was resolved to make the possession of Isabella an unalterable condition, before he would grant Matilda to his wishes.

The marquis was not surprised at the silence that reigned in the princess's apartment. Concluding her, as he had been advertised,* in her oratory, he passed on. The door was a-jar; the evening gloomy and overcast. Pushing open the door gently, he saw a person kneeling before the altar. As he approached nearer, it seemed not a woman, but one in a long woollen weed,* whose back was towards him. The person seemed absorbed in prayer. The marquis was about to return, when the figure rising, stood some moments fixed in meditation, without regarding him. The marquis, expecting the holy person to come forth, and meaning to excuse his uncivil interruption, said, Reverend father, I sought the lady Hippolita.—Hippolita! replied a hollow voice: camest thou to this castle to seek Hippolita?—And then the figure, turning slowly

round, discovered to Frederic the fleshless jaws and empty sockets
of a skeleton, wrapt in a hermit's cowl. Angels of grace, protect
me!* cried Frederic recoiling. Deserve their protection, said the
spectre. Frederic, falling on his knees, adjured the phantom to take
pity on him. Dost thou not remember me? said the apparition.
Remember the wood of Joppa! Art thou that holy hermit? cried
Frederic trembling—can I do aught for thy eternal peace?—Wast
thou delivered from bondage, said the spectre, to pursue carnal
delights? Hast thou forgotten the buried sabre, and the behest of
heaven engraven on it?—I have not, I have not, said Frederic—
But say, blest spirit, what is thy errand to me? what remains to be
done? To forget Matilda! said the apparition—and vanished.

Frederic's blood froze in his veins. For some minutes he
remained motionless. Then falling prostrate on his face before
the altar, he besought the intercession of every saint for pardon.
A flood of tears succeeded to this transport; and the image of the
beauteous Matilda rushing in spite of him on his thoughts, he lay
on the ground in a conflict of penitence and passion. Ere he could
recover from this agony of his spirits, the princess Hippolita, with
a taper in her hand, entered the oratory alone. Seeing a man without motion on the floor, she gave a shriek, concluding him dead.
Her fright brought Frederic to himself. Rising suddenly, his face
bedewed with tears, he would have rushed from her presence;
but Hippolita, stopping him, conjured him in the most plaintive
accents to explain the cause of his disorder, and by what strange
chance she had found him there in that posture. Ah! virtuous
princess! said the marquis, penetrated with grief—and stopped.
For the love of heaven, my lord, said Hippolita, disclose the cause
of this transport! What mean these doleful sounds, this alarming
exclamation on my name? What woes has heaven still in store for
the wretched Hippolita?—Yet silent?—By every pitying angel,
I adjure thee, noble prince, continued she, falling at his feet, to
disclose the purport of what lies at thy heart—I see thou feelest
for me; thou feelest the sharp pangs that thou inflictest—Speak,
for pity!—Does aught thou knowest concern my child?—I cannot
speak, cried Frederic, bursting from her—Oh! Matilda!

Quitting the princess thus abruptly, he hastened to his own apartment. At the door of it he was accosted by Manfred, who, flushed by wine and love, had come to seek him, and to propose to waste some hours of the night in music and revelling. Frederic, offended at an invitation so dissonant from the mood of his soul, pushed him rudely aside, and, entering his chamber, flung the door intemperately against Manfred, and bolted it inwards.* The haughty prince, enraged at this unaccountable behaviour, withdrew in a frame of mind capable of the most fatal excesses. As he crossed the court, he was met by the domestic whom he had planted at the convent as a spy on Jerome and Theodore. This man, almost breathless with the haste he had made, informed his lord, that Theodore and some lady from the castle were at that instant in private conference at the tomb of Alfonso in St. Nicholas's church. He had dogged* Theodore thither, but the gloominess of the night had prevented his discovering who the woman was.

Manfred, whose spirits were inflamed, and whom Isabella had driven from her on his urging his passion with too little reserve, did not doubt but the inquietude* she had expressed had been occasioned by her impatience to meet Theodore. Provoked by this conjecture, and enraged at her father, he hastened secretly to the great church. Gliding softly between the aisles, and guided by an imperfect gleam of moonshine that shone faintly through the illuminated windows, he stole towards the tomb of Alfonso, to which he was directed by indistinct whispers of the persons he sought. The first sounds he could distinguish were—Does it, alas, depend on me? Manfred will never permit our union.—No, this shall prevent it! cried the tyrant, drawing his dagger, and plunging it over her shoulder into the bosom of the person that spoke—Ah me, I am slain! cried Matilda sinking: Good heaven, receive my soul!— Savage, inhuman monster! what hast thou done? cried Theodore, rushing on him, and wrenching his dagger from him.—Stop, stop thy impious hand, cried Matilda; it is my father!—Manfred, waking as from a trance, beat his breast, twisted his hands in his locks, and endeavoured to recover his dagger from Theodore to dispatch himself. Theodore, scarce less distracted, and only mastering the transports of his grief to assist Matilda, had now by his cries drawn some of the monks to his aid. While part of them endeavoured in concert with the afflicted Theodore to stop the blood of the dying princess, the rest prevented Manfred from laying violent hands on himself.

Matilda, resigning herself patiently to her fate, acknowledged with looks of grateful love the zeal of Theodore. Yet oft as her faintness would permit her speech its way, she begged the assistants to comfort her father. Jerome by this time had learnt the fatal news, and reached the church. His looks seemed to reproach Theodore; but turning to Manfred, he said, Now, tyrant! behold the completion of woe fulfilled on thy impious and devoted head! The blood of Alfonso cried to heaven for vengeance; and heaven has permitted its altar to be polluted by assassination, that thou mightest shed thy own blood at the foot of that prince's sepulchre!—Cruel man! cried Matilda, to aggravate the woes of a parent! May heaven bless my father, and forgive him as I do! My lord, my gracious sire, dost thou forgive thy child? Indeed I came not hither to meet Theodore! I found him praying at this tomb, whither my mother sent me to intercede for thee, for her—Dearest father, bless your child, and say you forgive her.—Forgive thee! Murderous monster! cried Manfred—can assassins forgive? I took thee for Isabella; but heaven directed my bloody hand to the heart of my child!—Oh! Matilda—I cannot utter it—canst thou forgive the blindness of my rage?—I can, I do, and may heaven confirm it! said Matilda—But while I have life to ask it—oh, my mother! what will she feel!—Will you comfort her, my lord? Will you not put her away? Indeed she loves you—Oh, I am faint! bear me to the castle—can I live to have her close my eyes?

Theodore and the monks besought her earnestly to suffer herself to be borne into the convent; but her instances were so pressing to be carried to the castle, that, placing her on a litter,* they conveyed her thither as she requested. Theodore supporting her head with his arm, and hanging over her in an agony of despairing love, still endeavoured to inspire her with hopes of life. Jerome on the other side comforted her with discourses of heaven, and holding a crucifix before her, which she bathed with innocent tears, prepared her for her passage to immortality. Manfred, plunged in the deepest affliction, followed the litter in despair.

Ere they reached the castle, Hippolita, informed of the dreadful catastrophe, had flown to meet her murdered child; but when she saw the afflicted procession, the mightiness of her grief deprived her of her senses, and she fell lifeless to the earth in a swoon. Isabella and Frederic, who attended her, were overwhelmed in almost equal sorrow. Matilda alone seemed insensible to her own situation: every thought was lost in tenderness for her mother. Ordering the litter to stop, as soon as Hippolita was brought to herself, she asked for her father. He approached, unable to speak. Matilda, seizing his hand and her mother's, locked them in her own, and then clasped them to her heart. Manfred could not support this act of pathetic piety. He dashed himself on the ground, and cursed the day he was born. Isabella, apprehensive that these struggles of passion were more than Matilda could support, took upon herself* to order Manfred to be borne to his apartment, while she caused Matilda to be conveyed to the nearest chamber. Hippolita, scarce more alive than her daughter, was regardless of every thing but her: but when the tender Isabella's care would have likewise removed her, while the surgeons examined Matilda's wound, she cried, Remove me? Never! never! I lived but in her, and will expire with her. Matilda raised her eyes at her mother's voice, but closed them again without speaking. Her sinking pulse, and the damp coldness of her hand, soon dispelled all hopes of recovery. Theodore followed the surgeons into the outer chamber, and heard them pronounce the fatal sentence with a transport equal to phrensy—Since she cannot live mine, cried he, at least she shall be mine in death!—Father! Jerome! will you not join our hands? cried he to the friar, who with the marquis had accompanied the surgeons. What means thy distracted rashness? said Jerome: is this an hour for marriage? It is; it is, cried Theodore: alas, there is no other! Young man, thou art too unadvised,* said Frederic: dost thou think we are to listen to thy fond transports in this hour of fate? What pretensions hast thou to the princess?

Those of a prince, said Theodore; of the sovereign of Otranto. This reverend man, my father, has informed me who I am. Thou ravest, said the marquis: there is no prince of Otranto but myself now Manfred by murder, by sacrilegious murder, has forfeited all pretensions. My lord, said Jerome, assuming an air of command, he tells you true. It was not my purpose the secret should have been divulged so soon; but fate presses onward to its work. What his hot-headed passion has revealed, my tongue confirms. Know, prince, that when Alfonso set sail for the Holy Land—Is this a season for explanations? cried Theodore. Father, come and unite me to the princess: she shall be mine—in every other thing I will dutifully obey you. My life! my adored Matilda! continued Theodore, rushing back into the inner chamber, will you not be mine? will you not bless your—Isabella made signs to him to be silent, apprehending the princess was near her end. What, is she dead? cried Theodore: is it possible? The violence of his exclamations brought Matilda to herself. Lifting up her eyes she looked round for her mother—Life of my soul! I am here, cried Hippolita: think not I will quit thee!—Oh! you are too good, said Matilda—but weep not for me, my mother! I am going where sorrow never dwells.— Isabella, thou hast loved me; wot* thou not supply my fondness to this dear, dear woman? Indeed I am faint!—Oh! my child! my child! said Hippolita in a flood of tears, can I not withhold thee a moment?—It will not be, said Matilda—Commend me to heaven—Where is my father? Forgive him, dearest mother— forgive him my death; it was an error—Oh! I had forgotten— Dearest mother, I vowed never to see Theodore more—Perhaps that has drawn down this calamity—but it was not intentional— can you pardon me?—Oh! wound not my agonizing soul! said Hippolita; thou never couldst offend me.—Alas, she faints! Help! help!—I would say something more, said Matilda struggling, but it wonnot* be—Isabella—Theodore—for my sake—oh!—She expired. Isabella and her women tore Hippolita from the corse; but Theodore threatened destruction to all who attempted to remove him from it. He printed a thousand kisses on her clay-cold hands, and uttered every expression that despairing love could dictate.

Isabella, in the mean time, was accompanying the afflicted Hippolita to her apartment; but in the middle of the court they were met by Manfred, who, distracted with his own thoughts, and anxious once more to behold his daughter, was advancing to the chamber where she lay. As the moon was now at its height, he read in the countenances of this unhappy company the event he dreaded. What! is she dead? cried he in wild confusion—A clap of thunder at that instant shook the castle to its foundations; the earth rocked, and the clank of more than mortal armour was heard behind. Frederic and Jerome thought the last day was at hand. The latter, forcing Theodore along with them, rushed into the court. The moment Theodore appeared, the walls of the castle behind Manfred were thrown down with a mighty force, and the form of Alfonso, dilated to an immense magnitude, appeared in the centre of the ruins. Behold in Theodore, the true heir of Alfonso! said the vision: and having pronounced those words, accompanied by a clap of thunder, it ascended solemnly towards heaven, where the clouds parting asunder, the form of saint Nicholas was seen; and receiving Alfonso's shade, they were soon wrapt from mortal eyes in a blaze of glory.

The beholders fell prostrate on their faces, acknowledging the divine will. The first that broke silence was Hippolita.* My lord, said she to the desponding Manfred, behold the vanity of human greatness! Conrad is gone! Matilda is no more! in Theodore we view the true prince of Otranto. By what miracle he is so, I know not—suffice it to us, our doom is pronounced! Shall we not, can we but dedicate the few deplorable hours we have to live, in deprecating the farther wrath of heaven? Heaven ejects us—whither can we fly, but to yon holy cells that yet offer us a retreat?—Thou guiltless but unhappy woman! unhappy by my crimes! replied Manfred, my heart at last is open to thy devout admonitions. Oh! could—but it cannot be—ye are lost in wonder—let me at last do justice on myself! To heap shame on my own head is all the satisfaction I have left to offer to offended heaven. My story has drawn down these judgments: let my confession atone—But ah! what can atone for usurpation and a murdered child? a child murdered in a consecrated place!———List, sirs, and may this bloody record be a warning to future tyrants!

Alfonso, ye all know, died in the Holy Land—Ye would interrupt me; ye would say he came not fairly to his end—It is most true—why else this bitter cup which Manfred must drink to the dregs?* Ricardo, my grandfather, was his chamberlain*—I would draw a veil over my ancestor's crimes—but it is in vain: Alfonso died by poison. A fictitious will* declared Ricardo his heir. His crimes pursued him—yet he lost no Conrad, no Matilda! I pay the price of usurpation for all! A storm overtook him. Haunted by his guilt, he vowed to saint Nicholas to found a church and two convents if he lived to reach Otranto. The sacrifice was accepted: the saint appeared to him in a dream, and promised that Ricardo's posterity should reign in Otranto until the rightful owner should be grown too large to inhabit the castle, and as long as issue-male from Ricardo's loins should remain to enjoy it.—Alas! alas! nor male nor female, except myself, remains of all his wretched* race!—I have done—the woes of these three days speak the rest. How this young man can be Alfonso's heir I know not—yet I do not doubt it. His are these dominions; I resign them—yet I knew not Alfonso had an heir—I question not the will of heaven— poverty and prayer must fill up the woeful space, until Manfred shall be summoned to Ricardo.

What remains is my part to declare, said Jerome. When Alfonso set sail for the Holy Land, he was driven by a storm on the coast of Sicily. The other vessel, which bore Ricardo and his train, as your *lordship* must have heard, was separated from him. It is most true, said Manfred; and the title you give me is more than an out-cast can claim—Well, be it so—proceed. Jerome blushed, and continued. For three months lord Alfonso was wind-bound in Sicily. There he became enamoured of a fair virgin named Victoria.* He was too pious to tempt her to forbidden pleasures. They were married. Yet deeming this amour incongruous with the holy vow of arms by which he was bound, he was determined to conceal their nuptials until his return from the crusado, when he purposed to seek and acknowledge her for his lawful wife. He left her pregnant. During his absence she was delivered of a daughter: but scarce had she felt a mother's pangs, ere she heard the fatal rumour of her lord's death, and the succession of Ricardo. What could a friendless, helpless woman do? would her testimony avail?—Yet, my lord, I have an authentic writing.—It needs not, said Manfred; the horrors of these days, the vision we have but now seen, all corroborate thy evidence beyond a thousand parchments. Matilda's death and my expulsion—Be composed, my lord, said Hippolita; this holy man did not mean to recall your griefs. Jerome proceeded.

I shall not dwell on what is needless. The daughter of which Victoria was delivered, was at her maturity bestowed in marriage on me. Victoria died; and the secret remained locked in my breast. Theodore's narrative has told the rest.

The friar ceased. The disconsolate company retired to the remaining part of the castle.* In the morning Manfred signed his abdication of the principality, with the approbation of Hippolita, and each took on them the habit of religion in the neighbouring convents.* Frederic offered his daughter to the new prince, which Hippolita's tenderness for Isabella concurred to promote: but Theodore's grief was too fresh to admit the thought of another love; and it was not till after frequent discourses with Isabella, of his dear Matilda, that he was persuaded he could know no happiness but in the society of one with whom he could forever indulge the melancholy that had taken possession of his soul.

APPENDIX

GOTHIC CONTEXTS

THESE extracts—both of which were published in 1762—show how mid-century commentators attempted to rethink the Gothic not in contrast to the classical, but by paralleling and comparing the cultural context of the ancient world with medieval Europe. *Anecdotes of Painting in England* was Horace Walpole's first public formulation of a Gothic sensibility, in which he reassesses the Gothic in relation to architecture. Richard Hurd's *Letters on Chivalry and Romance*, meanwhile, endeavoured to do the same for literature and in doing so demarcated the place of medieval romance poetry in the popular imagination. Both extracts reveal, therefore, the assimilation and domestication of the Gothic of the Middle Ages for eighteenth-century readers and connoisseurs; two years later, Walpole wrote *The Castle of Otranto*.

From Horace Walpole, *Anecdotes of Painting in England*, 4 vols (Twickenham, 1762), i. 105–13.

CHAPTER V.
State of Architecture to the end of the Reign of HENRY VIII.

IT is unlucky for the world, that our earliest ancestors were not aware of the curiosity which would inspire their descendants of knowing minutely every thing relating to them. When they placed three or four branches of trees across the trunks of others and covered them with boughs or straw to keep out the weather, the good people were not apprized that they were discovering architecture, and that it would be learnedly agitated some thousand of years afterwards who was the inventor of this stupendous science. In complaisance to our inquiries they would undoubtedly have transmitted an account of the first hovel that was ever built, and from that patriarch hut we should possess a faithful genealogy of all it's descendants: Yet such a curiosity would destroy much greater treasures; it would annihilate fables, researches, conjectures, hypotheses, disputes, blunders and dissertations, that library of human impertinence. Necessity and a little common sense produced all the common arts, which the plain folks who practiced them were not idle enough to record. Their inventions were obvious, their productions usefull and clumsy. Yet the little merit there was in fabricating then being soon consigned to oblivion, we are bountifull enough to suppose that there was design and system in all they did, and then take infinite pains to digest and methodize those imaginary rudiments. No sooner is any aera of an invention invented, but different countries begin to assert an exclusive title to it, and the only point in which any countries agree is perhaps in ascribing the discovery to some other nation remote enough in time for neither of them to know any thing of it. Let but France and England once dispute which first used a hatchet, and they shall never be accorded 'till the chancery of learning accommodates the matter by pronouncing that each received that invaluable utensil from the Phoenicians. Common sense that would interpose by observing how probable it is that the necessaries of life were equally discovered in every region, cannot be heard; a hammer could only be invented by the Phoenicians, the first polished people of whom we are totally ignorant. Whoever has thrown away his time on the first chapters of general histories, or of histories of arts, must be sensible that these reflections are but too well grounded. I design them as an apology for not going very far back into the history of our architecture. Vertue [George Vertue] and several other curious persons have taken great pains to enlighten the obscure ages of that science; they find no names of architects, nay little more, than what they might have known without inquiring; that our ancestors had buildings. Indeed Tom Hearne, Brown Willis, and such illustrators did sometimes go upon more positive ground: They did now and then stumble upon an arch, a tower, nay a whole church, so dark, so ugly, so uncouth, that they were sure it could not have been built since any idea of grace had been transported into the island. Yet with this incontestable security on their side, they still had room for doubting; Danes, Saxons, Normans, were all ignorant enough to have claims to peculiar ugliness in their fashions. It was difficult to ascertain the periods when one ungracious form jostled out another: and this perplexity at last led them into such refinement, that the term *Gothic Architecture*, inflicted as a reproach on our ancient buildings in general by our ancestors who revived the Grecian taste, is now considered but as a species of modern elegance, by those who wish to distinguish the Saxon style from it. This Saxon style begins to be defined by flat and round arches, by some undulating zigzags on certain old fabrics, and by a very few other characteristics, all evidences of barbarous and ignorant times. I do not mean to say simply that the round arch is a proof of ignorance; but being so natural, it is simply, when unaccompanied by any gracefull ornaments, a mark of rude age—if attended by misshapen and heavy decorations, a certain mark of it. The pointed arch, that peculiar of Gothic architecture, was certainly intended as an improvement on the circular, and the men who had not the happiness of lighting on the simplicity and proportion of the Greek orders, were however so lucky as to strike out a thousand graces and effects, which rendered their buildings magnificent, yet genteel, vast, yet light,[1] venerable and picturesque. It is difficult for the noblest Grecian temple to convey half so many impressions to the mind, as a cathedral does of the best Gothic taste—a proof of skill in the architects and of address in the priests who erected them. The latter exhausted their knowledge of the passions in composing edifices whose pomp, mechanism, vaults, tombs, painted windows, gloom and perspectives infused such sensations of romantic devotion; and they were happy in finding artists capable of executing such machinery. One must have taste to be sensible of the beauties of Grecian architecture; one only wants passions to feel Gothic. In St. Peter's one is convinced that it was built by great princes—In Westminster-abbey, one thinks not of the builder; the religion of the place makes the first impression—and though stripped of it's altars and shrines, it is nearer converting one to popery than all the regular pageantry of Roman domes. Gothic churches infuse superstition; Grecian, admiration. The papal see amassed it's wealth by Gothic cathedrals, and displays it in Grecian temples.

I certainly do not mean by this little contrast to make any comparison between the rational beauties of regular architecture, and the unrestrained licentiousness of that which is called Gothic. Yet I am clear that the persons who executed the latter, had much more knowledge of their art, more taste, more genius, and more propriety than we chuse to imagine. There is a magic hardiness in the execution of some of their works which would not have sustained themselves if dictated by mere caprice. There is a tradition that Sir Christopher Wren went once a year to survey the roof of the chapel of King's college, and said that if any man would show him where to place the first stone, he would engage to build such another. That there is great grace in several places

---

[1] For instance, the façade of the cathedral of Rheims.

even in their clusters of slender pillars, and in the application of their ornaments, though the principles of the latter are so confined that they may almost all be reduced to the trefoil, extended and varied, I shall not appeal to the edifices themselves—It is sufficient to observe, that Inigo Jones, Sir Christopher Wren and Kent, who certainly understood beauty, blundered[2] into the heaviest and clumsiest compositions whenever they aimed at imitations of the Gothic—Is an art despicable in which a great master cannot shine?

Considering how scrupulously our architects confine themselves to antique precedent, perhaps some deviations into Gothic may a little relieve them from that servile imitation. I mean that they should study both tastes, not blend them: that they should dare to invent in the one, since they will hazard nothing in the other. When they have built a pediment and portico, the Sibyll's circular temple, and tacked the wings to a house by a colonnade, they seem *au bout de leur Latin*. If half a dozen mansions were all that remained of old Rome, instead of half a dozen temples, I do not doubt but our churches would resemble the private houses of Roman citizens. Our buildings must be as Vitruvian, as writings in the days of Erasmus were obliged to be Ciceronian. Yet confined as our architects are to few models, they are far from having made all the use they might of those they possess. There are variations enough to be struck out to furnish new scenes of singular beauty. The application of loggias, arcades, terrasses and flights of steps, at different stages of a building, particularly in such situations as Whitehall to the river, would have a magnificent effect. It is true, our climate and the expence of building in England are great restrictions on imagination; but when one talks of the extent of which architecture is capable, one must suppose that pomp and beauty are the principal objects; one speaks of palaces and public buildings; not of shops and small houses—but I must restrain this dissertation, and come to the historic part, which will lie in small compass. [. . .]

I have myself turned over most of our histories of churches, and can find nothing like the names of artists. With respect to the builders of Gothic, it is a real loss; there is beauty, genius and invention enough in their works to make one wish to know the authors. I will say no more on this subject, than that, on considering and comparing it's progress,

---

[2] In Lincoln's-Inn chapel, the steeple of the church at Warwick, the King's-bench in Westminster-hall, &c.

the delicacy, lightness and taste of it's ornaments, it seems to have been at it's perfection about the reign of Henry VI. as may be seen particularly by the tombs of the archbishops at Canterbury. That cathedral I should recommend preferably to Westminster to those who would borrow ornaments in that stile. The fretwork in the small oratories at Winchester, and the part behind the choir at Glocester would furnish beautifull models. The windows in several cathedrals offer gracefull patterns; for airy towers of almost filigraine we have none to compare with those of Rheims.[3]

From Richard Hurd, *Letters on Chivalry and Romance* (London, 1762), 61–8.

LETTER VIII

WHEN an architect examines a Gothic structure by Grecian rules, he finds nothing but deformity. But the Gothic architecture has it's own rules, by which when it comes to be examined, it is seen to have it's merit, as well as the Grecian. The question is not, which of the two is conducted in the simplest or truest taste: but, whether there be not sense and design in both, when scrutinized by the laws on which each is projected.

The same observation holds of the two sorts of poetry. Judge of the *Faery Queen* by the classic models, and you are shocked with it's disorder: consider it with an eye to it's Gothic original, and you find it regular. The unity and simplicity of the former are more complete: but the latter has that sort of unity and simplicity, which results from it's nature.

The Faery Queen then, as a Gothic poem, derives its METHOD, as well as the other characters of it's composition, from the established modes and ideas of chivalry.

---

[3] Some instances of particular beauty, whose constructions date at different aeras from what I have mentioned, have been pointed out to me by a gentleman to whose taste I readily yield; such as the nave of the minster at York (in the great and simple style) and the choir of the same church (in the rich and filigraine workmanship) both of the reign of Edward III. The Lady-chapel (now Trinity-church) at Ely, and the Lantern-tower in the same cathedral, noble works of the same time: and the chapel of bishop West (also at Ely) who died in 1533, for exquisite art in the lesser style. These notices certainly can add no honour to a name already so distinguished as Mr. Gray's; it is my own gratitude or vanity that prompts me to name him; and I must add, that if some parts of this work are more accurate than my own ignorance or carelessness would have left them, the reader and I are obliged to the same gentleman, who condescended to correct, what he never could have descended to write.

It was usual, in the days of knight-errantry, at the holding of any great feast, for Knights to appear before the Prince, who presided at it, and claim the privilege of being sent on any adventure, to which the solemnity might give occasion. For it was supposed that, when such a *throng of knights and barons bold*, as Milton speaks of, were got together, the distressed would flock in from all quarters, as to a place where they knew they might find and claim redress for all their grievances.

This was the real practice, in the days of pure and antient chivalry. And an image of this practice was afterwards kept up in the castles of the great, on any extraordinary festival or solemnity: of which, if you want an instance, I refer you to the description of a feast made at Lisle in 1453, in the court of Philip the Good, Duke of Burgundy, for a crusade against the Turks: As you may find it given at large in the memoirs of *Matthieu de Conci, Olivier de la Marche*, and *Monstrelet.*

That feast was held for *twelve* days: and each day was distinguished by the claim and allowance of some adventure.

Now laying down this practice, as a foundation for the poet's design, you will see how properly the Faery Queen is conducted.

—"I devise, says the poet himself in his Letter to Sir W. Raleigh, that the Faery Queen kept her annual feaste xii days: upon which xii several days, the occasions of the xii several adventures happened; which being undertaken by xii several knights, are in these xii books severally handled."

Here you have the poet delivering his own method, and the reason of it. It arose out of the order of his subject. And would you desire a better reason for his choice? [. . .]

This Gothic method of design in poetry may be, in some sort, illustrated by what is called the Gothic method of design in Gardening. A wood or grove cut out into many separate avenues or glades was amongst the most favourite of the works of art, which our fathers attempted in this species of cultivation. These walks were distinct from each other, had, each, their several destination, and terminated on their own proper objects. Yet the whole was brought together and considered under one view by the relation which these various openings had, not to each other, but to their common and concurrent center. You and I are, perhaps, agreed that this sort of gardening is not of so true a taste as that which *Kent and Nature* have brought us acquainted with; where the supreme art of the Designer consists in disposing his ground and objects into an *entire landskip*; and grouping them, if I may use the term, in so easy a manner, that the careless observer, tho' he be taken with the symmetry of the whole, discovers no art in the combination. [. . .]

This, I say, may be the truest taste in gardening, because the simplest: Yet there is a manifest regard to unity in the other method; which has had it's admirers, as it may have again, and is certainly not without it's *design* and beauty.

EXPLANATORY NOTES

Like all editors, I am conscious of drawing on the work of previous scholars, most notably W. S. Lewis's excellent edition of *The Castle of Otranto* (London: Oxford University Press, 1964) with notes by Joseph W. Reed, revised by E. J. Clery in 1996. In particular, I have drawn on Reed's notes for Italian and French sources; in such cases, my debt is recorded by signing the notes 'JWR'. Michael Gamer's edition (London: Penguin, 2001) is useful for the reception of *Otranto*, Robert Mack's (London: Dent, 1993) for republishing *Hieroglyphic Tales*, and Frederick S. Frank's (Peterborough, Ontario: Broadview, 2003) for republishing *The Mysterious Mother* (see also Paul Baines and Edward Burns, *Five Romantic Plays, 1768–1821* (Oxford: Oxford University Press, 2000)); these editions are referred-to by editor. Although Walpole's reading copy of Shakespeare was likely to have been Nicholas Rowe's 1709 edition, for ease of reference I have used *The Oxford Shakespeare: The Complete Works*, gen. eds Stanley Wells and Gary Taylor (Oxford: Clarendon Press, 1988). All biblical citations are from the Authorized Version (Oxford and New York: Oxford University Press, 1997). *OED* refers to *Oxford English Dictionary* and *ODNB* to *Oxford Dictionary of National Biography*, both in online editions, and definitions from Samuel Johnson's *Dictionary of the English Language* are taken from the first edition (London, 1755–6). Quotations from Lewis's monumental edition of *Horace Walpole's Correspondence*, ed. W. S. Lewis et al., 48 vols (London: Oxford University Press, 1937–83), are noted as '*Correspondence*'.

TITLE PAGE OF THE FIRST EDITION

1 *William Marshal, Gent.*: an engraver of the same name is mentioned in a letter from William Cole to Walpole (2 August 1764; *Correspondence*, i. 71).

Onuphrio Muralto: a half-translation of the name Horace Walpole (a possible source first suggested by Walter Scott); Walpole also mentions a musician, one Onofrio, in a letter to George Montagu (17 May 1763; *Correspondence*, xi. 73).

Tho. Lownds: Thomas Lowndes (1719–84), printer and bookseller.

TITLE PAGE OF THE SECOND EDITION

3 *A Gothic Story*: this subtitle was added to the second edition. By naming his novel Gothic, Walpole proposes it as an alternative to orthodox neo-classical literary taste, alerting the reader not simply to its medieval setting, but to the politics and ideology of the Whig Party that pervade the text (see Introduction, pp. xii–xvi, xxiii).

Epigraph: the epigraph, based on Horace's *De Arte Poetica*, was added to the second edition. Walpole slightly misquotes Horace's lines, '*vanae* |

fingentur species, ut nec pes nec caput uni | reddatur formae' (ll. 7–9). W. S. Lewis argues that the misquotation was deliberate, Walpole altering the lines from 'idle fancies shall be shaped [like a sick man's dream] so that neither head nor foot can be assigned a single shape' to 'nevertheless head and foot are assigned to a single shape' (Lewis, *Otranto*, pp. xii–xiii). If so, the lines look forward to the *disjecta membra* of Alfonso the Good coming together, and also make a claim of artistic unity for the romantic plot.

PREFACE TO THE FIRST EDITION

5 *the library of an ancient catholic family in the north of England*: most critics assume that Walpole is suggesting that the manuscript of *The Castle of Otranto* was discovered in this distant location well away from the metropolitan Protestant Whiggism of the south (see Introduction, p. xiii). However, it is strongly implied that it was actually a *printed* version that was found in the library. The antiquarian conceit of the found document was at its height in the 1760s.

Naples, in the black letter . . . 1529: Walpole matches northern English Catholicism with the southern remoteness of Catholic Naples, while also invoking the Visigothic heritage of Italy. The 'black letter' refers to Gothic typeface, thus. In the eighteenth century this fount was associated with Bibles, broadside ballads, Parliamentary Acts, and English antiquity. The date 1529 is a reminder of the Reformation, which began in Germany in 1517, and in England in the 1530s.

purest Italian: see Hamlet's comments on *The Murder of Gonzago*: 'The story is extant, and writ in choice Italian' (III. ii. 250–1). Like Shakespeare, Walpole suggests that Mediterranean politics are passionate and murderous; in doing so he draws on Aristotelian climate theory, and subtly challenges the prevalent eighteenth-century antiquarian taste for the classical culture of Imperial Rome and the neo-classical Renaissance.

not long afterwards: Walpole's tale has some features in common with the history of the Hohenstaufen dynasty, rulers of the Kingdom of Sicily (including the southern part of the peninsula, where Otranto is located). Frederick II, Holy Roman Emperor and leader of the fifth Crusade (1228–9), was locked in rivalry with the papacy over the control of Italy until his death in 1250; for many years it was believed by his supporters that he would one day return. His successor Conrad was stranded in Germany, and Frederick's illegitimate son, Manfred of Taranto, became viceroy in the Southern Italian kingdom, defeating the papal army at Foggia in 1254. Conrad died on his way through Italy, and his heir, the infant Conradin, remained in Germany. In 1258 Manfred exploited rumours of the death of the child to declare himself King. The Pope, determined to eradicate the Staufen line, persuaded Charles of Anjou to oppose the usurper, and in 1266 Manfred was defeated and killed at the battle of Benevento. Unlike his fictional namesake, King Manfred, with his wife Helena, had four sons, who were kept in chains by the conqueror until they died. [JWR]

Arragonian kings in Naples: Peter III of Aragon, King of Spain, had laid claim to Southern Italy in 1282 by virtue of his marriage to a daughter of King Manfred. He took the island of Sicily, but the establishment of Aragon in Naples did not come until Alfonso V captured the city in 1442. Spanish rule, interrupted by various contests and conflicts, continued into the eighteenth century. [JWR]

[moderated however by singular judgment]: an example of parathesis, a clause or phrase contained within square brackets (also known in the period as 'crotchets'). Parathesis is a distinctive feature of *Otranto*'s punctuation, and, like the variable dashes, gives the narrative the air of a playtext. The schoolmaster John White defines a parathesis as 'a seperate Discourse explanatory of something relating to the Subject discoursed upon' (*The Country-Man's Conductor in Reading and Writing True English* (Exeter, 1701), 69). In the Preface, Walpole substitutes square brackets for the usual parentheses, (thus).

Luther: Martin Luther (1483–1546), architect of the Protestant Reformation.

6 *flowers*: ornaments, embellishments (Johnson).

rules of the drama: the dramatic unities laid down by Aristotle (*Poetics*, chapters 6–8), as interpreted by neo-classical critics. Unity of action dictates that a plot consist of a single narrative, unity of place that it takes place at a single location, and unity of time that events onstage unfold in real time, or within a period of twenty-four hours. See Samuel Johnson's remarks on Shakespeare: 'Whether Shakespeare knew the unities, and rejected them by design, or deviated from them by happy ignorance, it is, I think, impossible to decide, and useless to inquire. . . . As nothing is essential to the fable, but unity of action, and as the unities of time and place arise evidently from false assumptions, and, by circumscribing the extent of the drama, lessen its variety, I cannot think it much to be lamented, that they were not known by him, or not observed' ('Preface', *Plays of Shakespeare*, 8 vols (1765), i. 25).

passions: Walpole highlighted the centrality of the passions to Gothicism in his *Anecdotes of Painting in England* (1762): 'One must have taste to be sensible of the beauties of Grecian architecture; one only wants passions to feel Gothic' (see Introduction, pp. xxiii–xxiv, xxvii, and Appendix).

conduce: promote an end (Johnson).

the sins of fathers are visited on their children to the third and fourth generation: 'for I the LORD thy God am a jealous God, visiting the iniquity of the fathers upon the children unto the third and fourth generation of them that hate me' (Exodus 20: 5; see also Exodus 34: 7, Numbers 14: 18, and Deuteronomy 5: 9).

7 *the censure to which romances are but too liable*: romances were medieval tales of adventure and the supernatural. Such reading material was held responsible for inflaming the imagination and disordering the reason, and hence many educationalists, particularly female commentators, warned readers against these books. Samuel Johnson claimed that his inability to

fix on any stable career was due to reading too many romances as a young boy (James Boswell, *Life of Johnson*, ed. G. B. Hill, rev. L. F. Powell (Oxford: Clarendon Press, 1934–50), i. 49). Reading romances could even lead to a life of crime. Stephen Burroughs claimed that dwelling on the adventures of *Guy of Warwick* had blown 'the fire of [his] temper into a tenfold rage . . . at that early period of life, when judgment was weak', the result being the 'very pernicious consequences, in the operations of my after conduct': i.e. theft, robbery, counterfeiting, adultery, arson, and manslaughter (*The Memoirs of Stephen Burroughs* (Hanover, 1798), 10).

7 *variety and harmony*: an ironic comment, but see Walpole's Francophobic comments to Hannah More in his letter of 14 October 1787 (*Correspondence*, xxxi. 256).

the theatre: Walpole directs his readers to attend to the drama and theatricality of the text—dialogue is rapid and naturalistic, stage directions appear in square brackets, and props and special effects abound. Ironically, the novel's five-act structure almost adheres to the dramatic unities.

some real castle: Walpole had begun Gothicizing his 'little cottage' Strawberry Hill in 1749, and his extravagant home is undoubtedly the primary inspiration here. Notwithstanding this, Walpole's education at Eton College and King's College, Cambridge, were also influences (*Correspondence*, vi. 145). At the time of writing Walpole was not aware that there was an actual castle at Otranto, but in 1786 he was delighted to receive a sketch of the building (*Correspondence*, xxxii. 177).

PREFACE TO THE SECOND EDITION

9 *received by the public*: the first edition of 500 copies sold out in four months, necessitating this second edition.

two kinds of romance, the ancient and the modern: see Introduction, pp. xxxiv–xxxv.

drama: Walpole again alerts readers to the dramatic features of his narrative.

rules of probability: Horace's *On the Art of Poetry* endorses Aristotle's *Poetics* by noting that plot and character must be credible and within the bounds of probability (ll. 379 ff.). This became a cornerstone of neoclassical criticism as it established how poetry, drama, and fiction could be didactic and thereby morally improving. See Nicholas Rowe's criticism of the casket episode in *The Merchant of Venice* as being 'a little too much remov'd from the Rules of Probability' (*Works of Mr. William Shakespear*, 6 vols (1709), i, p. xx); see also Henry Fielding, *The History of Tom Jones, A Foundling* (1749), book 8, chapter 1.

10 *My rule was nature*: three and a half weeks before publication of the second edition, Cole wrote to Walpole, 'I, who know your facility and ease in composing, am not so much surprised at the shortness of the time you completed your volume in, as at the insight you have expressed in the nature

and language, both of the male and female domestics. Their dialogues, especially the latter, are inimitable and very Nature itself' (17 March 1765: *Correspondence*, i. 92).

affections: states of mind (Johnson).

sublime: Walpole's introduction of the sublime reveals his debt to Edmund Burke's influential *A Philosophical Enquiry into the Origin of our Ideas of the Sublime and the Beautiful*, first published in 1757 (see Introduction, pp. xxii–xxiii, xxxv–xxxvii), which in turn drew on Longinus' treatise *On the Sublime*, widely available after 1739 in William Smith's popular translation, and John Baillie's Lockean *Essay on the Sublime* (1747).

That great master of nature, Shakespeare, was the model I copied: Shakespeare was the epitome of English Gothic literature, in contrast to neo-classical taste: he mixed tragedy and comedy, high and low characters, and disregarded the dramatic unities. *Hamlet* is a key influence on *Otranto*; there are allusions to *Cymbeline*, *King Lear*, *Macbeth*, *Richard III*, and *The Taming of the Shrew* (see notes below); and the atmosphere of plays such as *Julius Caesar* haunt the action (see Introduction, pp. xxvi–xxvii, xxx). Shakespeare's reputation as a 'natural' genius began in his lifetime (see, for example, Francis Beaumont's *The Knight of the Burning Pestle*, 1607–8) and was cemented by John Milton's famous lines in 'L'Allegro' on hearing 'sweetest Shakespeare fancy's child, | Warble his native wood-notes wild' (ll. 133–4).

omitted, or vested in heroics: by the eighteenth century, the stage tradition of Shakespeare had become independent from the scholarly reading text, and the versions performed were extensively rewritten by Nahum Tate, Colley Cibber, and David Garrick (among others) to ensure that they were in keeping with contemporary expectations. Interestingly, elements of these adaptations remained in performances up to the middle of the twentieth century (see, for example, *Richard III*, dir. Laurence Olivier (1955), with extra dialogue and revisions by Cibber and Garrick).

11 *a little boy measuring his thumb*: apocryphal, but the stupendous size of the Colossus at Rhodes foreshadows the magnitude of the statue of Alfonso the Good.

Voltaire: the pen-name of François-Marie Arouet (1694–1778), a leading figure of the Enlightenment. From 1726 to 1729, he lived in exile in England. After his return to France, he became an influential disseminator of English culture, publishing commentaries on the work of Shakespeare and other poets and playwrights, as well as Newton and Locke, all at that time almost unknown in the rest of Europe. In his view, Shakespeare was a primitive, capable of poetry of surpassing genius, but lacking the art of the great French dramatists of the seventeenth century, Corneille and Racine. This opinion of their relative merits is reiterated in his edition of the collected works of Corneille, *Le Théâtre de Pierre Corneille avec des commentaires*, published in twelve volumes in 1763. The complaint that there is 'scarcely a tragedy by Shakespeare where one doesn't find the jokes of coarse men side by side with the sublimity of heroes' appears in the preface to *Le Cid*, in *The Complete Works of Voltaire*, ed. Theodore Besterman et al. (Geneva, Banbury, and Oxford: Voltaire Foundation, 1968–), liv. 38–9. [JWR]

11 *Corneille*: Pierre Corneille (1606–84), founder of French classical tragedy. His tragicomic play *Le Cid* (1637) precipitated a debate on the protocols of neo-classical drama, which he subsequently observed more closely. Corneille exercised a powerful influence on Restoration English literature and criticism through the plays of John Dryden.

this mixture of buffoonery and solemnity is intolerable: Voltaire means the English and Spanish drama, not Corneille (see 'Remarques sur *Le Cid*'). Walpole later sent a copy of the second edition to Voltaire with an elaborate apology (21 June 1768: *Correspondence*, xli. 149–50; also xxxv. 435).

twice translated the same speech in Hamlet . . . latterly in derision: the famous soliloquy from *Hamlet* beginning 'To be, or not to be' (III. i. 58–92), translated first in *Lettres philosophiques*, originally published in English as *Letters Concerning the English Nation* (1733), in Letter XVIII 'On Tragedy'; secondly in *Appel à toutes les nations de l'Europe* [pp. 34–9] (1761). Both the translations, with commentary, are reproduced in Besterman (ed.), *Studies on Voltaire and the Eighteenth Century*, liv: *Voltaire on Shakespeare* (Geneva: Voltaire Foundation, 1967). [JWR]

Enfant prodigue: Voltaire's play *L'Enfant prodigue*, *The Prodigal Son* (1736), which itself mixed high drama with comedy.

history has been grossly perverted: Walpole's *Historic Doubts on the Life and Reign of King Richard the Third* (1768) was a piece of Ricardian revisionism that endeavoured to restore the reputation of the last Plantagenet king.

the same person: see Voltaire's preface to *Le Comte d'Essex*, in *Commentaires sur Corneille*, *Complete Works*, lv. 1002. [JWR]

12 *On y voit un melange . . . le mieux traité*: 'We find there a mixture of seriousness and jesting, of the comic and the pathetic; often even a single incident produces all these contrasts. Nothing is more common than a house in which a father is scolding, a daughter—absorbed in her emotions—weeping; the son makes fun of both of them, some relatives take different sides in the scene, etc. We do not infer from this that every comedy ought to have scenes of buffoonery and scenes of touching emotion: there are many very good plays in which gaiety alone reigns; others entirely serious; others mixed; others where compassion gives rise to tears: no genre should be ruled out: and if someone were to ask me which genre is best, I would reply, the one which is best handled.' From 'Préface de l'éditeur de l'édition de 1738' of Voltaire's play *Mérope* (1736); *Œuvres complètes de Voltaire*, ed. Louis Moland, new edition (Paris: Garnier, 1883), iii. 443. The preface to *L'Enfant prodigue* was written by Voltaire himself, as Walpole suspected. [JWR]

Maffei: Scipione, Count (1675–1755), an Italian scholar whose tragic drama *Mérope* (1713) was a great success and rapidly went through many editions. Voltaire wrote his own play on the subject and prefaced it with a letter to Maffei reflecting on differences in dramatic practice among European nations. [JWR]

Tous ces traits . . . espece de simplicité: 'All these features are naïve: all are appropriate to the people you bring on stage, and the manners you give them. These natural familiarities would have been, I believe, well received in Athens; but Paris and our audience demand a different kind of simplicity.' From 'A M. Le Marquis Scipio Maffei' prefixed to *Mérope* (1743); *Œuvres Complètes*, iv. 188. [JWR]

13 *a discussion of the espece de simplicité*: although Walpole quotes Voltaire, he actually implies that *simplicité* should be understood in its derogatory sense—not 'simplicity', but 'silliness'.

parterre: the part of the ground floor of a theatre in front of the orchestra (*OED*); another reminder of theatricality.

difficiles nugæ: laboured trifles; see Martial, *Epigrams*, ii. 86. 9.

singled out to defend in Racine: see '[Remarques sur] Bérénice, tragédie', in *Commentaires sur Corneille, Complete Works*, lv. 941. [JWR]

Rosencraus: this spelling of Rosencrantz is consistently used in the second Quarto edition of Shakespeare's play and appears in a handful of eighteenth-century versions.

ichnography: the groundplot (Johnson); i.e. the ground-plan (*OED*).

the prince of Denmark and the grave-digger: see *Hamlet*, V. i. 65–211.

a second time: referring to Voltaire's two translations of the 'To be, or not to be' speech (see note, above).

14 *whatever rank their suffrages allot to it*: Walpole invokes the Enlightenment vision of the 'republic of letters' by noting that his readers, whatever their intellectual status, have already endorsed the novel.

15 *Sonnet . . . LADY MARY COKE*: the dedicatory sonnet was added to the second edition and is a daring archaism. Sonnets were little regarded at the time; Shakespeare's sonnets, for example, did not receive serious scholarly attention until Edmond Malone edited them in 1780 (*Supplement to the Edition of Shakspeare's Plays published in 1778*, 2 vols). Johnson indicates the low esteem of the form in his *Dictionary*, commenting that 'It is not very suitable to the English language, and has not been used by any man of eminence since *Milton*'. Walpole's sonnet is experimental, written in iambic tetrameter rhyming abab cdcd eefaaf. His dedicatee, Lady Mary Coke (1726–1811), was an aristocrat and socialite, as well as a humourless and tempestuous drama queen. She corresponded with Walpole, who observed to Horace Mann in 1773—shortly before they inevitably fell out in 1775—that:

> she has a frenzy for royalty, and will fall in love with and at the feet of the Great Duke and Duchess. . . . However . . . Lady Mary has a thousand virtues and good qualities: she is noble, generous, high-spirited, undauntable, is most friendly, sincere, affectionate, and above

any mean action. She loves attention. . . . I have often tried to laugh her out of her weakness, but as she is very serious, she was so in that, and if all the sovereigns in Europe combined to slight her, she still would put her trust in the next generation of princes. Her heart is excellent, and deserves and would become a crown . . . (*Correspondence*, xxiii. 530–1).

Walpole intimates that the innovative excesses and spectacular melodrama of *Otranto* mirror her notorious capriciousness.

THE CASTLE OF OTRANTO

17 *Manfred . . . Matilda . . . Conrad . . . Isabella*: the name Manfred is not un-usual. Manfred is the father of Tancred in James Thomson's play, *Tancred and Sigismunda, A Tragedy* (1745), and Voltaire described the thirteenth-century reign of the Holy Roman Emperor Frederick II and his supposed dispatch by Manfred, King of Sicily. Following a popish plot to poison him, 'Frederick was obliged to take Mahometans for his guard. It is said, however, that these could not secure him against the furious revenge of Manfred, one of his bastards, who strangled him in his last illness' (*The Works of M. de Voltaire*, tr. Tobias Smollett et al., 25 vols (1761), ii. 73). Subsequently, Voltaire observed of the German king, Conrad IV, a son of Frederick II: 'I find it confidently asserted by most authors, that this Conrad was poisoned by his brother Manfreddo, or Mainfroi, Frederick's natural son; but I do not see that any one of them have brought the least proof of this assertion. Manfred seized upon this kingdom, which of right belonged to his nephew Conradin, son to the emperor Conrad, and grandson to Frederick I' (ii. 157).

Matilda: a familiar Old English name, derived from the Empress Matilda of England (1102–67). Matilda was the name of the reputed wife of Geoffrey Chaucer, and appears as a nun in Spenser's *The Faerie Queene*. In *Odes on Various Subjects, Humbly Address'd to the Right Honourable the Lord Walpole* (1741), by 'A Gentleman of the Inner-Temple', Matilda is named as a virtuous maid in the tragic pastoral 'The Passion of Alexis' (21–3); she also appears in passing in William Mason's 1752 play *Elfrida, A Dramatic Poem* (25).

Conrad: in Shakespeare, possibly alluding to the virtual nonentity Conrade (*Much Ado About Nothing*). See also Conrad IV of Germany, above.

Isabella: in Shakespeare, the virginal and chaste sister of Claudio whom Angelo attempts to debauch (*Measure for Measure*).

precipitation: tumultuous hurry (Johnson).

Hippolita: in Shakespeare (and Chaucer), Hippolyta is Queen of the Amazons, defeated by and married to Theseus (*A Midsummer Night's Dream*).

sterility: barrenness, want of fecundity, unfruitfulness (Johnson). The word could apply equally to women (e.g. *The Tragedy of King Lear*, I. iv. 257); even so, doubt is cast on Manfred's potency.

18 *terror and amazement*: constituents of Burke's sublime; moreover, Burke argues that 'No passion so effectually robs the mind of all its powers of acting and reasoning as fear' (42).

casque: a helmet (Johnson).

proportionable: commensurate in size (*OED*); the gigantic is, according to Burke, 'very compatible with the sublime' (162).

19 *partial*: inclined to favour without reason (Johnson).

insensibility: torpor (Johnson).

wretched: miserable, unhappy (Johnson).

20 *St. Nicholas*: probably St Nicholas of Myra, a fourth-century bishop and a popular saint in the Latin Church. He was revered for saving children, including the resurrection of several boys who had been prepared to be sold as pork by an innkeeper; he also reputedly saved three sisters from prostitution by providing each with a bag of gold. Hence he is both the patron saint of children and associated with market places and urban commerce—pawnbrokers advertise their business by suspending three golden globes outside their premises. Most of the relics of St Nicholas are held by the Basilica di San Nicola at Bari, 125 miles north of Otranto. Robert Mack, however, plausibly suggests St Nicholas I (the 'Great'), a ninth-century pope who championed Christian morality in the face of the worldliness, corruption, and plotting of secular rulers, especially on the issue of marriage laws (Mack, *Otranto*, 142).

gripe: grasp, hold, seizure of the hand (Johnson).

obeisance: a bow, a courtesy, an act of reverence made by inclination of the body or knee (Johnson).

jealousy: vehemence of feeling, solicitude (*OED*).

poignarded: stabbed, especially to death, with a poniard, a small, slim dagger (*OED*).

vulgar: plebeian, the common people (Johnson).

mob: crowd, a tumultuous rout (Johnson).

21 *ejaculations*: the hasty utterance of words expressing emotion (*OED*).

kept prisoner under the helmet itself: a bizarre incarceration that recalls the perverse ingenuity of medieval tortures and Catholic martyrdoms.

22 *enjoined*: ordered, prescribed (Johnson).

wanted: lacked (Johnson).

twilight: the action takes place in obscurity, from twilight to impenetrable darkness.

23 *part*: business, duty (Johnson).

24 *prime of his age*: attention is drawn to Manfred's potency, which may be in doubt.

date: end, conclusion (Johnson).

25 *the portrait of his grandfather . . . uttered a deep sigh and heaved its breast*:
Walpole wrote to Cole on 9 March 1765 that 'When you read of the picture quitting its panel, did not you recollect the portrait of Lord Falkland
all in white in my gallery?' The picture was painted by Paul van Somer
(1576–1621) (*Correspondence*, i. 88; see also Walpole's *Description*, 51). The
Critical Review observed that this detail was perhaps an anachronism: 'We
cannot help thinking that this circumstance is some presumption that the
castle of Otranto is a modern fabrick; for we doubt much whether pictures
were fastened in pannels before the year 1243' (19 January 1765, 50–1).

pannel: a wooden board or similar rigid material (as opposed to a canvas)
used as a surface for painting in oils or distemper (*OED*; this was the preferred spelling until the mid-nineteenth century).

Do I dream?: 'Or do I dream? Or have I dreamed till now' (*The Taming of
the Shrew*, Induction 2, 68).

Lead on! cried Manfred; I will follow thee to the gulph of perdition: Hamlet
commands the ghost of his father, 'Go on, I'll follow thee' (I. iv. 63);
Horatio has already warned caution: 'What if it tempt you toward the
flood, my lord, | Or to the dreadful summit of the cliff' (I. iv. 50–1); see
also 'Master, go on, and I will follow thee | To the last gasp with truth and
loyalty' (*As You Like It*, II. iii. 70–1); *Coriolanus* (III. i. 91); and *Othello*
(III. iii. 93, V. ii. 287).

invisible hand: Samuel Johnson had inquired into the 'Cock Lane Ghost'
mystery, being a persistent and ghostly knocking (his dismissal was published in the *Gentleman's Magazine* for 1762: see *Boswell's Life of Johnson*,
i. 406–8n.). Note that the 'poltergeist' was first identified by the Reformist
Martin Luther as a Teutonic (and thereby a Gothic) phenomenon.

26 *a subterraneous passage*: Walpole's fascination with the labyrinthine and the
chthonic directs both the action and its setting.

contiguous: bordering upon (Johnson).

several intricate cloisters: in 1758, Walpole had written that he wished to
extend Strawberry Hill to include 'a gallery, a round tower, a larger cloister,
and a cabinet, in the manner of a little chapel (*Correspondence*, xxi. 238).
Work on the Cloister commenced in 1760, and was completed in 1763.

labyrinth of darkness: see Johnson's *Rasselas* (*The Prince of Abissinia*, 2 vols,
1759), which likewise features 'a long narrative of dark labyrinths' (ii. 48).

28 *totally dark*: as Burke notes, 'night increases our terror more perhaps than
any thing else' (67, also 142); see also Johnson's *Rasselas*: 'I am like a man
habitually afraid of spectres, who is set at ease by a lamp, and wonders at
the dread which harassed him in the dark, yet, if his lamp be extinguished,
feels again the terrours which he knows that when it is light he shall feel
no more' (ii. 141).

modestly: unassumingly (*OED*).

29 *essay*: attempt, endeavour; also a trial, an experiment (Johnson).

durance: imprisonment, custody, a prison (Johnson).

disculpate: to clear from blame or accusation, to exculpate (*OED*; not in Johnson and used very rarely in the century); Walpole also employs the word in *Historic Doubts on the Life and Reign of King Richard the Third* (1768), 122.

30 *Peace! blockhead*: Macbeth repeatedly insults the messengers that come to him ('The devil damn thee black, thou cream-faced loon! | Where gott'st thou that goose look?', *Macbeth*, V. iii. 11–12, and V. v. 33; see also *Julius Caesar*, I. i. 35).

Providence: the novel is pervaded by a divine destiny ('How came we ashore?' | 'By providence divine', *The Tempest*, I. ii. 159–60; also V. i. 192).

31 *resolute*: determined (Johnson).

Jaquez: in Shakespeare, Jaques is the melancholy commentator dallying in the Forest of Arden (*As You Like It*). The incongruous comic double-act of Diego and Jaquez is a deliberate mixing of high and low elements, of comedy with catastrophe.

32 *comprehensive*: apprehensive, a malapropism *avant la lettre* (the celebrated Mrs Malaprop first appeared onstage in Richard Brinsley Sheridan's *The Rivals*, 1775). Walpole is alluding to Dogberry, who makes the same mistake speaking to the First Watchman (*Much Ado About Nothing*, III. iii. 23).

Sot!: a blockhead, a dull ignorant stupid fellow, a dolt (Johnson; see *Twelfth Night*, I. v. 117, V. i. 195; and *Tragedy of King Lear*, IV. iii. 8).

wont: accustomed (Johnson).

two together: both together.

uught. any thing (Johnson).

33 *adjure*: swearing an oath in a prescribed form (Johnson).

his hair stood on end: 'And each particular hair to stand on end | Like quills upon the fretful porcupine' (*Hamlet*, I. v. 19–20), 'Your bedded hairs . . . Start up and stand on end' (*Hamlet*, III. iv. 112–13). The actor David Garrick had a mechanical wig for his performances of Hamlet that indeed made it appear that his hair was standing on end.

I saw his foot and part of his leg: Anna Laetitia Barbauld (née Aikin) proposes that Anthony Hamilton's 'Le Bélier' (1730) was a source for the giant (Introduction to Barbauld (ed.), *The British Novelists*, 50 vols (London: F. C. and J. Rivington, 1810), xii, p. ii). Antoine Hamilton (1646–1720) was an Irish Catholic and Francophile, who wrote a series of tales of the fantastic inspired by Antoine Galland's translation of *The Thousand and One Nights* (1704–17). Among these is 'Le Bélier', a romantic medievalist prosimetrum typical of the French Celtic revival. 'Le Bélier' does admittedly contain a giant and a castle, but it also includes talking animals and a Druid, and so the influence on *Otranto* is not significant. 'Le Bélier' was printed in English as 'The Ram' in 1849 (Count Anthony Hamilton, *Fairy Tales and Romances*, tr. M. G. Lewis, H. T. Ryde, and C. Kenney (London: Henry Bohn, 1849), 445–543). Satirical depictions of Robert Walpole as a giant, for example in the print *Idol-Worship* (1740), may also have contributed.

34 *revenue*: the action of returning to a place (*OED*, which lists this meaning as both obsolete and rare).

35 *series*: course (Johnson).

36 *exquisite*: excellent, consummate, complete (Johnson); Johnson's second meaning is 'consummately bad'.

   pallet-bed: a small bed, a mean bed (Johnson).

37 *Bianca*: in Shakespeare, the sharp-witted and loquacious mistress of Cassio, dismissed as a whore by Iago (*Othello*, IV. i. 92–4); Bianca Lancia was the mother of Manfred of Sicily.

   Donna Rosara: Madonna rosary; i.e. cast the veil.

38 *all men use their wives so, when they are weary of them*: 'They are but stom-achs, and we all but food. | They eat us hungrily, and when they are full, | They belch us' (*Othello*, III. iv. 102–4).

   moped: to confine or shut up in a place (*OED*, which gives this sentence as the earliest recorded usage); Johnson's definitions (to be stupid, to drowse, to be in a constant daydream; and to make spiritless, to deprive of natural powers) are also, however, suggested.

   orisons: a prayer, a supplication (Johnson; see *Hamlet*, III. i. 91–2).

39 *the almanack*: almanacs gave details of astronomical events and moveable feasts (such as Easter), an astrological prognostication for the year, and a month-by-month 'kalendar' of days of the week that included fixed fes-tivals such as saints' days.

   great saint Nicholas: there is no tradition of the Feast of St Nicholas (6 December) being a propitious date for love divination.

   there's no resisting one's vocation: 'Why, Hal, 'tis my vocation, Hal. 'Tis no sin for a man to labour in his vocation' (*1 Henry IV*, I. ii.104–5).

   idle babbling humour: 'Heaven cease this idle humour' (*The Taming of the Shrew*, Induction 2, 12); 'Let not our babbling dreams affright our souls' (*Richard III*, V. vi. 38).

   This castle is certainly haunted!: the line suggests Elsinore Castle in *Hamlet* (see also *Richard II*, III. ii. 154).

40 *If they are spirits in pain, we may ease their sufferings by questioning them*: another allusion to *Hamlet*. Horatio commands the ghost of King Hamlet: 'If there be any good thing to be done | That may to thee do ease and grace to me, | Speak to me' (*Hamlet*, I. i. 111–13).

   beads: prayer, rosary beads.

   restless: without sleep (Johnson).

41 *sift*: to examine, to try (Johnson); 'Well, we shall sift him' (*Hamlet*, II. ii. 58).

make a property of him: Johnson defines 'to property' as, 'to seize or retain as something owned, or in which one has a right; to appropriate; to hold', and remarks that 'this word is not now used'; hence, exploit.

simpleton: trifler (Johnson).

Jerome: named for St Jerome, fourth-century theologian and hermit who prepared the Latin translation of the Bible, the Vulgate.

convent: like *monastery*, an assembly of religious persons, i.e. not confined to nuns (Johnson).

Speak quickly, said Matilda; the morning dawns apace: 'More light and light it grows' (*Romeo and Juliet*, III. v. 35; see also *Romeo and Juliet*, II. i. 221).

42 *A by-stander often sees more of the game than those that play*: probably proverbial before Walpole's use (see 'Cosmopolita', *Letters on Popery: being A Vindication of the Civil Principles of Papists* (Dublin, 1775), 25: 'It has been observed . . .').

spark: a lively, showy man, commonly used in contempt (Johnson).

rhapsody: muddled collection of words (*OED*).

43 *fish out your secrets*: 'That "sort" was well fished for' (*The Tempest*, II. i. 109).

postern-gate: a small gate, a little door (Johnson).

talisman: a magical character (Johnson).

44 *another-guess mould*: a different kind of matter (Johnson).

dower: dowry, that which the wife brings to her husband upon marriage (Johnson).

ought: see *aught*, above, which Johnson notes 'is sometimes, improbably, written *ought*'.

45 *good-liking*: approval, good-will (*OED*).

I do not use: I am not accustomed (Johnson).

[Manfred's colour changed]: 'colour' meaning freshness, or appearance of blood in the face (Johnson). The parathesis here suggests a stage direction.

46 *bearded*: opposed to the face, openly defied (Johnson).

Cant: a whining pretension to goodness, in formal and affected terms (Johnson).

oratory: a private place, which is deputed and allotted for prayer alone, and not for the general celebration of divine service (Johnson).

47 *reposes*: places (Johnson).

48 *a crown that can never pass away*: 'his dominion is an everlasting dominion, which shall not pass away' (Daniel 7: 14).

related to me in the fourth degree: collateral consanguinity was calculated by counting each degree of kinship back to a common ancestor. In common law every genealogical step was counted, in canon law only the steps after the common ancestor were included. In practice, then, a brother and sister are related in the second degree in common law and the first degree in canon law; an uncle and niece are related in the third degree in civil and the second degree in canon law; and a great uncle and niece in the fourth degree in civil law and the third degree according to canon law. Manfred's claim suggests that he is deliberately confusing common and canon law to strengthen his case, but it is still unconvincing (see Sir Samuel Toller, *The Law of Executors and Administrators* (London: A. Strahan, 1800), 62).

48 *dispensation*: an exemption from law, a permission to do something forbidden (Johnson).

fulminated: thundered (Johnson).

49 *over-reached*: deceived (Johnson); also defined as gone beyond, circumvented.

traverse his views: oppose his intentions, designs (Johnson).

50 *Theodore*: the name is possibly influenced by Theoderic the Great, the Gothic King of Italy. Its literal meaning is 'gift of God'.

51 *boarded*: laid or paved with boards (Johnson).

52 *boon*: a grant, a benefaction (Johnson).

shrieve: to hear at confession (Johnson: *shrive*); a deliberately archaic spelling, later adopted by Samuel Taylor Coleridge for the 1798 version of 'The Rime of the Ancyent Marinere' ('O shrieve me, shrieve me, holy Man!', l. 607).

53 *discovered the mark of a bloody arrow*: an identifying birthmark. Such indices of the body have obvious biblical and classical sources (Cain, Odysseus), and are a staple of early modern ballads (e.g. 'Valentine and Ursine', in Thomas Percy, *Reliques of Ancient English Poetry*, 3 vols (1765), vol. iii, Book III), and Shakespearean drama, such as *Cymbeline*. The motif was revived in the eighteenth century, reflecting anxieties over legitimacy and inheritance and hence the succession of political power. However, as E. J. Clery observes, 'Walpole employs the device with an ironic twist, since the rise of Theodore up the social scale entails the demotion of his beloved, Matilda, and contributes to the final tragedy' (*Otranto*, 122).

giving a loose to: giving free rein to.

Manfred's heart was capable of being touched: despite his Mediterranean tendencies, Manfred also displays the sentimental responses of an English man of feeling; he is not remorselessly evil.

54 *abject*: one without hope, a man whose miseries are irretrievable (Johnson).

speak: pronounce (Johnson).

the dust whence we sprung, and whither we must return: 'Earth to earth, ashes to ashes, dust to dust' (*Book of Common Prayer*); 'And yet to me what is this quintessence of dust' (*Hamlet*, II. ii. 309–10); 'Alexander died, Alexander was buried, Alexander returneth into dust . . .' (*Hamlet*, V. i. 204–5); and 'Fear no more the heat o' th' sun . . . come to dust' (*Cymbeline*, IV. ii. 259–76).

55 *brazen*: brass (Johnson).

56 *wicket*: a small gate (Johnson).

herald: an officer whose business it is to register genealogies, adjust ensigns armorial, regulate funerals, and anciently to carry messages between princes, and proclaim war and peace (Johnson).

57 *interposition*: intervenient [intercedent] agency (Johnson).

saucy: insolent (Johnson).

Frederic marquis of Vicenza: in Shakespeare, Duke Frederick is the usurper of his brother, Duke Senior (*As You Like It*).

defies: challenges (Johnson).

warder: a truncheon by which an officer forbade fight (Johnson); Johnson quotes Shakespeare ('Sound trumpets, and set forward combatants! | Stay, the King hath thrown his warder down', *Richard II*, I. iii. 117–18), but *OED* quotes this sentence as an example of the signal for the commencement of hostilities in a battle or tournament. In other words, casting down the warder is a challenge.

league: three miles.

issue: progeny, offspring (Johnson).

58 *taken the cross and gone to the Holy Land*: joined the Crusades.

espousing her himself: Walpole promotes Manfred's zeal for legitimacy and succession rather than his incestuous lust.

adjust: put in order, settle (Johnson).

59 *management*: dealing (Johnson).

the holy princess Sanchia of Arragon: probably Walpole has confused the daughter of Sancho of Aragon (in the eleventh century) and the daughter of Sancho I of Portugal (in the thirteenth). St Sancia of Portugal (d. 1229) founded a convent at Cellas and took the veil herself there. Her brother had at one time urged her to marry her nephew in order to make peace between Spain and Portugal. [JWR]

hasted: hurried (Johnson).

60 *the cavalcade arrived*: W. S. Lewis suggests that Walpole's sources were Sir William Segar's *Honor, Military and Ciuill* (1602) and Sylvanus Morgan's *The Sphere of Gentry deduced from the Principles of Nature* (1661), both richly illustrated (*Otranto*, p. xii), although it has been suggested that this is a comical episode. Nevertheless, such a fascination with antiquarian detail is also evident in Percy's *Reliques*, published less than two months after the first edition of *Otranto*, and already in print by the autumn of 1764.

harbingers: fore-runners (Johnson).

wands: staff of authority (Johnson).

led horse: a sumpter horse, that carries the clothes or furniture (Johnson); a spare horse, led by an attendant or groom (*OED*).

60 *the arms of Vicenza and Otranto quarterly*: a heraldic division of a shield into four quarters, indicating not only marriage between two houses but also a dynastic entitlement. The shield of Henry V, for instance, quartered the leopards of England with the *fleurs de lys* of France, thus reflecting the English claim to the French throne that was still part of the British monarch's official title when Walpole was writing. Here, the quartering is of course a challenge to Manfred's position. Walpole's interest in heraldry was evident throughout the interior decorations of Strawberry Hill: the library ceiling, for example, was emblazoned with coats of arms related to the Walpole dynasty.

telling his beads: i.e. rosary beads.

beavers: the parts of helmets that cover the face (Johnson); i.e. visors; in *Hamlet*, the ghost of the King is described as having his beaver up (I. ii. 228).

cartel: a writing containing, for the most part, stipulations between enemies (Johnson).

61 *gage*: a pledge, any thing given in security (Johnson).

hospital: a place for shelter or entertainment (Johnson).

preternatural: unnatural, supernatural (*OED*).

62 *ween*: think, imagine, form a notion, fancy (Johnson).

re-demand: demand back (Johnson); demand return of (*OED*).

63 *vitious*: corrupt, wicked, opposite to virtuous (Johnson).

the decision of unknown mutes: referring to the brotherhood of silent knights.

choler: anger, rage (Johnson).

disgusted with the world: the condition of being profoundly wearied by the world was later named *Weltschmerz* by the German Romantic poet Jean Paul (Richter) (1763–1825).

64 *a man of many sorrows*: 'a man of sorrows' (Isaiah 53: 3).

ambition, alas, is composed of more rugged materials: 'Ambition should be made of sterner stuff' (*Julius Caesar*, III. ii. 93; see also *Macbeth*, ii. iv. 28).

viceroy: he who governs in place of the king with regal authority (Johnson).

68 *the effect of pent-up vapours*: a deliberately ludicrous explanation, possibly alluding to satirical writing of the earlier part of the century such as Jonathan Swift's *Tale of a Tub* (1704), in which certain bodily 'pent-up vapours' are held responsible for inspiring religious enthusiasm. Despite Walpole's mockery of rational exposition, later Gothic writers deliberately debunked apparently supernatural episodes—most notably Ann Radcliffe in her novel *The Mysteries of Udolpho* (1794). Walter Scott preferred Walpole's 'bold assertion of the actual existence of phantoms and apparitions' that seemed to him 'to harmonize much more naturally with the manners of feudal times and to produce a more powerful effect upon the reader's mind, than

any attempt to reconcile the superstitious credulity of feudal ages with the philosophic skepticism of our own, by referring those prodigies to the operation of fulminating powder, combined mirrors, magic lanterns, trap-doors, speaking trumpets, and such like apparatus of German phantasmagoria' (*Lives of the Novelists*, 2 vols (Philadelphia: H. C. Carey and I. Lea, 1825), ii. 133–4). See Hamlet's observation, 'it appears no other thing to me than a foul and pestilent congregation of vapours' (II. ii. 304–5).

suit: i.e. of armour.

swear himself eternally her knight: 'in those turbulent feudal times a protector was necessary to the weakness of the [female] sex, so the courteous and valorous knight was to approve himself fully qualified for that office' (Richard Hurd, *Letters on Chivalry and Romance* (1762), 42).

69 *regardless*: heedless, negligent, inattentive (Johnson).

repair: to betake himself (Johnson).

gloomiest shades: Walpolean 'gloomth' (see Introduction, pp. xvii–xviii); Johnson repeatedly defines 'gloom' and its cognates as 'obscurity'.

pleasing melancholy: the cult of melancholic poetry was typified by Thomas Warton's *The Pleasures of Melancholy* (1747): 'O wrap me then in shades of darksome pine, | Bear me to caves by desolation brown, | To dusky vales, and hermit-haunted rocks!' (14).

the caves: caves played a metaphorical and symbolic role in the imagination, common to both biblical parable and classical myth (David at the cave of Adullum, for instance, and the Cyclops' Cave of *The Odyssey*), and linking more recent romantic legend (Shakespeare's *Cymbeline*, and the Arthurian *Merlin: A Poem*, by Jane Brereton (1735), 4) with the lure of the grotto (Pope's 'Cave of Spleen' episode in *The Rape of the Lock* (1714), canto III, and 'The Witch of Wokey' in Percy's *Reliques*, vol. i, Book III).

70 *approve*: prove, show (Johnson).

what would a censorious world think of my conduct?: Isabella retains an awareness of decorum typical of a sentimental heroine (see Introduction, p. xxxv).

74 *dreamed*: Frederic presents his original dream as a portent that foreshadows the features of the novel's plot: incarceration, dire threat, holy prophecy, and immense artefacts.

Joppa: Yafo, Japho, Jaffa; now part of Tel Aviv-Jaffa. Jaffa is an ancient port in Israel, mentioned several times in the Old Testament. It became a focus for the Crusades, being taken in the First Crusade in 1100, recaptured by Saladin in 1187, and retaken by Richard I *Coeur-de-Lion* in 1192. Frederick II left two inscriptions on one of the city's walls in 1229, describing himself to be 'Holy Roman Emperor'.

75 *corse*: a dead body (Johnson, who observes that it is 'a poetical word').

enormous sabre: the appearance of gigantic arms to complement the colossal armour hints at coming vengeance.

76 *glosing*: flattery, insinuation, or specious show (Johnson: *gloze*).

76 *Why do you fix your eye-balls thus?*: see Hamlet quizzing Horatio on the ghost of his father ('And fixed his eyes upon you?', II. ii. 231), his dialogue with the ghost himself ('Make thy two eyes like stars start from their spheres', I. v. 17). See also Macbeth's cry as he contemplates the apparition of Banquo: 'Thou art too like the spirit of Banquo. Down! | Thy crown does sear mine eyeballs' (IV. i. 128–9).

78 *corsairs*: the cruisers of Barbary, or Muslim privateers, notorious for raiding Mediterranean coasts; some of their sorties ranged as far as the north coast of Devon in England.

   rover: a robber, a pirate (Johnson).

   desert: individual qualities considered with respect to rewards or punishment (Johnson).

   warm: zealous, ardent (Johnson).

80 *attitude*: the posture or action in which a statue or painted figure is placed (Johnson).

   dole: provisions or money distributed in charity (Johnson).

81 *filial*: pertaining to a son or daughter (*OED*; Johnson confines his definition to the male).

82 *heaven purposes*: see Providence, above; 'The heavens give safety to your purposes' (*Measure for Measure*, I. i. 73).

83 *assassin*: a murderer, one that kills by treachery, or sudden violence (Johnson).

84 *never, never behold him more*: 'Thou'lt come no more. | Never, never, never, never, never' (*The Tragedy of King Lear*, V. iii. 283–4).

86 *burthen*: burden (Johnson).

   morning office: a morning service in the Christian Church (*OED*, quoting this sentence).

   Will heaven visit the innocent for the crimes of the guilty?: in contrast to the faith shown in the workings of Providence, here divine justice is doubted and appears more savage.

87 *while a father unfolds a tale of horror . . . sensations of sacred vengeance*: see the account given by the ghost of Hamlet's father (especially I. v. 7 and I. v. 25).

   shade: the soul separated from the body; so called as supposed by the ancients to be perceptible to the sight, not to the touch (Johnson).

   The Lord giveth, and the Lord taketh away: 'the LORD gave, and the LORD hath taken away' (Job 1: 21).

89 *lance her anathema*: transfixing with a violent curse of excommunication and therefore damnation.

   three drops of blood fell from the nose of Alfonso's statue: although some commentators mistake this for comedy, it is a moment of significant historical allusion, referring to the 'severe nosebleeds' of James II that helped to thwart his attempts to raise an army against the invasion of William of Orange in 1688 (*ODNB*), and hence redirected the royal bloodline. It is a reminder therefore of the historical destiny of the Whigs and the constitutional settlement of Protestantism in England. It is also unnervingly reminiscent of the auto-cannibalistic nosebleed in *The Farther Adventures of Robinson Crusoe* (1719; p. 187).

meddling friar: 'Tis a meddling friar; | I do not like the man' (*Measure for Measure*, V. i. 127–8).

90 *they wither away like the grass, and their place knows them no more*: 'For they shall soon be cut down like the grass, and wither as the green herb' (Psalms 37: 2; see also Isaiah 40: 6; 1 Peter 1: 24). See 'You were as flowers, now withered' (*Cymbeline*, IV. ii. 287; see also Ophelia's lament in *Hamlet*, IV. v. 182–4).

91 *his reliance on ancient prophecies*: a reminder of Macbeth's dependence on the Witches' prophecies (IV. i. 95–116).

92 *oriel window*: a large polygonal recess with a window, projecting from a building, usually at an upper storey, and supported from the ground or on corbels (*OED*).

vulnerary herbs: herbs useful in the cure of wounds (Johnson).

by my halidame: a common oath: see *Two Gentlemen of Verona* (IV. ii. 132); our blessed lady (Johnson: *halidom*).

affectioned: had an affection for (a rare transitive use, *OED*).

93 *though I am poor, I am honest*: 'My friends were poor but honest; so's my love' (*All's Well That Ends Well*, I. iii. 191).

94 *Francesco*: in Shakespeare, two minor characters are named Francisco (*Hamlet*, *The Tempest*).

95 *I fear my hair*: 'My very hairs do mutiny, for the white | Reprove the brown for rashness, and they them | For fear and doting' (*Antony and Cleopatra*, III. xi. 14).

watchet-coloured: pale-blue (Johnson); famously, there is a Blue Bedchamber at Strawberry Hill.

rubbing the ring: i.e. the ring given to her by Manfred.

suborned: procured by secret collusion (Johnson); induced to commit a crime or misdeed, especially by bribery or other corrupt means (*OED*).

96 *staggered*: cast into doubt (Johnson).

the principality of Otranto . . . contingent reversion of it with Matilda: Frederic is tempted to take the title immediately by force rather than taking the risk of succeeding to the title by marrying Matilda.

97 *advertised*: been informed, given notice of (Johnson, who notes 'it is now spoken with the accent upon the last syllable; but appears to have been anciently accented on the second').

weed: garment, cloaths, habit, dress (Johnson).

98 *Angels of grace, protect me!*: 'Angels and ministers of grace defend us!' (*Hamlet*, I. iv. 20; see also V. ii. 313).

99 *inwards*: within (Johnson).

dogged: hunted as a dog, insidiously and indefatigably (Johnson).

inquietude: disturbed state (Johnson).

100 *litter*: a kind of vehiculary bed (Johnson).

101 *Isabella . . . took upon herself*: Isabella becomes an increasingly independent character.

thou art too unadvised: 'It is too rash, too unadvised, too sudden' (*Romeo and Juliet*, II. ii. 160).

102 *wot*: will, a spurious archaism.

wonnot: will not be (*OED*).

103 *The first that broke silence was Hippolita*: like Isabella, Hippolita now displays self-determination.

104 *drink to the dregs*: a popular image in hymns and sermons. See Isaac Watts's 'Song of Moses and the Lamb; or, Babylon Falling': 'The Cup of Wrath is ready mixt, | And She must drink the Dregs' (Isaac Watts, *Hymns and Spiritual Songs* (1707), 55).

chamberlain: probably the lord chamberlain of the household who has the oversight of all officers belonging to the king's chambers, rather than the servant who has care of the chambers (Johnson).

A fictitious will: the threat of textual forgery becomes manifest.

wretched: calamitous, afflictive (Johnson).

Victoria: *OED* records that the word was 'employed as a shout of triumph', as well as designating the classical goddess Victory.

105 *The disconsolate company retired to the remaining part of the castle*: as in a five-act Shakespearean tragedy, there is a melancholy diminuendo as the final lines are uttered (see, for example, 'We that are young | Shall never see so much, nor live so long', *Tragedy of King Lear*, V. iii. 301–2).

each took on them . . . the neighbouring convents: 'The Duke hath put on a religious life | And thrown into neglect the pompous court' (*As You Like It*, V. iv. 179–80); see also the repetition of 'Get thee to a nunnery' and 'To a nunnery, go' in *Hamlet* (III. i. 123–52).

*The
Oxford
World's
Classics
Website*

www.worldsclassics.co.uk

- Browse the full range of Oxford World's Classics online

- Sign up for our monthly e-alert to receive information on new titles

- Read extracts from the Introductions

- Listen to our editors and translators talk about the world's greatest literature with our Oxford World's Classics audio guides

- Join the conversation, follow us on Twitter at OWC_Oxford

- Teachers and lecturers can order inspection copies quickly and simply via our website

www.worldsclassics.co.uk

American Literature

British and Irish Literature

Children's Literature

Classics and Ancient Literature

Colonial Literature

Eastern Literature

European Literature

Gothic Literature

History

Medieval Literature

Oxford English Drama

Philosophy

Poetry

Politics

Religion

The Oxford Shakespeare

A complete list of Oxford World's Classics, including Authors in Context, Oxford English Drama, and the Oxford Shakespeare, is available in the UK from the Marketing Services Department, Oxford University Press, Great Clarendon Street, Oxford OX2 6DP, or visit the website at www.oup.com/uk/worldsclassics.

In the USA, visit www.oup.com/us/owc for a complete title list.

Oxford World's Classics are available from all good bookshops. In case of difficulty, customers in the UK should contact Oxford University Press Bookshop, 116 High Street, Oxford OX1 4BR.

	Late Victorian Gothic Tales
JANE AUSTEN	**Emma**
	Mansfield Park
	Persuasion
	Pride and Prejudice
	Selected Letters
	Sense and Sensibility
MRS BEETON	**Book of Household Management**
MARY ELIZABETH BRADDON	**Lady Audley's Secret**
ANNE BRONTË	**The Tenant of Wildfell Hall**
CHARLOTTE BRONTË	**Jane Eyre**
	Shirley
	Villette
EMILY BRONTË	**Wuthering Heights**
ROBERT BROWNING	**The Major Works**
JOHN CLARE	**The Major Works**
SAMUEL TAYLOR COLERIDGE	**The Major Works**
WILKIE COLLINS	**The Moonstone**
	No Name
	The Woman in White
CHARLES DARWIN	**The Origin of Species**
THOMAS DE QUINCEY	**The Confessions of an English Opium-Eater**
	On Murder
CHARLES DICKENS	**The Adventures of Oliver Twist**
	Barnaby Rudge
	Bleak House
	David Copperfield
	Great Expectations
	Nicholas Nickleby
	The Old Curiosity Shop
	Our Mutual Friend
	The Pickwick Papers